The Measure of Life

By

Judith Works

Copyright Notice
This is a work of fiction. Names, characters, places, and incidents are either the product of the author's imagination or are used fictitiously, and any resemblance to actual persons living or dead, business establishments, events, or locales, is entirely coincidental.

The Measure of Life
COPYRIGHT © 2024 by Judith Works

All rights reserved. No part of this book may be used or reproduced in any manner whatsoever without written permission of the author or The Wild Rose Press, Inc. except in the case of brief quotations embodied in critical articles or reviews.

Contact Information: info@thewildrosepress.com

Cover Art by *Lea Schizas*

The Wild Rose Press, Inc.
PO Box 708
Adams Basin, NY 14410-0708
Visit us at www.thewildrosepress.com

Publishing History
First Edition, 2024
Trade Paperback ISBN 978-1-5092-5779-9
Digital ISBN 978-1-5092-5780-5

Published in the United States of America

Dedication

To Glenn, my household god

Praise for The Measure of Life

Who can resist a novel set in Rome with details of places, recipes and restaurants that make the mouth water, and cultural anchors only a writer who has lived in Italy can accurately infuse into a story. The Measure of Life is an emotionally resonant saga that takes the reader from a young woman's early missteps in love and life, through secrets kept with excruciating consequences. Through twists and plot turns Judith Works takes us to a satisfying finale, a redemption, and a redefinition of love and family. - Harriet Cannon, author of *Exit South*.

The Measure of Life is a book about conflict and choices, and how one moment of weakness creates a domino effect of events that lasts a lifetime. Trapped in a tepid marriage as an expat in a foreign country, practical and dependable Nicole uncharacteristically gives in to her attraction for an Italian medical student who provides her with Italian lessons, which affects her entire family. This story is filled with unforgettable characters, gorgeous settings, delicious food, simmering romance, and family drama. - Laura Moe, author of *Breakfast With Neruda*

Seattle transplant, Nicole Carlisle is a 26-year-old expat trapped in a passionless marriage to an older man who relocates them to Rome. In Rome she meets the love of her life, her language teacher, the intoxicating Signor Alessandro. Nicole is catapulted into a secret world of insatiable desire, a true affair of the heart that threatens her marriage and alters life as she knows it. As she balances her two irreconcilable lives she learns the language, falls in love with Rome and deeper into her secret affair. From an unexpected pregnancy to a death her world spirals out of control teeming with secrets, betrayal, family drama, and a dash of espionage. Nicole's journey ultimately leads her to forgive the secrets of others as she discovers the true power of lasting love. - Mindy Halleck, author of *Return to Sender*

Judith Works' fascinating true-to-life story hits the reader directly in the heart. The intimate details of life in Rome and the emotional impact of a family dealing with problems of communication, upheaval and betrayal will ring true to those who have lived an expat experience. To counterbalance the difficulties there are also the joys as the main character Nicole discovers when she meets her Italian lover. Throughout the first half of the book, I wanted to skip ahead to discover how they solved their problems. The realistic descriptions of life in Rome, the visit to the Protestant cemetery and the Etruscan tombs of Cerveteri, the sudden and violent thunderstorms that Rome experiences are spot on. – Mary Jane Cryan, author of *The Painted Palazzo*

Truly what is the measure of a life? Nicole is on a journey to find out. Relocating from Seattle to enchanting Italy, she struggles to raise children within a stale marriage. In stark contrast to her relationship with her husband, the vibrant sights, sounds, and soul of Rome leap off the pages, and also into Nicole's empty heart. Now she discovers passion and its consequences. As a reader I'm spellbound as Nicole finds her way through many twists in life. Shocking what you don't know about a person. – Wendy Kendall, author of *Kat Out of the Bag*

"I knew the fire of that hearth burned before its Lares no more——it went out long ago, and the household gods had been carried elsewhere."

Villette
Charlotte Bronte

PART I

CHAPTER ONE

Despite the cold Roman winter, perspiration ran down my back and my face burned with heat. In my hurry I stumbled on a cobblestone, scuffing my shoe and nearly falling. It was twenty minutes past the hour when I found the bar.

Young men and women sat outside surrounded by textbooks and espresso cups. All wore heavy jackets with scarves around their necks and sunglasses propped up on their hair, looking young and carefree as if the future held only success. Intent on their conversations, no one looked up.

The man I needed to find must be inside. I peered through the glass before yanking open the heavy door to enter the crowded, smoke-filled room. At first, I didn't see anyone likely. Then a man in a black sweater half rose from his table. I raised a hesitant hand in acknowledgement. Stay or leave?

He smiled. I waved back.

"Good morning, signorina. Are you Miss Nicole?" He stood.

I walked toward the table with a smile painted on my face. I liked his accent, the way my name rolled off his tongue. "Yes. Are you Signor Alessandro? I am happy to meet you. Please forgive me for my lateness." I hoped he understood my words in English.

Alessandro grinned. "Everyone is always late in

Rome. Let me help with your *cappotto* and what would you like to drink? Would you like a *cornetto*? This place has best in Rome. I like filled with how-you-say thick milk."

I explained the words meant either cream or custard and requested a cappuccino along with the *cornetto*. He draped my coat on the chair back before heading to the bar. I sat and turned sideways so I could watch him. He looked a few years older than me, perhaps twenty-eight or twenty-nine. He was tall and muscular, with dark curly hair and a confident walk.

The thought of exchanging Italian and English language lessons dissolved into something more hazy, more attractive.

When he brought my order and another cappuccino for himself, I couldn't stop myself from glancing down at my sweater in the hope he couldn't detect my wildly thumping heart. I'd read about love at first sight in novels but never believed it. It couldn't be love though; we'd hardly spoken. Maybe it was lust. Yes, lust at first sight. That had to be a thing, right? *Grow up*, I told myself. I'm married with two kids. Yet…

And then I hated the dull beige turtleneck sweater I chose for our first meeting. My scuffed shoe added to my unfashionable appearance.

After he sat back down, I leaned forward and took a tiny bite of the *cornetto* to avoid the possibility of crumbs on my chest. "*Buono.*" Even if it wasn't the right word, the pastry was indeed the best I'd tasted. Nothing like the enormous and often heavy croissants in Seattle. I sprinkled sugar into the cappuccino foam. The coffee aroma mixed with the scent of his aftershave transported me away from the responsibilities at home. My sole focus was on the present, with him. I wanted to touch his clean-shaven cheek but picked up a paper napkin to blot a nonexistent custard spot before lifting my cup. My lips burned with a heat I'd never known. *Get a grip,* I told myself, but he seemed so full of life, so at ease. So not like Martin.

Alessandro broke the silence. "I am happy to meet you. How you are in Rome? In Italian *per favore.* Then I will tell some about me in English and you ask questions. After, we make plan if this will work. I have one hour before class."

Our eyes locked for an instant before I broke the spell to stir my cappuccino. He did the same, the only noise at our table the soft clinking of spoons against heavy china cups decorated with a coffee company logo. The background noise of muffled conversations entranced me into feeling we were the only two actively present in the moment.

One of us had to speak up. So, using grade-school words, I told him about arrival in Rome a month earlier, dutifully emphasizing husband and children. I asked about restaurants. I didn't ask about places people our age would like: American-style bars or discos, jazz or pop concerts. I was a mother. I gave up those things for a life with Martin, who cared little about life outside of work.

Alessandro responded in English, speaking equally slowly. He said he didn't have time or money for fine restaurants because he was in medical school. Then he added, "People with money go to Pierluigi in the center. My father took the family there once when I finished my first year."

I couldn't picture Martin treating us to a fancy

restaurant now like he'd done when we were dating.

I did my best to tell Alessandro I'd been in Rome for five weeks. He didn't need to know that Martin was away in Milan at an intensive language school for his job, leaving me alone with two children and no idea how to go about anything in the beautiful but chaotic city.

I asked if Alessandro was originally from Rome.

"My family is from the city near the Mare Adriatico, called Ascoli Piceno where my father is a radiologist. My mother is *professoressa* of Italian literature. I go to New York next year for resident in big hospital for cardiology."

His eyes lit up as he spoke. The energy was contagious. The more he talked, the more I wanted to continue the conversation, to remain at the small table even though I needed to shop before the children came home from school. I asked about English-speaking doctors in Rome, especially pediatricians. How domesticated I sounded. Matronly—a deadly description when you're twenty-six.

He said it was best to call the American consulate for names. Speaking of my family sobered me. The conversation became too personal, but I'd led it there. I grew aware of the background babble filling the space beyond our table mixed with my uncharted desires.

"Sorry, I need to go."

"Wait. Please." He extended his hand resting it momentarily on my sleeve, sending a warm sensation coursing through my body. "I must learn so much before I go to New York. I need your help."

Being needed, and told I was needed, lured me back in. I should have hesitated, knowing this could lead to something more than a tutoring session. "All right." I had something in mind. "Next meeting I want you to tell me about the Italian poets, the ones your mother teaches." The hell with being a matron.

He ran his hand through his hair and furrowed his brow for a second or two. "Poets?"

"Yes, I'd like to learn about Italian culture."

After a moment, he said, "I will ask my mamma what book. And I want to know about life in America. Is it like the movies we see?"

"Sometimes." *Sleepless in Seattle* popped into my head—a complete fantasy I'd seen before we left. As every Seattleite knew, the boat ride scenes were shot in the wrong location. Anyway, it wasn't the right film to talk about. It was too romantic.

I buttoned my coat and said, "*Arrivederci* until next week." I caught a glimpse of his face as he searched his briefcase for something, before I closed the door. Heat rose from my belly as a sharp wind blew me along the street as if my red coat was a spinnaker.

****

The days until our next meeting ticked by, not as slowly as I feared because I was scrambling to make sure the children were settling in, find my way around the neighborhood, and learn how to shop when many of the vegetables were unknown and the labels on packages were obscure. I'd always loved to cook but now I was often flummoxed, and it was easier to go out for a pizza at a nearby place. Despite buying a chart to convert measurements from those I used in Seattle, I continued to be confused and ended up with strange results for the dinner table. I should have arranged to exchange conversation with some middle-aged Italian housewife instead of a young man when I'd checked the bulletin board at a nearby language school and found a card from a person who wanted to work on his English with someone who wanted conversational Italian.

****

At least my thoughts about Alessandro were diverted by the arrival of our furniture. The movers—both stocky older men dressed in blue overalls and jackets—showed up two weeks after Martin had left. One wore a hat made of newspaper folded like a toy boat.

The men hefted out the company furniture and replaced it with boxes and crates of our own, lugging the heavier furniture to wherever I pointed. There was the dresser, night tables, and our bed. I could see two distinct indentations, one larger than the other in the mattress. They were further apart than I remembered. We'd slept spooned together early on but it hadn't lasted long enough to make an impression.

When the last box was heaved into the apartment, I signed a document I couldn't read and held my front door open, saying *grazie* to the movers. It was one of my modest selection of Italian words. I used it liberally along with a smile.

My sense of accomplishment continued when Sophie came home from her kindergarten. I'd gone to meet the van that transported her and other children back and forth. She'd been calm since the day Martin left when she'd clung to his pant leg screaming, "Daddy, daddy," until he pried her fingers away.

Today, she talked about her kindergarten as she ate her usual cookies and milk before I put her down for her nap. Her room, now arranged as it was in Seattle, beckoned her to climb into the familiar bed with her pink unicorn comforter. I closed the door to avoid waking her as I unpacked and hung clothes. After about thirty minutes, I peeked to make sure all was well. Sophie was sitting on the floor dismembering her teddy. Clumped stuffing lay scattered and one button eye had rolled under the bed.

"Oh, honey, look what happened to Threadbear." I gasped and put my hand over my mouth.

She snuggled in my lap and hid her head as I cradled her. Thumb in her mouth, she held out the other hand out to grasp the now headless one-legged bear with its plush long since worn off from too much love.

"Shall we find a needle and thread and nurse him back to health? Then you can help me unpack." Sophie snuffled, gave a tentative smile and disentangled herself from my arms. I gathered the disconnected pieces and found my sewing kit to stitch it into a semblance of its former self.

If only I could have used a needle and thread to mend Sophie's woes. To destroy Threadbear, her constant companion, frightened me. She'd always been what some would call difficult: colicky and determined not to sleep for months after she was born, fond of the word "no" as she grew. But my pediatrician said she met all milestones, and she'd grow out of her bad humors. I'd have to watch her closely after this incident and if she didn't calm down soon, find a specialist to consult. But how would I find one in Rome?

At least I could be thankful for Tyler, the only one of us who'd settled in immediately as he rapidly made friends at his school and picked up Italian with no effort. As I fretted about Sophie, he was wolfing down three peanut butter and jam sandwiches in succession after he'd helped me arrange furniture when he'd come home late in the afternoon.

Martin called in the evening, but his mood told me now was not the time to discuss Sophie and the teddy bear incident. I told him the movers did a good job and the kids were okay. He asked no more questions.

CHAPTER TWO

I arrived at the bar ten minutes early. Alessandro was already there with a slim volume in his hand. He leaped up when he saw me and helped me with my coat again. My emotions shifted into overdrive.

"I found at old book place." His smile was slightly crooked. The small imperfection only increased my enchantment despite telling myself to avoid distraction and focus on learning Italian.

Our hands brushed as he handed me the book. His was warm and soft but my fingers felt singed by lightning as I accepted the old leather-bound book. The cover had a large black ink stain. I couldn't stop my nose wrinkling from the musty smell as I leafed through a few sepia-toned pages, the print set in a format for poetry. I handed it back, careful to avoid his hands and eyes.

I'd been eager to learn more about poetry during my one year at university, but never heard of Giacomo Leopardi, the name on the first page. Marriage at the end of my freshman year, followed by an immediate pregnancy put an end to poetic thoughts and other daydreams. I'd been in a hurry to start life as I saw it.

"I know nothing about Italian poetry." But I knew poetry could be hazardous. It might make me think about things I'd put aside and now wanted back.

"Leopardi is famous poet. I read you the poem in Italian and then try to translate. You fix what I say.

Okay? Like we say *va bene* I think. It was written around 1820 and its name is 'Infinity.' I do now. Then you do different poem." He turned to a page bookmarked with a receipt from the bar.

"*Sempre caro mi fu quest'ermo colle, e questa siepe…*"

His voice was soft, the Italian liquid and warm. He must have practiced the recitation, so perfect were his words. I understood some and was captivated, however I willed myself against it. When he finished, I was silent, trying to ignore the fervent desire rushing through my body.

"I'm sorry, I bore. Shall I do in English? It will ruin the poem." He looked disappointed, as though I considered him a failure.

"I'm not bored. It was beautiful. And, yes, let's try English. Let me look at the lines while you speak. Hope I know some of the words." I kept my head lowered to disguise my heated face.

Alessandro moved his chair around the table to sit close. I inhaled his woodsy scent.

"The solitary hill is always dear to me, and the…oh I don't know this word…closes out my view…"

Unable to concentrate, I stopped listening, unnerved by his nearness. My throat was thick. I caught myself leaning forward with eyes closed before I came to my senses. I opened them to see his own eyes near mine, so close I could see amber flecks in the brown of his iris. Overcome with emotions, I grabbed my coat. I stuttered, "I need to go. Sorry."

I heard him say "next week" before I was out the door. I shivered as I boarded a nearby tram. Visions of Alessandro swirled around my head, an apartment with a table set with two glasses and a bottle of wine, flickering candles, and a big iron bedstead with a mattress so old it sagged in the middle to keep lovers together. Visions of making long and leisurely love on our own soft island.

Stop this, it's only a silly crush, I told myself over and over. But in fact, a thunderbolt had zapped me.

****

At least a comforting diversion appeared a few days later when I heard scraps of Italian conversation floated up from the lobby as I struggled with the locks on our apartment front door after shopping. A female voice conversed with the *portinaia*, a widow dressed in black who sat at her station in the building entrance to watch comings and goings and did odd jobs for tips. The conversation ended, and I heard slow footsteps ascending the wide marble steps. I looked over the stairwell railing to watch an amply figured woman lugging shopping bags approach. She paused on the landing below to rest. After a minute, she continued until arriving at my doorway on the fourth floor. She put the bags down.

"Hello!" she puffed. "I could have taken the elevator, but I need the exercise. I'm Maggie. I've been wondering who moved into the empty apartment since I got back from visiting my family up north last week. Are you new to Rome?"

"Yes. I'm Nicole, Nicki for short." I was so relieved to hear English, I almost hugged her. "And, yes, we're new. The place is still a mess after our furniture arrived but would you like to come in for coffee or tea?" I gushed at the prospect of a friend like a kid getting a bike for her birthday.

Maggie peered into my apartment still stacked with boxes and said, "Let me host please. I'm on the floor above. I'd love to have a chat."

"Oh gosh, that would be great!"

"Grand. See you in a tick." She picked up her bags and turned toward the last flight of stairs.

****

I pulled the scrunchie from my hair to shake it out and washed up before knocking on her door. Maggie welcomed me into a penthouse apartment. It looked like some I'd seen in home décor magazines.

"Wow! This is super." I sounded like the hick I was.

She smiled at my enthusiastic admiration of the paintings on the walls and Persian rugs on the parquet floor. "Orazio, he's my husband, inherited these old things from his parents. Family treasures, you know." She gestured for me to sit on a blue-velvet sofa before continuing.

"I've been here for donkey's years now. Moved from Ireland when I was just a slip of a thing. Still get back to see all my brothers and sisters every year." She paused and then said, "Do you have children?"

"Two, Tyler—he's my stepson—is thirteen. Sophie's five."

"My girls are twenty-four and nineteen, the boys are sixteen and my baby, Ludo, is about the age of your Sophie. He was a genuine surprise, I must say! A wonderful surprise. And now I have a wee grandchild." She paused, before saying, "Oh sorry, I'm rattling on. Anyway, just to say, I wanted to get away from village life but never dreamed I'd end up in Rome. Many twists in life aren't there?"

"You're right for sure." I put on my best smile as if

I could cope with anything when inwardly I wanted to have a good cry to resolve my inner turmoil.

"Indeed. That's Rome. Love it and hate it on the same day. Now how about tea? You can tell me about your family." She recited the varieties in her pantry. I selected Irish Breakfast. She bustled off while I stood at the French doors leading to a large terrace wondering what it would be like to be married to an Italian. Would he be a mama's boy like I'd read about?

Maggie's family life and mine were true opposites, family ties and children and grandchildren, which judging from her remarks was her abiding interest and concern. I was an only child and Martin had been orphaned at a young age.

After Maggie returned with our tea, I sunk into her luxurious sofa again and said, "I was so happy when my husband, Martin, got a job offer here for two years."

Maggie then alluded to a first marriage to an Italian and meeting Orazio shortly after the divorce. "So many of us girls from the country married Italians right off the bat. We were so young and naïve and they were so handsome."

I was all ears, but after her expectant pause, I felt obligated to offer at least another minimal contribution. "We've been married six years. He's in the defense industry and had to go to a language school in Milan for his work. I wish I was there too." I couldn't say the eighteen-year age gap between us was lengthening as if it was calculated in dog years. More and more I longed for a do-over, especially now.

I turned the conversation back to my lack of Italian. "I'm trying to learn but am afraid it will take forever. When I shop, I end up pointing or fumbling with my little dictionary. It's embarrassing. Sometimes I buy weird things. And I really want to learn to cook Italian while we're here." I confessed to serving horse meat thinking it was beef, making her chuckle.

"There are many language schools around and I know there are Italians who would like to exchange Italian conversation for English. It helped me when I first arrived. Before I met Fausto, my first husband. The one who didn't work out. Bad in bed, to say the least."

She winked before continuing. "And maybe you should think about a cooking school. There are many here catering to tourists and expats."

"I found someone to help, but the person knows nothing about cooking." Maggie raised her eyebrows at my obvious evasion but didn't comment.

When I put my cup back in its saucer to leave, Maggie said, "Wait a moment." She turned to her kitchen and returned with a thick book in hand.

"It's an extra copy. It's been my favorite cookbook ever since I gave up soda bread and corned beef in favor of spaghetti and risotto."

I looked at the title: *L'Arte di Mangiar Bene,* The Art of Eating Well—Maggie translated—rather different from the ones I'd soon unpack from a shipping crate. I'd always loved to cook and harbored pipe dreams of becoming the new Alice Waters, but *Joy of Cooking* was as far as I'd gotten.

Touched by the gesture, I said, "Next time, it's my turn."

We'd become friends immediately, but it was much too early to reveal any matters of the heart.

****

Despite my new friend and the constant effort to

juggle family demands, my thoughts were consumed by Alessandro mixed with fantasies about love and sexual fulfillment. I'd had similar but vague thoughts about Martin before we'd married, but the thoughts about Alessandro were vivid, thoughts which percolated to the surface inspired by the romance of Rome and the couples I'd watched as they sat in cafes or walked in the parks where I took Sophie to play. The beautiful parks with orange trees, cypress, and umbrella pines. Always lovers strolling hand in hand or embracing, mirroring the erotic statues and paintings in the museums I visited after shopping.

Before Martin, my previous experience with sex was limited to fumbling with a pimply kid in the afternoons at his house, an activity neither bothered to continue after a month. At least Martin didn't fumble during our engagement or the following year. And then it seemed a barrier between us was raised. Was it innocent but difficult Sophie, was it me, or some unknown factor?

Definitely, I told myself. I would not succumb to an affair, wouldn't go to the bar again to avoid making domestic life even more difficult than it was. Definitely. But when the day arrived, my nerve endings frizzed with anticipation. I gave in, telling myself he wouldn't be there after I'd fled the week before.

Yet there he was at the same table. We looked at each other, silent, until I said, "The term you were looking for in English is 'hedgerow.' Now, where were we?" I hoped my tone was business-like.

We worked—heads close—translating for thirty minutes. When I couldn't handle the nearness any longer, I said, "You wanted to hear about American food.

Here's a story." I sat up straight. He did too but he continued to incline his head toward me to listen. The distance I should have wanted didn't materialize and I was glad.

"There used to be places where you could drive into a kind of parking lot where there was a speaker. You could order hamburgers and a root beer over an intercom and a waitress on roller skates would serve them on a tray hooked to the window of your car door."

He looked puzzled but politeness made him say, "I hope there will be something like that when I go." His smile was genuine.

We continued with innocuous simple conversation until I looked at a clock on the wall filled with photos of people who must have been famous patrons.

"Can I have your phone number in case I cannot come next time?"

"Very sorry but I do not have a phone. My *padrona* will give message."

I didn't offer mine and he didn't ask. So far, he'd made no remark I could interpret as encouraging me beyond language lessons. I was simultaneously relieved and disappointed.

CHAPTER THREE

Restless nights spent brooding about betraying Martin, even if only in my thoughts, and worrying about Sophie compelled me to compose a message for Alessandro: I was too busy with family to meet any more. But I couldn't bring myself to call his landlady even though we had no future. I would only be in Rome for less than two years. He was a medical student, intending on cardiology and would be leaving for an residency in a year or so. But I thought of a friend's advice at my Seattle going-away party.

"Have some fun Italian style," she'd said. I decided to follow it, and, instead of breaking off, the meetings with Alessandro became the fixed point around which my week revolved. His presence both soothed and excited me.

In the time between trying to study Italian through newspapers and the endless job managing in Rome, I continued to take the children to parks, archeological sites and museums on weekends. When they were in school, I walked the city alone, listening to church bells mixing with the cacophony made by buses, cars, scooters, and motorinos roaring through the narrow streets. I was enchanted with the fountains and obelisks, antique shops, coffee bars in piazzas and small shops filled with handmade shoes and handbags like those in a fashion magazine. I wasn't sure how much Martin earned, but for the first time we weren't short of money. Using my expanding vocabulary, I bought high-style sunglasses, sandals and a scarf like Sophia Loren wore in films, and designer silk ties for Martin. Tyler picked his own clothes but I bought dresses for Sophie in the lavish shops specializing in clothes for children even though she resisted entering, wanting instead to be bribed with a gelato first.

But Martin's money didn't make a full life. While I was grateful for the opportunity to sample Rome's cultural and emotional richness, Alessandro had filled the empty emotional hole in my existence.

One day, I discovered the San Clemente church with its crazy-quilt of architectural styles, one built atop the other echoing the city's history. The intense and glowing mosaic colors in the top layer reminded me of Alessandro who radiated a life force drawing me ever nearer despite my recognition of danger. I avoided the confessionals on my way to the level below the main church.

There, the faded, cardboard flat, and rigid figures of the medieval frescoes echoed Martin's demeanor. But the altar at the lowest level, with the carving of the ancient god Mithras killing a bull, was beyond my ability to comprehend. Disturbed by thoughts about the two men combined with a rite involving blood and death, I shivered as I climbed back to the warm sunlight and headed to Maggie's front door hoping for easy small talk.

****

"I'm glad you caught me. I was about to pick up the dry cleaning but it can wait. Come on in." Maggie held her door open wide. She'd quickly become my anchor and guide to all domestic things in Rome.

Now she brewed espresso and poured two cups. "How are you doing? I haven't seen much of you lately."

"It's hard here. I've found there's no double tasking." I glanced into my tiny cup to see a perturbed face reflected until steam blurred the image. I regretted that I'd bothered her. "I'd better go so you can do your shopping before the stores close for siesta."

"You aren't taking my time and you only arrived. I'm always happy to see you. Sit a while." After a drink of coffee, she said, "I know so many other women whose husbands are all-consumed by their work. I would hate to think you will have spent your stay in Rome without meeting people who are your age, not middle-aged like me, content with family."

"It's difficult with two children. And especially Sophie. She's bright and loves school but is a loner. I don't think she has friends. I've talked to her teacher who doesn't seem concerned but I am." I tried not to remember the incident where she'd torn her constant companion Threadbare apart.

"My Francesca—the one in Parma—was like your Sophie, but everything is fine now, thank the Good Lord. Don't worry so much. Get out when you can. Rome's too wonderful to waste time worrying. Kids are resilient."

"Thank you. You are a lovely soul." I caught myself twisting my wedding ring around my finger.

"There's more, isn't there?"

"Yes." I looked at my shoes.

Maggie placed her hand over my rings. "Tell me, if you want to."

The door to this confessional opened and I couldn't resist entering. "It's just...well, Martin and I don't get along much anymore, haven't for several years and it's become even worse since we arrived. I was sure we would be better in a new environment, and I wanted to live in Europe. But sometimes he's angry and I think he blames me; other times he's spaced out like he's far away. And he travels for work all the time for the defense company. Now I look forward to his absence even though I think it affects the children."

"Oh, my dear, I'm sorry to hear this." She took my hand.

Now I couldn't shut up. "Maybe some of it comes from Martin being orphaned as a kid. He doesn't seem to know how to be an easygoing dad like I'd hoped. And, to make things even more complicated, you remember I mentioned finding someone to exchange Italian and English conversation with?"

"And—"

"It's working out differently than I expected. And I'm having a tough time dealing with it." I could feel a flush radiating up from my neck as I tried to sit still on her sofa as portraits of Orazio's stern-looking ancestors glared at me.

"Tell me if you wish."

I sat back to tell Maggie the story. After, I said, "There's no advice you can give me, I know, but I needed to talk to help find my way."

"I wouldn't presume to advise or criticize, and you remember I told you about my first marriage, so you mustn't think you're the only one who has had uncomfortable choices to make. I hope you don't define yourself as a caretaker, an appendage. You *will* find your way, I'm sure because Rome is so full of opportunities. And I'll be here to listen if you need."

So adult and sensible. Just what I needed. I was

determined not to become an appendage to a distant husband and thus fell into a double life rather than make a choice.

****

Alessandro and I met twice a week. To control my raging emotions, I stayed away from subjects which could be misconstrued as provocative. I asked questions about Rome and told him about life in the United States. I honored his request to tell him how patients like to be spoken to in America by imagining how I would want to be told.

I struggled, wanting to be with him—not to talk about the newspaper headlines or hamburgers but to learn the details of his life and his hopes for his future. Not cardiology but other matters of the heart. It wasn't hard to sense he too was finding our meetings ever more difficult as he began a sentence on some innocuous subject then stuttered to a halt. As the space between our discussion topics lengthened, the tension increased.

One day he said, "Nicole, you never talk about you, what you want in life. Let's not talk about American food anymore." He placed his warm hand over mine. I could feel his pulse beating at the same rapid pace, throbbing throughout my body.

I wanted to tell him I needed love, comfort, and encouragement but couldn't articulate the words. I wanted to say it was important to be a good mother, and I wanted to say some time I'd make up for dropping out of school—become a professional like most of my friends who'd gone on to graduate and start careers.

To break the dangerous spell, I reached for my coffee with the other hand, but accidentally knocked over the cup, spilling it on the table. He withdrew his hand to wipe the mess away.

"Will you come again next week?"

I mumbled, "Yes." He gathered his books and hurried away. I was rooted to the chair, my mind racing with anticipation I could not tamp down.

****

When I got back to our apartment Martin was home. "Where were you?"

"Working on my Italian. I need the language if you want me to manage here."

"There's laundry in my suitcase."

I could feel my face contort in anger. He looked alarmed and added, "Nice to be home. What's for dinner?" It didn't quell my rage. It was easier to manage without his presence and I hoped he'd be off again soon.

CHAPTER FOUR

I forced myself to help with Sophie's reading, attend Tyler's soccer games and school events, and cook Martin's favorites, beefsteak and baked potatoes, when I wanted to serve *pasta fagioli, spaghetti alla carbonara,* and *Carciofi alla Giudea,* dishes I tried to make from the cookbook Maggie had given me. No matter how much I crammed into the day, the nights were interminable, my mind a spinning galaxy filled with thoughts about Alessandro, our next meeting, versus my obligations to the project I'd so willingly and naively taken on: my widower husband and the two children.

****

Alessandro held the poetry book again when I arrived at the exceptionally-noisy bar. He was so beautiful everything else faded into the background.

As I slipped my arm out of my jacket, Alessandro said, "It's a beautiful day. Why don't we go to the Villa Borghese for a walk?"

Spring 1994 had already arrived in Rome on this early March Monday, not like Seattle, which would still be encased in dreary wet weather. Sun flooded in from the window illuminating the bar and its occupants. I knew it was a risk but I said, "Yes, let's," anyway. Martin was traveling again.

The park was deserted except for a few joggers and nannies chatting while their charges ran around. We walked the statue-lined path to the lake to look at the little temple to Asclepius, the Greek god of healing, on the water's edge. A man rowed a small boat while his female passenger leaned against a cushion. The slow splash of the oars made gentle ripples on the otherwise still waters. I watched the woman dangle her fingers in the lake. When she lifted her languid hand, I could see it was devoid of a wedding ring but the drips from her fingers made little rings of their own in the water.

I glanced at Alessandro to see his gaze was fixed on the couple. He must have felt my need, the need I'd tried to disguise. He turned to me.

"Nicole?"

"Yes." I meant to make the word a question rather than a statement.

He took my hand. The touch heated my entire body. He leaned close to my ear. "You must know I'm in love with you. I've tried so hard not to be but you are in my mind day and night."

Lost in his confession and his brown eyes' fathomless pools, I fell ever downward into a pit from which there was no escape. But I didn't want to escape. "I know what you're going to say, but I'm afraid. Please don't say more. It's wrong." I put my finger on his lips to quiet them, but my touch was too tender to stop him. Or me.

"My apartment isn't far. It's small, like a closet, I'm sure nothing like where you live. But please."

I looked away from him to watch the couple in the boat. The woman leaned toward the man; her arm now outstretched as if to stroke his cheek. Their boat rocked. I turned back toward Alessandro, unable to resist the burning message of desire coursing through my body.

We walked in silence along the path toward a residential area with him holding my hand as I stumbled, vision unfocused. We climbed three flights to his apartment. I leaned against him on the threshold with eyes closed as he fumbled with the lock before opening the door.

I opened my eyes to see a small room, one corner reserved for cooking with a hotplate and tiny refrigerator, another with a desk and chair. Medical texts were strewn everywhere. A student's garret.

Alessandro swept the books off the bed before he returned to the doorway to take me in his arms. I trembled as another sensation of heat washed over me, my body aching with desire. Tears of happiness rolled down my cheeks. He held my face in both hands as he kissed the tears before slowly undressing me, first the jacket. Then my dress. I kicked off my shoes. He paused before removing my lingerie, kissing me tenderly before he continued. I stood still, eyes locked onto his. When I was free from the confining clothing, I unbuckled his belt.

We fell onto the bed, bodies as one, ravenous for each other. The world spun away. Solely this room, this bed, this man remained as my senses exploded into a spiral nebula of pleasure. An ecstasy I never knew could exist.

Afterward, I was silent as I watched him brew espresso. A fine gold chain around his neck lay against his honey-colored skin and the brown mole on his lower back. When I looked at his broad shoulders tapering to a narrow waist, muscular hips and legs, his body reignited my passion. He returned to the rumpled bed with two tiny cups, the fragrance of the coffee joining with his aftershave, the smell of his body, and of lovemaking. I knew I would never again drink espresso without remembering the moment.

We did not need to talk as we wordlessly explored the delights of each other's bodies until an hour later when I saw the bedside clock reminding me I needed to leave soon. After one last caress, I found my discarded clothes.

"Please, don't leave yet." He took my hand to stay me.

I fell back in his arms. We lay side by side, for a few moments until he raised himself with one elbow. "Nicole, will you come to me again?"

"I will come here every Monday and Thursday, if you want."

"I want so much."

I desperately desired to spend the night, to dine at a small trattoria while sitting outside in the warm evening sharing a meal of the tender little Roman artichokes in oil followed by *Spaghetti alle Vongole Veraci* made with the freshest baby clams still in their shells, and *panna cotta* surrounded by tiny wild strawberries and currents for dessert. We'd finish a bottle of pinot grigio and share an espresso before strolling in fountain-graced piazzas with other lovers before returning to his apartment. A life I'd dreamed about since my friends had gone off on their junior year abroad and sent postcards of castles and palaces while I was newly married with an infant.

But I knew none of this dream could ever come true and instead, I blindly stumbled home to my lonely apartment.

****

Our affair continued throughout the spring. Several

times when Martin was away, I toyed with asking Maggie to babysit after school so I could spend the day with Alessandro. But I could not do it. Betraying my husband was bad enough. Taking time from the children's lives was too much.

Even so, she picked up on my confusion during our coffee times. One day she said, "Don't get hurt my dear."

"Not to worry," I hoped my words conveyed conviction to Maggie and to me, even though I was alternately ashamed and thrilled with the affair. I was undone by my need for love, for sex, to have my body melt into his as time was both suspended and rushing simultaneously. Italian lessons were forgotten except for the language of love from the poets and from Alessandro himself.

When we were satiated on those few stolen times, we shared wine or coffee at a nearby bar where he'd softly run a finger over the tender inside of my wrist as if checking my pulse while we chatted about nothing in Italian and English, searching for the right word in either language to express love. We never spoke of our future because there wasn't one. We were encased in a magical soap bubble—thin, prismatic, fragile. It would inevitably burst.

****

One May morning, I woke to an unexpected sensation. Something was different. I became queasy after coffee hit my stomach with a thud. I made it to the bathroom without a moment to spare. "It can't be," I thought, "I'm on the pill."

I looked at the packet to convince myself I'd taken them regularly. Half the pills from the previous month and all from this month were still in the blister pack. I looked at the mess in the sink. How could I have been so careless? Or maybe it was an unconscious desire for another child, one from a man who embodied what I desired in life, that had defeated my good judgment.

Tyler's face was in a book while he devoured toast loaded with butter and jam. He ran a damp finger around the plate to gather crumbs before he shut the book and put the plate in the sink.

"Bye, Nicole," he squeaked in his changing voice before he skipped down the stairs two at a time to the bus stop.

Sophie, ever more independent, had fixed a bowl of cereal without spilling but lingered in the kitchen, finger in mouth, staring at me. I was sure the child's sensitive antennae picked up my shock. I took her hand to walk down the stairs to the pickup spot for the kindergarten's van.

"Kiss, please," Sophie said as she raised her arms to me. I happily obliged.

The apartment was quiet, the day already unseasonably warm. Perspiration formed around my hairline and between my breasts. Carrying a baby through the hot Roman summer would be unpleasant, but the thought of another child made me happy and I could deal with my future when we returned to Seattle. But what would Martin do? Surely not divorce me, the housekeeper and mother to his two children.

The past several years I'd made repeated efforts to bridge the gap between us. I wanted to recover the time I'd felt enveloped in love when I agreed to marry the handsome widower with a small son. All those divine dinners and walks in West Seattle and the Arboretum we shared. But soon his enthusiasm muted. Once, when we'd gone to bed, I said: "Martin, don't you love me?"

And he'd mumbled, "Of course I do," before he pretended to breathe slowly as if he was asleep. True, he'd come home with flowers the next day, but the gesture was too insignificant to heal the wound and left me wondering if he had a mistress. I'd never asked again but whatever his problem was, it was clear something was up. But what?

Recently, maybe sensing my newfound sensuality, he'd taken me to dinner or approached me at bedtime. Our intimacy, if it could be called such, made me want Alessandro even more. Could my pregnancy be the result of Martin's exertions? I hoped not. I wanted it to be Alessandro's baby, a reminder of our love and a child in whose eyes I would always see him. *Martin would just have to deal with it,* I told myself.

I had a momentary vision of moving with the children to New York to be with Alessandro when he departed Rome. Martin might consider it kidnapping, a possessiveness toward the children as proof of his virility but little more. How could I be married for years to someone I now recognized I barely knew but feel I'd known Alessandro all my life?

But could Alessandro as a medical resident possibly manage a sudden ready-made family with two children he'd never met and another on the way? I put the absurd fantasy aside. Besides, we'd all be back in Seattle in about eighteen months and I could make plans including Martin or not in my personal life. Whatever happened, I'd never leave Tyler and Sophie, nor attempt to tear them away from their father.

But how *would* Martin react to the pregnancy? He'd never expressed happiness at having Tyler and Sophie.

He wasn't cruel, just distant as if he didn't know how to be a father. So often Tyler looked to me for validation of his projects and activities. Sophie, who openly craved her father's attention tried in every way to keep him to herself, hanging on his arm, climbing into his lap, even blocking his way. Sometimes he responded and would read her a story or listen to her prattle on. Other times he ignored her. It was distressing.

Martin was often lost in his thoughts and endured broken sleep, sometimes crying out in a nightmare. Maybe he feared further loss after his parents died in a car accident when he was five. He was in the car when it skidded on black ice and ended upside down in a ditch. He said he was shuffled off to a fanatically religious aunt until he escaped to join the Army and get shipped to Vietnam. And then there was his first wife's death. All he'd told me was her name was Yvette, daughter of French planters who'd fled their rubber plantation during the war. They married in 1978. But she died of cancer in 1986.

****

I sat on the edge of the bathtub to calm down. *Be practical,* I told myself. What about a doctor? What was an OB-GYN called here? I wished I was back in Seattle where everything was simple.

I bought a pregnancy test at the local pharmacy. Too distracted to do the grocery shopping I knocked on Maggie's door. "I…I just wondered if you were up for a coffee?"

"Oh dear, I'm sorry but my grandson Ludo needs some help for a school project so I can't today."

I felt Maggie's scrutiny before she opened the door wider and said, "Is something wrong?"

"No, I just hoped for some company. How about next week? At my place." I must have succeeded in hiding my need.

"Yes, I'll plan on it." She took one more look at me before I could turn away.

I returned to the quiet apartment and lit a candle Maggie had given me in the hope it would be soothing. The shutters were down and I sat in the half-dark watching the flame flicker, the sandalwood scent perfuming the air. When I snuffed the wick, a trail of smoke from the spent flame curled upward, as if to pass on an obscure message. I examined the lazy coils, trying to decipher the meaning. In the end there wasn't any.

I cleaned already clean cupboards until Sophie came home. Not only was she unusually clingy, but Tyler noticed my mental absence.

When he returned from orchestra practice, he asked "Are you okay? I mean…" His words trailed off but the concern on his face was obvious. I tousled his hair and said it was just a headache. No way would I allow myself to feed his fear he might lose another mother through illness or departure from the family.

****

I took the test kit to the garbage container on the street below our apartment the following morning after my hopes and fears were confirmed. The day was brilliant, warm and sunny, perfect to welcome the existence of a Roman baby. I walked the ancient cobbled streets to organize my mind. I'd tell my parents during our weekly phone call after Martin had digested the news. I hoped they'd be happy to have another grandchild although I had to wonder if they would even pay attention, with Dad's continuing love affair with

Kentucky bourbon and Mom's enabling, alternating between fluttering around him to beg him to go to AA or doping up on tranquilizers to calm herself. He was a senior manager at the biggest hardware store in Seattle, founded during the 1898 Gold Rush. A crate of tools fell from a height and sheared off his forearm when he was inspecting their warehouse years earlier. He couldn't adjust to the prosthesis and the pain never passed, leading him to self-medicate with alcohol. Something I'd have to face when I got back to Seattle next year along with the fact I didn't think either of them had ever approved of my marriage although they never said anything. It almost made me feel middle-aged dealing with parents and children.

I stopped at a café near the Colosseum for an overpriced panino with a glass of sparkling water. Tourists competed with each other for a place to sit, sprawling in exhaustion as soon as they found one. Lost in my own world again, the tourists blended into the Roman scene. They didn't help provide any answer to the most immediate dilemma: Should I tell Alessandro or just break the relationship without giving a reason? If I did give him my news, how would he react—happy, horrified, indifferent? For a fleeting moment I dreamed he begged me to leave Martin and go with him to New York. Ridiculous.

I returned to the apartment to sweep the terrace. At least there would be a positive outcome until the next round of dust from crumbling monuments or a sirocco carrying dead locusts blew in from North Africa. Then I showered, put on fresh makeup and did my hair before Martin returned from work. He didn't notice.

"How was your day? You look tired." We were at

the dinner table eating pot roast.

"Busy day at the office. As usual."

"I finally got the terrace cleaned."

"Any more of this?" He held out his plate. Tyler followed his lead.

I cleared the table the moment he put his fork down after the second helping. Furious at him and at myself for marrying him, a glass slipped from my hand. It shattered on the terrazzo floor. Tyler hurried into the kitchen to offer to help but I waved him out. I needed to be alone.

Night had fallen and my reflection in the kitchen window stared back. An angry face. I told myself to relax, to remember if I hadn't married Martin, I wouldn't have met Alessandro. It was pointless to blame Martin for who he was. The baby had to be Alessandro's, conceived in love, not boredom. In any case, I'd have to tell Alessandro. The affair was over.

I called his landlady to let him know I'd meet him at the bar instead of his apartment.

****

Hoping for some comfort, I knocked on Maggie's door. She gave me a kiss on both cheeks as usual, then stepped back a pace.

"Tell me, dear."

"I…" I put my hand on my belly without thinking.

"Are you pregnant?"

The perceptive question solved my fear of making some histrionic announcement or keep stuttering. "Yes, but how did you know?"

"Orazio always said he could see it in my eyes, but I think it's because you had your hand on your stomach last week and again now."

I put my hand in my jeans pocket. "Martin is going

to be really upset. And, you know what, I don't care." A semi-lie if there is such a thing. "He didn't want more children."

"What about your friend? Have you told him?"

"Not yet, and I don't know how. I'm sure it's his. I mean, I want it to be his. But I don't know how to tell either of them."

"Obviously, you won't be able to hide the fact for long. The new child is the most important thing. It will need love, love no matter what."

"I know. Everything is so confusing now." I broke down and wept. Maggie put her arms around me as we sat awkwardly side-by-side.

"Don't worry, all will work out and you will have a new child to nurture and bring you happiness."

If only it was so simple.

****

Instead of the usual shower, I ran a bath the day I would use careful and gentle words when I met Alessandro at the bar to give him the news. I let the water flow until the deep tub was full and sunk down to my neck, washcloth draped over my face. How much longer did I have before I told Martin? I sat up to look at my belly, my breasts. Maybe a little thickening, but the real change wouldn't show for a few more weeks. Martin would be upset, although how upset remained to be seen. The real issue was Alessandro, my lover, the father.

I rinsed off and prepared to face a day like no other. I arrived at the bar early and ordered a *camomilla*. The cup rattled in the saucer when I carried it to the table. Unable to concentrate, I couldn't get the teabag from its wrapper to dunk it in the hot water. Every few seconds I glanced at the door. Maybe he wouldn't come. Problem solved. But I needed to see him one last time to tell him I would love him forever.

His figure was surrounded by radiant sunlight when he opened the door to the bar. I sucked in my breath as he neared the table with a bewildered expression.

"Nicole?"

"I have to tell you something." I paused to take a sip to prepare for the next sentence. The astringent taste made my mouth pucker. There was no point in evasion and I needed to get it over, my anxiety swamping my plan for a careful, gentle approach. I blurted, "I'm pregnant. I can't see you anymore. I can't leave the other children. I should never have begun this, this…affair."

I watched the color drain from his face. I'd made an utter mess of the situation. Without giving him a chance to speak, I fled to the sidewalk in tears.

From a distance I heard him say, "Wait. Please, Nicole, wait." Wary of tripping, I walked as fast as I could, but he caught up and stopped in front to face me. "Stop, please. Don't run away. I want to know about you. And the baby. Don't turn away from me. It's lovely news. We'll figure something out." He stroked my wet cheek with the back of his hand before I could turn away.

The pedestrians who crowded the sidewalk parted and then merged again as if we were merely a rock in a river. I remained with my face turned away, unable to look in his eyes for fear I'd relent. He cupped my chin to raise my face to his. "Please return. We must talk about this."

"It's over. It had to end anyway. I'm sure the baby is yours, and I will always love you. Always." I shook off his hand and continued to the tram stop. He didn't follow but I could hear him say, "Nicole, Nicole, let me know when…" After I boarded the tram, I saw him standing where I'd left him. He looked desolate.

"Oh, God, what have I done to him? Why did I even tell him?" I realized I spoke aloud when an old woman in black turned around to stare at me.

"*Con calma, signorina,*" the woman said before ringing the bell to descend at the next stop.

I watched the arthritic woman struggling with her grocery bags as she hobbled away from the tram. I wept for the old woman, for myself, for Alessandro, and for the baby who would never know its father.

Tears soaked my face as I stumbled back to the empty apartment.

CHAPTER FIVE

The American consulate gave me a list of English-speaking obstetricians. I made an appointment with an Englishwoman, gray-haired and well-loved to judge from the photos of smiling mothers and toothless babies sporting bows on their bald heads lining her office's walls. After the exam she said, "I'm so happy for you and your husband. You are about two months along now."

"Where does one go to have babies here?"

"There's a clinic called Saint Gerard Majella I recommend. It's named for a patron saint of pregnancy. It's on Via Alessandria. I anticipate your due date in mid-December."

I gasped at the street name.

My emotions rocketed around like a pinball machine, veering from desire for another child and worry about Martin's reaction.

****

One evening, after the children had already scurried from the dinner table, I leaned over him to serve coffee. He put out his hand for the cup, but his head jerked back, gaze focused on my abdomen. His eyebrows shot up before they sunk into a scowl.

"Surely it's not true." He put out his hand as if to touch my stomach.

I stepped back a pace, defiance and guilt battling in

my head. "It's true."

"And you know I don't want another."

We glared at each other until Martin broke the silence with a loud voice. "So, whose is it?"

"Keep your voice down." Fortunately, Tyler was engrossed with a noisy soccer match on the TV in his room. Sophie was in hers with the door shut. "We do have sex once in a while, or don't you remember?"

"Bullshit. You've been looking all too pleased with yourself lately. I ask you again, who-is-the-father?"

I faltered in my determination to win the face off, "I'm not sure."

He scoffed, "So you've found consolation to escape my supposed faults?"

"I found it because of me. I didn't intend to hurt you."

Martin stood so fast it was as though a rocket had exploded under him. He shoved his chair away from the table. It fell over, legs in the air as if in submission. "How dare you? You've humiliated me."

"Tell me, Martin—what do you want from me? I'm like your housekeeper. I've had no independent life. What kind of a marriage is that? I care for the children I adore and will never neglect them. I don't know if you're the father or not. What the hell difference does it really make to you. You're never here!"

Martin turned away without righting the chair. He stopped and turned back, taking a few paces toward me, raising his hand and pointing a finger in my face. "What more do you want from me? I pay for your life here. I pay for the children's needs. You damn well know what I want. Peace. Peace and quiet at home. All I ever asked for." He was shouting. "And remember, coming here is what you wanted. So, do whatever you want, you…you…but you'd better…" He spluttered to a stop before saying, "I'll throw you out if you even have one thought about taking *my* children away. That's what kind of difference it makes." His face drained from red to white, almost ghostly, his eyes glazed.

I stood my ground still holding the coffee cup. "Do you really care for the children? Sometimes it doesn't seem like it."

"How could you say such a thing! They are my own and I love them."

"Then show it."

I saw his eyes water. A moment later he turned away and I heard the apartment door slam as he left without a jacket or hat. I poured the half-full cup of cold coffee into the sink and returned to the dining table to prop my head in my hands tightly in an unsuccessful attempt to hold my thoughts still.

Where had he gone? Why couldn't he show love after the first year or so? What would he do when he returned? Would I come home from shopping tomorrow to find the locks changed? If he made life hell, I'd have no choice but to return to Seattle before his contract was up and somehow begin life as a single parent with the new baby. Maybe I could take Sophie, but likely Martin would never let Tyler go. I might have to live with my parents who would look at me and think, "I told you so," while I dealt with whatever their problems were now. Oh God!

The next morning Martin came home to pack a suitcase, saying he was off on a business trip somewhere. When he returned days later, he appeared to ignore the situation. I was baffled at his passive-aggressive behavior keeping me off balance. I eventually concluded he needed me to continue domestic services while he was in Rome in return for ignoring a child he didn't want—his idea of peace. When we returned to Seattle, I could make a decision about my future which would not be a continuation of our current relationship whatever I'd thought, or more likely didn't bother to think, six years earlier.

I'd been so enamored at first.

We'd met at a jazz concert at the University of Washington in 1988 at a time when I was intent on breaking out on my own and not knowing how. Martin was a prince in waiting, sitting next to me at the concert, a charming and handsome man. Sophisticated. A widower with a small boy and charisma. So self-assured as he talked about his success as a real-estate agent after returning from Vietnam, and how he enrolled in law school on the GI Bill. How impressed I'd been when he told me he'd interned at a big law firm in Seattle the previous summer and planned to work for them after graduation the following year.

I'd wanted to make my life sound interesting. But what had there been to say? I was a freshman with a job as a part-time secretary, bored at home and undecided on a major but leaning toward English Lit for lack of any other idea. I'd gone through pledge week and was rejected. The rejection stung more than anything so far in my life.

Martin appeared at just the right time to help sooth my vulnerability. He seemed so interested in me. Maybe he was then.

"I just love to cook," "I wish I had a brother," "Wow—you're on law review," "Tyler is such a good kid." I'd offered adoration on a platter with my gushing words. Martin ate it up and I'd basked in his attention.

Now it was hard to remember the fun we'd had early on: pizza with Tyler, listening to jazz in local nightspots, picnics at Gas Works Park, watching the salmon run at the Ballard Locks, or our visits to Longacre to watch the horse races. Once he bet on a sure loser and won $1500. He gave me half, saying, "Go shopping for something you'd like."

I'd felt so secure with my man but there was no basking now, no little-girl dependency.

One evening I caught a questioning look in Tyler's eyes during dinner. He'd been withdrawn although Sophie told us about her school day as he sat fooling with a broccoli chicken casserole. Afterwards, I followed him into his bedroom and sat on a corner of his bed while he fiddled with a model airplane.

"Tyler, hon, do you want to talk? You know I'm always here for you."

Tyler shrugged, keeping his face turned toward the plane.

"Please don't be upset. It's just Dad has a lot of responsibilities at work. And I'm going to have a baby in December. I don't know if it's a girl or a boy."

"Whatever." He picked up the model to glue the wings to the body.

I wanted to put my arms around his adolescent body but knew he'd shy away—a boy not yet ready to deal with adult situations like his stepmother and his father having sex or disagreeing.

"Remember, I will always love you. And if you're feeling bad you know we can talk things over whenever you want."

He briefly inclined his head in my direction, almost as a benediction. I left, quietly closing the door to his room.

I wasn't sure what or how to tell Sophie but when I tried to give her a cuddle one day a couple of months later, she said, "You're so fat. I can't get close any more."

"It's how mommies get as the baby grows just like when I had you and Tyler's mother had him. You'll have a sweet little brother or sister to play with."

Sophie wriggled away. "Don't want anybody."

I watched her face scrunch up. Tears followed. "Honey, I have enough love for all of you." My efforts at soothing her were unsuccessful.

"Don't want, don't want," she wailed and ran to her room. I heard her throw her precious books on the floor. I waited until quiet prevailed before tip-toeing into the room. I held out my arms but she ignored me, her arms folded, mouth turned down in her usual sulk.

How would Sophie, a child who refused to play with dolls and desperate for her father's attention, adjust to what she'd see as a living competitor in the apartment, especially one who would have to share her bedroom? My parenting books said minor exhibitions of jealousy were normal. What was minor? The teddy bear incident shortly after arrival in Rome came to mind.

I enrolled Sophie in several summer day camps and spoke with the camp counselors who agreed to keep watch. Fortunately, she enjoyed the opportunities, and according to the counselors, played with other children.

Tyler was invited for holidays by a succession of friends whose parents owned homes in the mountains or the seaside to escape the scorching summer heat. The air in Rome felt as though it had already been breathed by others as it stagnated in the apartment with the shades drawn tight. And there were mosquitos lurking. Tiny bats stirred at twilight but didn't get them all. I bought mosquito coils. They smoldered in the bedrooms with their faint chemical odor warding off the whine of the insects looking for blood.

Life carried on as the months dragged toward my due date. School began again. Martin operated on his own schedule and the apartment was silent during the day. My disc player had disappeared during the move and I bought a radio to listen to Italian pop songs. Maybe the baby heard them too.

To occupy the time, I concentrated on the recipes from *The Art of Eating Well,* the book Maggie had gifted me. Every day I'd open the pages at random and pick a pasta, main dish, or dessert. I'd become proficient in converting measurements, using grams instead of ounces, liters and milliliters for liquid measurements, Centigrade for Fahrenheit. I could order an *etto* and knew how many slices of prosciutto there should be. But I also began to subconsciously measure the people in my life: Martin and Alessandro, Sophie and Tyler, Maggie and me, the traits and characteristics of us all for good or ill.

When my contractions began, Martin drove me to the private clinic on Via Alessandria. My little girl's birth was easy, not like Sophie's, which had extended for over twenty hours. It was as if the baby was happy to enter the outside world to see what would happen next. I wished I knew some Italian lullabies to croon as I nursed her.

We remained at the clinic for four days, the Italian medical system less in a hurry to send new mothers and babies home. Martin visited once after the birth. He didn't carry flowers. I watched him as he observed the baby's face.

"Martin, what shall we name her?"

"I don't care. You choose."

Maggie's youngest daughter was named Maria Pia. I'd toyed with the name for my baby but it was just too much in Martin's face. "I'll name her Jenna after my grandmother."

"I'll be back tomorrow after work to collect you." But despite his cool words, he did touch the baby's tiny pink cheek for a moment.

****

Martin and I retrieved the older children from Maggie. Sophie refused to look at either me or Jenna. Tyler smiled at the baby and held her gingerly for a few minutes.

I wanted to set up the bassinet in our bedroom to ease Sophie's acceptance but Martin objected, saying he needed his sleep.

"I'll put the bassinet in the living room and sleep there."

"I'll take the hide-a-bed in my office instead. You can stay in the bedroom."

The small gesture of concern for me surprised and relieved me.

I called my mom later to tell her about the birth. She was thrilled the baby was named after her own mother and demanded photos to show her friends as soon as I could get them in the mail. She asked after Sophie and Tyler but didn't mention Martin, another relief.

****

Christmas arrived. The children seemed happy with

their new toys and Martin said he was pleased with the wallet and designer silk tie I'd bought last fall and stashed away. Maggie invited us to dinner complete with turkey, Brussels sprouts, and potatoes with a whiskey-soaked fruitcake covered in marzipan and icing for dessert. Martin loved it, and Sophie and Tyler laughed at the Christmas crackers with the little charm, tissue paper hat, and fortune. Mine said, "You will enjoy good health and financial independence."

****

About a month later, the two older children were in their own rooms after dinner and I played peek-a-boo with Jenna in a living room chair when Martin came home late from work. I could smell alcohol.

"Just so you know, they've asked me to stay on indefinitely and I've agreed. Tyler's doing well and I'm sure Sophie will too now she's in first grade. And I'm earning good money finally and I'll get home leave every year." He smiled as he leaned over my chair. "It's Rome for us now."

After I gathered my wits, I burst out, "How could you do this without talking to me? What about what *I* want? Don't you care? It's hard here with everything I have to do. What if I don't want to stay? What then, Martin?" The realization he must have been negotiating this for some time without bothering to talk to me was infuriating.

"If you want to hire someone to help out, do it. Or go back to Seattle with your baby, but remember, you go without *my* children." His words were tight, bitter, so different from his earlier casual words.

"And who would take care of Tyler and Sophie? Who? Tell me. And Jenna might be yours."

"Oh, get real, Look at her."

I didn't need to glance at Jenna in my arms for confirmation. She started to bawl, loud and long, unwilling to accept my effort to comfort her.

"You can tell the children. I'm not going to." I know it sounded petty but I just couldn't have gotten the words out in an adult way.

Through the open doors, I heard him give the news and the reactions. Tyler said, "Cool! I'll tell Nino and Raj tomorrow." Sophie said, "Miss Dodson will be happy. *She* likes me."

I'd willed myself to hang on for a few more months until Martin's contract was finished. It would be so much easier to live in Seattle, and despite Rome's banquet of attractions, the return home would speed healing my heart and maybe end my nights spent thinking of Alessandro while I fed Jenna.

Now it was Rome with family or Seattle with just Jenna. I needed to do the right thing for the children who, judging from their overheard responses, were happy to stay in Rome. Tyler loved his school and friends and the excursions all over Europe. Sophie's first-grade teacher, like her kindergarten teacher, said she was somewhat reserved around other children but was an academic star far ahead of her classmates. I could not bear to leave them. Jenna was half-Italian and deserved to be immersed in her heritage, even if she didn't know it. Someday I'd have to tell her.

I'd try once more to talk to Martin, get him to agree to make an effort to renew our earlier happy days; even suggest marriage counseling. I'd never expected I'd be the center of his universe but I didn't expect I'd be like planet Pluto either, downgraded to a nearly invisible speck in his life even before my fall from grace over the affair.

At breakfast the next morning, I said, "Martin, we must try harder for the children's sake. Would you agree to marriage counseling?"

"Look, I'm providing for you and the children, *all* of them, so let it be, will you?" He turned his attention to his office diary, flipping pages back and forth. "Got to go. Meetings again." He dumped the rest of his breakfast in the trash.

I took my coffee to the terrace to decide about my future. The fragrance from the lemon blossoms and the whisper of silver olive leaves gave me the answer: I must build my own life here until the two oldest could be on their own. Then I would leave with a clear conscience.

CHAPTER SIX

Jenna was six months old when she started on solid food. I delighted in the variety available beyond *pasta per bambino* in the local supermarket. Determined to have her be a true Italian at least in the food category, I toted home soft mixtures of chicken, veal, trout, rabbit or prosciutto, but skipped ostrich and horsemeat.

I donated my maternity clothes to a nearby Catholic church in hopes whoever got them would be blessed with an easy pregnancy and birth of a wanted child. The sense of closure was contrasted with a need to show Alessandro his beautiful daughter. When I looked at Jenna's golden soft skin, brown eyes and hair, I remembered his half-heard cry as I'd boarded the tram to run away: "Let me know." I assured myself enough time had passed so I wouldn't have trouble if we met. Still, I hesitated to contact him with all my "what ifs": he wouldn't see us, he'd already left for his residency, or would agree from curiosity, not fondness or love.

Taking a chance anyway, I called his landlady to say I'd like to meet him and would bring a new friend. The woman, who remembered my voice, agreed to convey the message. I bit my nails waiting for a response. The landlady called back after several days to say he wanted to meet. I said we would be near the lake in the Villa Borghese at ten the next day.

Alessandro was already in the park when we arrived.

I saw him in the distance scanning every passerby. His face lit up when he spotted us. He hurried in our direction and air-kissed me on each cheek in a formal gesture, one reserved for encountering friends on the street. Then he stepped away to look at Jenna.

"May I?"

"Yes, of course. I named her Jenna."

As he bent to gather his child, I could see tears trickle down his face. The slanting sunlight made them opalescent. He cradled the bonneted head and smiled when she gave a little kick with her tiny patent-leather shoes. I'd bought the shoes on a lark when I happened to walk by a store with a show window filled with delicious, extravagant baby clothes. The Mary Janes would never be walked in, but would serve as a memento of Jenna's early life. And the scene with Alessandro as a proud father.

We sat side by side on a bench, Jenna content in Alessandro's arms. I stared at the lake's shimmering reflection of the temple of Asclepius, wishing the ancient healer could bind my heart's wounds.

"How are your studies?" I dared not look at him.

"I leave for New York next month to be resident. I will return in three years or maybe more. After that, I hope to get a teaching post at La Sapienza and establish my studio. And you?"

"I am busy with all my children." So far, I hadn't come up with a satisfactory way to fulfill my objective of personal growth so what would I be in three years except older?

"Will I see you again? And Jenna?"

"I made a decision, and I must keep to it."

There was an uncomfortable silence until I added, "I

have my camera. Would you like me to take a photo of you and Jenna?" I held my breath hoping I hadn't cornered him.

I sensed the brief hesitation as he weighed the correct response—forget he ever had a child, or receive a photo acknowledging her existence with whatever consequences it might bring. He said yes and posed in front of the lake and its temple. I kept my eye on the viewfinder, afraid I'd fall into his arms and lock the three of us together if l let my attention waiver. I made sure the sun was behind me when I focused the lens. As I snapped the picture, Jenna raised one of her chubby legs in another small kick, her little face lit with joy at being alive. The shoe flew off as she kicked again. I retrieved it from the grass.

Silence surrounded us as we looked at the baby instead of each other. It lasted so long I was compelled to break it. "I should go. It will be time for Jenna's lunch soon. I'll have the photo developed and leave it at your landlady's apartment. Goodbye, Alessandro. I do wish you the best. I know you will be an excellent doctor." The Mary Jane dangled from my hand.

"Thank you for bringing the baby. She's a darling and I'm thrilled to see her. I'm sure she will have a charmed life with you and your family. Should she be in need you can contact me. I will do my best." He gave me the name of the teaching hospital in New York.

It was so formal I almost extended my hand, forcing him to do the same out of politeness. Worried I'd make a fool of myself, I dropped the camera back in my handbag and retrieved Jenna from his arms to place her in the stroller. She whimpered. I did not look back as we moved away on the graveled path toward a bus stop. The wheels of the stroller crunched on the stones, deadening the sound of my own halting sobs.

I took the roll containing the negative of Alessandro and Jenna, to the nearest photo shop and asked the clerk to develop two copies. When I retrieved them a few days later, I placed one in an envelope and took the tram to his apartment building to deliver the photo at a time when Alessandro would be in class. The landlady, delighted to be involved in what must be a romantic drama, said, "Your young man asked me to give this to you."

I took the package in both hands. It was wrapped in plain brown paper and tied with string but there was no name on it.

"I was in love once and I hope you two find a way out of whatever labyrinth you're in now." The woman placed a hand on Jenna's head and said in a soft voice, "*Ciao, tesoro.*" Jenna smiled and babbled.

"Yes, she's my treasure." I put the unopened package in my bag to privately experience the emotions it might unleash.

I sat on the terrace later to undo the paper to find the fragile book by Leopardi. It was easy to remember Alessandro's hesitation as he translated the *Infinity* poem into English. There was no inscription but I didn't need any to understand he wanted to give me a memory of a time when we loved without thinking about consequences. I found my copy of the photo of him holding Jenna to use as a bookmark for the poem.

****

A few months later, I took Jenna out for a walk to visit a bakery Maggie said made an especially excellent version of the thick-crusted Roman bread I loved. On the way, I passed what looked like a junk shop among the other small businesses: a bar, dry cleaner, a video rental place, and a shoe shop.

I stopped to look in the junk shop window on the way home. It was too dusty to see through with any clarity. Intrigued, I tried the door. It swung open with a creak but the interior was so dimly lit I assumed the clerk was absent. When my eyes adjusted, I saw an elderly man dressed in a threadbare suit sitting at the back with his face in a book. The book rested on a carved and battered table. His chair was high-backed and imposing, overwhelming his small size, as if the scene was an illustration from a fairy tale. He looked up as Jenna cooed, pushing his glasses to the top of his thick white hair.

"*Posso entrare?*"

"*Prego, signora.*" He gestured for me to enter.

I parked the stroller near the door and picked up Jenna to take a brief look around the space. It smelled of dust and disuse, of musty books and the old man's shaving lotion overtopped by my fresh bread's life-fulfilling aroma.

My intention was to return home to try a slice before the loaf cooled, but as I browsed, I grew fascinated by the objects. Portraits of elegant people dressed in eighteenth- and nineteenth-century clothes hung askew on the walls, gold-leaf frames chipped. They reminded me of Maggie's unloved paintings. Some tables held remains of old china dinner services, mostly Italian, but also some French and English marks I recognized. Fragile Venetian wine glasses, one or two remainders of what must have been sets of twelve or twenty-four, rested next to tarnished silver serving platters with engraved family crests. Many shelves held books. I picked out a few to browse. They were in Italian, Latin, German, English, Greek, and other languages I didn't recognize. The oldest were leather bound, the bindings worn and discolored from myriads of hands holding them over the years.

When Jenna sneezed, I turned toward the door to take her home.

"Might I hold her for a minute before you leave?" The old man's English was cultured and formal.

I hesitated to hand Jenna to an unknown person, but after looking at his kindly face, said. "Yes, for a moment." I put her into the man's open arms.

He held Jenna with care while he hummed a lullaby, a song I assumed he'd sung to his children and grandchildren long ago. Jenna's eyes drooped. I circled back every few minutes. After the third pass, he said, "Please don't be concerned. I loved having my grandchildren when they used to visit." He continued with the song ever more softly.

Embarrassed, I turned back to the treasures. One table held old terracotta jugs and bowls painted in traditional designs, all chipped or cracked. Another held oil lamps with mirrors to reflect light and wick-trimming tools hanging from chains. A group of terracotta figurines rested next to them. Their draped clothes were those worn by ancient Romans. I loved the absurd hairstyles worn by haughty empresses. But the men's faces looked like many I saw on the street. The shopkeeper could be a descendant.

I picked up a sculpted head, about eight inches tall. It was finely modeled, a beardless youth with short curly hair, wide brow and straight nose. It was as if a replica of Alessandro rested in my hands. I put it back on the table with care and turned back to the books, putting the living being out of my thoughts. Several shelves held books written by expatriates. I found one by a woman named Iris Origo—a biography of Leopardi. I asked its price.

After telling me the modest price, he said, "Marchesa Origo was a most fascinating woman. She wrote many books. My favorite is *Allegra*, about Lord Byron's illegitimate daughter. As if any child could be called illegitimate. All children are God's gift."

The old man continued, his face lighting at the reminiscence, "I met her once long, long ago. She was the kind of woman whose hand a man would kiss in homage. Her autobiography is titled *Images and Shadows.* I could find it for you if you wish. Oh signora, all women should have romance to keep them young and beautiful like she was." He bowed slightly from his seated position to avoid disturbing Jenna.

Images and shadows, my life since I'd come to Rome with what had become a shadow marriage temporarily eased by an affair leaving me with an indelible image of Alessandro.

"Please, I'd love to read an autobiography by a woman you met."

The old man moved stiffly from his chair to pass drowsy Jenna back to me. He walked to a shelf where he ran his forefinger over the spines until he found a dusty copy of the book. "Anything else, signora?"

I saw his longing for connection so I placed Jenna in the stroller so I could look for a romantic trinket to complement the books and remain with him a few minutes longer. I found a chipped Venetian goblet with gold dolphins on the stem and a ruby-red bowl. Then, as if my hand was on automatic, I picked up the sculpture of the young man's head.

When the parcels were wrapped, I placed them into the carry bag on the stroller while Jenna slept peacefully, little hands relaxed in a soft curl, mouth curved upward in a slightly crooked smile like Alessandro's. How sweet to be in a dream world. And how pleasant not to have pangs of loneliness upon waking.

****

The shop and its proprietor drew me back the following week. I introduced myself and asked his name. He produced a worn engraved calling card from his desk drawer and handed it over with a flourish.

I inspected the card, larger than an American business card. The words identified the bearer as one "Cavaliere Giulio Giovanni Battisti Boncompagni."

"I save this old card for sentimental reasons. It was a big and important family long ago. The *cavaliere* part is meaningless. My title before World War Two was "count." I don't used it. You can call me Julius. A bit like Caesar, although I never conquered anything in my life except my wife and she died thirty years ago."

"I'll call you *cavaliere*."

"Signora, you do me honor."

And so my visits to the fusty shop became a habit as regular as the visits with Maggie. The old man delighted in watching Jenna grow and how quickly she learned. He followed her as she took shaky baby steps and when she learned to run, careening around the laden tables. He read her children's stories in Italian and gave her sweets. Like a grandfather, he had no responsibilities but all the enjoyment.

One day I found an armchair placed in a corner near

his desk. It was richly upholstered in yellow damask but the cushion was in shreds from the many bottoms over the years. "For you, signora, when you read." Touched at the gesture, I sat while I sampled books. My conversations were limited to literature until he said, "Tell me, why is such a charming young woman like you here with me? Where is your lover?"

I looked up from a dog-eared copy of *Christ Stopped at Eboli*. The suit he'd worn every day, shiny with age, was put away for the summer. Instead, the old man wore a moth-eaten sweater vest over his striped shirt. He looked at me expectantly with his bushy gray eyebrows raised over inquisitive blue eyes. I saw the papery-thin skin around those eyes and the liver-spotted hands. He could be anyone's grandfather, including mine, neither of whom were alive when I was born.

"Oh, I'm in between right now. You're it for the present." I tried a bright smile and a jaunty tone.

"I do not believe this. I think you have lost someone most dear to you and you are sad. Heartbroken as you Americans say."

I could not help glancing at Jenna who was asleep in her stroller.

"He, the one you lost, is the father, isn't he? And he has gone away. You are lonely. Yes?"

I considered what to tell him: the truth, change the subject, or deny Alessandro. I'd told Maggie a few details but I found I wasn't yet through processing them. So, I told him about the man I loved, the pairing and parting, and how I was unable to forget him.

He listened without comment until I was finished with the story. He took my hand and said, "As long as I am here you may talk to me, but as for romantic love, you know I'm too old. You must find other pursuits until the right person comes for you."

I suppressed a laugh. He couldn't possibly believe I was interested in him as a lover. But when I looked at his hopeful expression, it was clear he needed me as much as I needed him.

"You're right. I do need more activities but I'll return to you for true friendship." His eyes crinkled as he smiled in acknowledgement of my promise.

****

The old man levered himself from his chair to welcome Jenna and me on another visit. After he queried me about what I'd done earlier in the morning and I'd admitted nothing productive, he said, "What were we talking about last time?"

"You were telling me about the Borgias. Lucrezia last week."

Our conversation kicked off, me with an old book in my hands about the famous family: popes, the murderous Cesare and the rest of them. When he tired, I said I'd read the next section for the day after tomorrow.

I was about to leave when he said, "Wait a minute, won't you please? I want to talk about *you*, not these crazy old families. Italian history is so complicated and bloody I get tired of it. Especially my own family. What about you and your husband?"

I wavered before giving in under his insistent gaze and bared my soul for a second time, praying he wouldn't reject me. "I made a terrible mistake when I married so young. I thought I was in love but it turned out I knew nothing about anything. We were fine the first year or so but something happened to change our lives— I'm not sure what. Martin drifted away and I guess I grew up and recognized being a subservient housekeeper wasn't what I wanted. I've always loved my stepson, but my husband doesn't love me, if he ever did." And then I added, "And I don't love him anymore, if I ever did." There, I said it.

He steepled his fingers and silently waited for more.

"I didn't fully recognize it until we came to Rome. Maybe it's all my fault. I encouraged him because I wanted to see Europe. But now I'm here for what seems like forever, and I'm drifting like the seaweed I used to see in the water when I went to the beach as a kid. I'm sad to say we're an unhappy family. Tyler mostly ignores his father; I can't seem to connect with Sophie and she's jealous of Jenna and has put up a fuss because she has to share her room. Martin is a cipher. I don't know if he loves any of us or he just doesn't know how to show it. He travels all the time, and now even when he's home, he's either in his office doing who knows what or out who knows where."

I could feel embarrassment's hot flush after I finished. "Oh, I'm terribly sorry for all this whining. I apologize. How selfish of me."

"I have a treat for us and you are not to be ashamed." He retrieved a brandy bottle and two small glasses from his desk drawer. "I've saved this for a special occasion. It's from my grandfather's cellar. Everything else is gone now." He poured a few drops into each glass and raised his. "To your health and happiness." After a pause, he added, "You aren't self-centered. You are honest with yourself and strong because you love your children. You recognize they need a mother who will take care of them until they become adults themselves. You can make a rewarding life here if you try."

I raised my glass to him before taking a sip. The warmth spread from my lips to the rest of me.

"You are a kind and gracious man. I love you dearly. And yes, I will try."

He smiled and found a handkerchief to wipe his rheumy eyes. "I'll help when I can."

CHAPTER SEVEN

When Jenna had abandoned her Linus blanket and entered the local *scuola materna*—nursery school—I tried to find a job with either an Italian company or a branch of an American one. First, I couldn't find anyplace needing my limited office skills, and even if I did, the company would need to prove to the government there wasn't an available Italian—an impossibility. Teaching English was an unattractive option with crowded classrooms and disinterested students.

Meanwhile, I concentrated on perfecting my Italian and bought a laptop to do newsletters for my English-speaking social groups. Including positive stories in the monthly letters was a way to keep my mind busy and entertain others who were sometimes overwhelmed with expat life.

My first column was about Roman colors: lavender wisteria, blue plumbago, magenta bougainvillea tumbling over walls; the apricot, tangerine, cantaloupe and blood orange of building facades; the spinach and eggplant colors of shutters; the scarlet poppies growing in untended spots; and the beautiful dark green cypress and umbrella pines. It got loads of good comments.

The next month I wrote about my favorite fountains, the following one about the obelisks punctuating the sky over the city, again to applause. I was growing a readership, although taken from a narrow pool. Not long after, I read about a new concept called blogging. Intrigued, I studied the process to launch my own blog. After a lot of false starts, I managed to post about the day I bought bread in the bakery Maggie recommended and ended up meeting the old man. I titled it *FIAT PANIS (Let There be Bread)*:

Once upon a time I met an old man out of a fairy tale. He was tiny and perched in a gigantic carved chair where he presided over a treasure trove of books and antiques. And it was the same day I first savored the goodness of real Roman bread, made the old-fashioned way. The kind of bread that's crispy brown on the outside and chewy inside. The kind baked in a wood-fired oven wafting a mouth-watering aroma out the door to compel you to follow the scent back to the bakery where fresh loaves await. But you must hurry or all will be sold before siesta.

I squeezed through the crowd toward the clerk to make my selection while imagining ancient Romans clustered at the baker's stall—the baker pulling the rounds of whole wheat spiced with poppy and fennel seeds from the hot oven while his wife handed them to house slaves who gossiped about their owners, and matrons who gossiped about the neighbors as they handed over a few coins.

I included colorful photos of the bakery and a loaf of fresh bread on my kitchen table along with frescoes of loaves from the ruins of Pompeii. And I promised to write more about the old man.

I chewed a few fingernails waiting to learn the response. I was amazed to see it attracted several hundred readers. My way forward was clear: capitalize on what had always interested me—food. Food I'd cook and food from places like bakeries. I'd been cooking since I was about twelve when I got a Betty Crocker children's cookbook, at summer camp and for my parents when mom had taken a tranquillizer.

This seemed like a great idea until I woke in the middle of the night to realize I didn't know where this would lead. But perhaps a path would open.

One day when the shopping was done, I chanced upon an old bookstore run by an Englishwoman and a calico cat. She introduced herself as Primrose and the cat as Orwell. We chatted about my culinary interests as I browsed. She pointed out a shelf filled with old food-stained regional cookbooks. I carried home a stack and a beautifully-bound book with works by various Italian poets like Dante and Petrarch. The *Infinity* poem by Leopardi was included. I'd already memorized it. It was the past but cooking became my present and, I hoped, future.

****

Maggie and I chatted about the subject of cooking as we often did and I asked if she knew of anyone who might help me to expand my repertoire of Italian dishes before I got too deep into the blogging. She did.

"Haven't seen her for a few years. Quite an interesting person—one of those people who still think they can get by with using titles abolished after World War Two but knows loads of people and can be charming. She calls herself Contessa Franca and is widowed. I think I still have her phone number somewhere." Maggie riffled through her desk and copied the name and number on a slip of paper.

A business-like woman answered in Italian and then English saying, "Cook with La Contessa."

I introduced myself and explained that while I was an experienced cook, I was interested in advanced lessons. The woman said a series of classes on her favorite dishes would begin the next month and the school was in the Castelli, the nearby hills. They would be once a week, a half day in the mornings for ten weeks. I signed up.

Life was filled with possibilities as I planned my schedule. I'd be home in the afternoon with Jenna and Sophie. Tyler was independent and I didn't worry about him. Martin was here or not as usual. We were like the proverbial saying about ships passing in the night, although he wanted sex occasionally and I complied reluctantly. Table talk was between Tyler, Sophie and me with Martin silent. I let it go and listened as Tyler enthused about his friends and Sophie told me how much her teachers appreciated her work.

****

One morning I drove up to the tiny hill town of Nemi, famous for wild strawberries. The cooking school was housed in one wing of an old palazzo. I parked in the courtyard and followed a sign to a large and modern room with six workstations set with an array of tools facing a long counter with range. It had a mirror above set at an angle so we could see the demonstrations. Long white aprons with an embroidered crest were placed on our stools. Several women were milling around. One, a petite elegantly turned-out woman in her early forties, welcomed me. She looked like one of the well-dressed Roman women I'd seen shopping on the Via Condotti. Her sunglasses were propped on top of her head holding henna-highlighted dark hair in place. A heavy gold bracelet and earrings, along with fabulous open-toed heels and a black suit instead of a chef's tunic completed the picture.

"You must be Signora Carlisle. You are so welcome. I am Contessa Franca." She beamed at me as if I was the single person she ever wanted to meet.

I warmed to her immediately despite the pretentious title.

When a few other women arrived, Franca clapped her hands and said, "We will put on our aprons now. We begin with the first in a series of my favorite recipes. Today we will learn how to do *Spaghetti alla Chitarra* with hearty sauce. It is a specialty of Le Marche."

"Guitar spaghetti?" At least it sounded intriguing. Franca had an assistant, a young woman, pass out square-sided boxes strung with what looked like fine piano wire, along with flour, eggs, and a bit of salt. Making pasta was something I'd never attempted.

We sifted the flour, measured the correct amount and made a nest for the eggs. My fellow cooks expertly cracked the eggs, one, two, three, four into the flour. I was nervous and half of egg number one ran down the side of the bowl; number two had bits of shell I had to pick out. The other two behaved. I saw the woman next to me give me the side-eye and I could feel my face heat up as I remembered Audrey Hepburn trying to crack eggs French style in the old movie *Sabrina*. I wiped my eggy hands on the apron and blended the ingredients.

Meanwhile, La Contessa was warning us to treat the dough with care or it wouldn't cook right. I failed again by mixing too vigorously because it fell apart when the time came to roll it out and press it into the strings with the rolling pin. The other students showed off their neat square-shaped pasta, ready to take home. I hid the crumbly mess under a paper towel.

It was time for a glass of wine. I wanted the bottle. After La Contessa told us about the history of the dish—traditional from the Abruzzo in the mountains east of Rome, she stopped by my workstation. "Don't worry, this is a difficult pasta and all the other students have been making pasta since they were children. I think it's an innate skill!"

She poured us a bit more wine and demonstrated how she made the sauce—a rich mixture of veal, pork and lamb with tomatoes. She cooked her pasta and served each of us a portion topped with previously-made sauce and some grated pecorino cheese. It was divine but way too complicated for my intended audience.

By the time the class was over I was worn out and disheartened. The other attendees left but Franca stopped me. "Why don't we chat a bit. I'd like to hear how you came to Rome and my cooking school. I normally have Italian women."

I told her a little—married, three children, wanting a project—and then waited for her story. She must have wanted someone to talk with because she spilled the words in rapid Italian.

"I grew up in Rome. Met this great chef, Ercole, when I took an art course in Florence; we married, he died in a car crash on the way to meet me at a resort to celebrate our anniversary. I decided to carry on with the food business."

"How shocking. I'm terribly sorry."

"It was five years ago now so I don't dwell on it quite so much. Anyway, to make a go of my idea for a school I used Ercole's background. He was distantly related to a minor branch of some obscure played-out noble family in Tuscany. We used to joke about it when I worked with him in the restaurant. Managed to get a Michelin star even. Anyway, after I lost him, I decided if I was going to go down, I'd go down fighting and I perfected a Florentine accent, designed the fake crest on the aprons, and opened this school. I dreamed up the Contessa thing for marketing. It worked."

I thanked the Lord I hadn't whined about my situation.

I longed to continue the chat but needed to get home. When I saw Maggie later, I thanked her for the tip and asked how they met. "She catered an event. It was a party when my oldest graduated from university. She's quite a character I must say but she's managed to overcome a raft of problems."

Just who I need was my thought. Bless Maggie. I loved her to bits but her life was circumscribed by husband and children and sometimes hard for me to imagine in relation to mine. Maybe the unsinkable countess could help me keep some positive direction.

I eagerly awaited the next week's meeting, hoping I'd not disgrace myself on the cooking end, and gain more information about the trauma she'd experienced and how she'd managed it if we chatted again after class.

****

The recipe sheet waiting by our workstations was titled: "How to make the addictive appetizer called *Olive Ascolane*—olives Ascoli style." I knew Ascoli Piceno is a small town near the Adriatic because it was where Alessandro's parents lived. Now I would think of him if I served the olives as an appetizer.

The thought held until I looked at the array of ingredients set before me and attempted to follow the directions. The idea was to stuff large olives before breading and frying. Franca demonstrated how she soaked breadcrumbs in stock, fried diced bacon and added ground pork, beef, tomato paste, and chicken livers before dumping all into a food processor with egg, Parmesan, and seasoning. Then she gave each of us a bowl of large olives to pit and a cup of the mixture to stuff them.

She'd made it look easy. I managed to remove the pits and leave the olives mostly whole before awkwardly forcing the mixture into the cavity and coating them with flour, egg, and breadcrumbs. Franca collected the results to deep-fry in olive oil. She passed the golden-brown antipasti for each of us to try while she gave a little of their history—ancient Romans served olives from Ascoli at every banquet, and in the eighteenth century, a genius chef came up with the idea to stuff them. The savory olives were absolutely addictive. I couldn't help licking my fingers before making some notes for a blog post.

The other students filtered out to chat in the courtyard, but I lingered inside again hoping to share an espresso and engage in another talk about life and all its permutations.

Franca was eager too. She removed her apron and said, "Got time for a coffee?" She waved a tiny cup back and forth. "There's a package of biscotti on the shelf above the cookbooks."

"I'll put them on the table outside."

The last student had left and I drew two French-style little chairs to a mosaic-tiled table. The wisteria was blooming overhead, dropping a few lavender petals to the table and cobblestones.

Franca appeared with our steaming bitter brew. No

sugar like a lot of life.

She took a sip and looked straight at me. Like with the old count, I couldn't resist.

"To be honest, I feel just totally discouraged with life and I want to take some control; be an independent person instead of a trailing spouse. There are years ahead of me here and three children who need me when I need my own goals. I need balance. I'm a nobody."

"So many women have this problem here. Tradition keeps their lives on hold."

"I'm like a weathervane trying to find a steady wind." I turned my face toward the drooping wisteria. What I wanted was approval, my own money, even just a few euros, and to have a separate identity from my family. Selfish, I guess.

"I'll tell you what I did after the shock of Ercole's death wore off. You might think about the idea. I made a list of my assets, both talents and money to capitalize on. And the constraints, of which there were many. It took quite a while to settle on the idea of a school and I made mistakes. Anyway, I'm sounding pushy, so please disregard if you aren't interested."

I was surprised at her openness. Except for the count, the Italians I'd met were always polite but distant.

"I've started writing a blog about Rome. In English for expats. Mostly food. Could you take a look some time and tell me if it might really be a start to something? Don't want to impose but…" I trailed off. I did want to impose.

After finishing the last drop of espresso, I said, "Any advice would be super." I'd never been good at taking advice, to be honest, so if I was going to find my way out of the thicket I'd planted, I would need to force myself

The Measure of Life

to be open.

Franca said she'd think about it and then dialed down the tenor of our conversation by telling me about some of the crazy patrons she'd had to deal with at the restaurant in Florence, like the rude American who marched into the kitchen to tell her how to cook pasta. He liked it soft, not al dente.

I returned home to contemplate Franca's suggestion to tot up assets and liabilities. What did I have going for me? My friends and acquaintances often solicited advice on navigating the expat life and I had cooking and child care skills but no experience in the business world. Helping expats was fine but I hadn't been around long enough to call myself an expert like those who'd lived here for ten or twenty years; setting up a child care business was out of the question when I was already busy with my own three. Cooking remained as the feasible option. I'd wait to see what Franca said before I did anything more.

I'd given her my contact information and website address and hoped she wasn't a procrastinator. She wasn't. She called me three days after the lesson.

"The blog is good although there's so much more you can do with it. Let's talk after the next lesson. We'll have lunch."

****

The next class was how to make various kinds of crostini using *Lardo di Colonatta*, a delicacy I'd never heard of. After that, Franca prepared a quick *spaghetti con alio, olio and pepperoncino*, and I tossed a salad. I wasn't very hungry because I'd eaten too many crostini samples laden with the Lardo, a traditional specialty from a cold Tuscan hill town near marble quarries. The thinly sliced pork fat is silky and luscious and loaded with calories. But who can resist *alio, olio and pepperoncino*?

We sat in the courtyard again. Between bites of pasta and sips of the last of the crisp white wine the class had as an accompaniment to the Lardo, Franca said, "What would you think about us working together? If you are willing to put in the effort to develop your blog and recommend my school to American expats, I could introduce you to some people."

"People?" I was hesitant.

"Being in the food business for so many years I know many local provisioners. And I know which ones are the best." Franca picked up on my concern. "Don't worry, this isn't the mafia."

I felt the deep red of embarrassment creep upward. I knew I was capable but what about working with someone I knew so slightly?

"Let me think. I mean, we just met."

"I've been wanting to expand my business and I can teach in English for your expats and tourists."

"I've never done anything like this before." My gut gurgled with signs of distress.

"We all start somewhere, *cara*. You can do it. I did."

I drove home in a daze to find Tyler had broken his arm in a soccer game.

****

Over the following weeks, Franca and the class worked our way through such eclectic delights as *Pasta con le Sarde* redolent with sardines, raisins, saffron, anchovies, and pine nuts; Risotto with black squid ink; stuffed Calamari, and other dishes with me trying to decide which ones my blog audience would warm to.

The final class was a lesson on how to prepare a grand dessert: Almond cake with pears and crème anglaise served with a sparkling Franciacorta. My mouth still waters when I think about it. Of course, I was seduced and told Franca our project was a "go."

****

With Franca's introductions I made in-depth explorations of markets, restaurants, and provisioners, taking notes and photos. I took a few business-oriented classes at John Cabot University. And I continued to thumb through the cookbook Maggie had given me when we first met. By now I'd added so many notes and propped it open to so many pages I had to hold it together with a rubber band.

I posted every three or four weeks. Several of the more popular posts were recipes for *Stracetti alla Rughetta*—paper-thin beef slices sauteed in olive oil served over tangy wild arugula; *Pasta e Ceci*—a thick winter soup of garbanzo beans, onions, tomato puree, and a small pasta called ditalini, seasoned with rosemary and chiles; and *Fiori di Zucca Fritti*—zucchini flowers stuffed with mozzarella for summer. More "likes" and positive comments poured in. I recommended provisioners I found reliable, along with cookbooks from my ever-growing collection. I posted photos of market stalls and described how I prepared a meal from the days' finds, always with both European and American measurements like grams and ounces. I planted an herb garden on my terrace: pots of rosemary, basil, oregano, parsley, and marjoram.

To find a greater audience, maybe even beyond Italy, the blog needed a better name than just my own. So, in homage to a basket of San Marzano tomatoes and a package of linguine resting on my counter for a post about how to cook one of my favorite dishes, *Pasta alla Puttanesca*, I christened the blog "When Pasta Met Tomato."

I got requests to talk at the women's clubs. I also led tours around Rome to new restaurants, and to artisan bakers, pasta, pastry, and cheese makers as well to those who made the myriad types of sausages available in my local *salumeria*. I continued to post recipes and photos, sometimes of food from Roman mosaics or Renaissance paintings. Franca or other friends tried out restaurants with me and I wrote reviews based on our thoughts. As my popularity increased, I charged a fee for the tours, hoping the tax authorities didn't notice. With the cost to hire knowledgeable instructors to give demonstrations and lectures, and buy ingredients, there was never going to be a significant profit.

****

Franca was an expert at encouragement especially when one of my posts flopped or an event ran off the rails. Her strength gave me someone to lean on. I called her Fearless Franca, my engine, while Motherly Maggie was my anchor.

My visits to the old count, Signor Boncompagni, in the junk shop continued but was for exercising my intellect. I often carried a container of whatever dessert I'd made to share as we talked. He liked the almond cake best. It was obvious his body was aging ever more rapidly, but his mind remained as sharp as ever as we discussed classics and history.

It amused me to have three such disparate Best Friends Forever: A fakey countess, a down-to-earth woman from Ireland profound, and a true count.

The Measure of Life

Maggie and I often shared a comfortable tea or coffee to laugh or moan about the never-ending challenges of Rome, and once in a while, family problems like good friends do.

One day, I'd crossed my line of tolerance with Rome—the bank tellers went on strike exactly when I was trying to cash a check after a wait in what Romans considered a line up, and the bus drivers followed suit leaving me with a long walk home. A thought crossed my mind while I trudged along. I invited Maggie for an *aperitivo*. When we settled, feet up, each with an Aperol spritz, I said: "What would you think about being my official taster? Jenna's too young, Sophie's too finicky, and Tyler too hungry to critique anything I put in front of him."

"I do know about critiquing after raising four children and now grandchildren. I'd love to."

"Let's go to the kitchen and try this ragù Bolognese. Do you think it could use a little more salt?" I handed Maggie a long wooden spoon.

"No, but it needs to simmer for at least another hour. Maybe more. And maybe another splash of white wine."

"White?"

"Yes, white for cooking this and red for drinking."

Thus our partnership began. Maggie served as sous chef, helping prepare *pomodori al riso*—rice-stuffed baked tomatoes served at room temperature in the summer, and *puntarelle*—a type of chicory prepared by stripping the leaves and soaking the shoots in cold water until they curl. I served it with a dressing of anchovy, garlic, vinegar, and salt emulsified with olive oil—and anything else we thought our followers would enjoy. We pored over comments on the blogs. As a result, we stopped working on traditional Roman recipes using the *quinto quarto*, the fifth quarter—offal—when some of our followers commented: "I don't eat rubber," "my husband dumped it in the garbage," or "the thought makes me want to throw up." No horsemeat either.

PART II

CHAPTER EIGHT

The years sped by as they do with all families: childhood's scraped knees and tears gave way to teenage acne and upsets, girl and boyfriends, sports events, and academics. I continued weekly phone calls with Mom to tell her about my life and attempt to assess her and Dad's well-being. Jenna often demanded to talk to Grandmother as she called her *nonna*, when I was on the phone. Our annual two-week home leave gave me a chance to visit my parents and give them time to enjoy Jenna and to help with home projects and medical appointments. As they grew older, Sophie sometimes agreed to visit but Tyler was off seeing his old pals from grade school.

Martin and I were civil, no fights, no remarks. Just "please" and "thank you" or "do you mind if…" It was heaven when he traveled and I had the bed to myself. I would have been happy if he'd slept in his office but he complained the folding hide-a-bed bothered his back even though he could easily afford a new one. He was always a restless sleeper, flinging his arms out and occasionally crying out or mumbling while he slept as if pursued by some demon.

More disturbing were the phone calls about twice a month. He'd grab the handset and rush to his office. Sometimes he looked shaken if he returned to the dinner table or living room, other times almost smug. "Just business," he'd say. I didn't like the thought of the armaments business with its greedy business dealings.

Martin assumed, correctly, the apartment, meals, and the children would be taken care of without his participation. But he gave me a generous allowance along with enough to pay the bills. The remainder was funneled to an investment account. "All is well," he said. I occasionally looked at the Italian and U.S. bank balances and the investment account. Everything looked fine although our investment account balances often changed in value. He assured me it was normal. I focused on my own business, halving the small profits with Maggie so I assumed he was correct.

Martin looked ever grayer and hunched as if bearing a heavy weight. He took the apartment elevator instead of the stairs. If it was out of service, he held onto the handrail to pull himself upward. I'd long since given up on encouraging him to take better care of himself and undergo tests when we were in Seattle on home leave. His aging paralleled my father, making me wonder at times if I'd originally been attracted to Martin because he subconsciously reminded me of Dad with all his problems.

Rather than embarrass Martin, I attended social events he said were obligatory. Some of the parties were hosted by the head of his firm's local office, Federigo Dante, a silver-haired aristocrat, as smooth and slippery as the heavy silk draperies in his magnificent apartment overlooking the Colosseum. Embassies from countries interested in buying military hardware hosted other events. At one party, I was seated next to a handsome diplomat from the French embassy. His accent and sparkling wit, so different from Martin's stodginess, appealed to me. And he was so handsome in his *smoking*, as Italians called tuxedos, I agreed to meet him for lunch at a hotel. But even though he insisted on calling me mademoiselle, his self-centered conversation and constant innuendos about my elderly husband during the meal made me sure I wasn't interested in casual sex, at least with him. A few other men attracted my attention, but no one could take Alessandro's place even after the passing years. After loving him, I'd put out the fire.

Once, I was sure I'd seen him walking with several others near the medical school. He was gesturing and saying something as the group, who looked young and eager, turned a corner in a whirl of white lab coats. Was it him with medical students? I couldn't be sure but it gave my soul a heavy blow, so much so I sat on an ancient chunk of marble in a nearby park to recover.

Tyler lost his childhood roundness and grew tall, lean, and muscular. Sophie and Jenna both grew into slender preteens and then teens. As a teenager, Sophie entered a Goth phase dressed in black complimented by chains, boots, and frightening makeup; Jenna left her clothes and books everywhere but was generally agreeable despite suffering a severe acne breakout when she was thirteen.

When Tyler was eighteen, he'd joined two other boys to backpack around Asia for a year before he entered university in France to study international relations. I missed him more than expected, my lively stepson always looking for adventure, and who'd brought levity to a rather blue household. After graduation, he'd traveled to Africa where he worked at a succession of charitable aid organizations involved in health care. I worried about him in distant and dangerous locations. I bought him a new mobile phone, but it was often difficult to connect. He called me in the middle of a weekday, Rome time, when he had a reliable connection. Sometimes I mentioned to Martin he'd called but more often I let it go.

My constant and never-ending worry was Sophie even after the Goth phase was abandoned. I could see she was unhappy, but I could not break through the impenetrable barrier she'd raised. As always, I gave her extra attention and praise and encouraged her to participate in activities with me. Instead, she'd continued her relationship with the now-ancient *portinaia* perched at the building entrance to the degree she helped her water the languishing scraggly plants in pots stained white by the calcium-laden water. When I passed by during off-school hours, the woman and Sophie would have heads together, snickering at some story. They'd pause talking until I was halfway up the stairs. My feelings about being a terrible mother intensified.

She'd remained at the top of her class throughout her school years, skipping a grade, graduating from high school at sixteen. For once, Martin and I had a substantive discussion and agreed Sophie should enroll at one of the colleges in Rome until she was eighteen. I admit I sighed in a combination of relief, worry, and exasperation as the front door slammed shut the day she moved to Boston University as a transfer student.

The relief didn't last long.

"Is Dad there?" Sophie asked when I answered her call on our land line.

"I'm afraid he's still at work. How are you?"

"I'm pregnant. You might want to buy me some baby clothes. Boy."

The Measure of Life

I was shocked into silence for a minute while I processed the news. "Oh Sophie, are you getting married, or going to continue with school, or...?"

"For sure there won't be a wedding. It was just some guy at a frat party. A mistake but I'm keeping it."

"Are you feeling well? Morning sickness? When is the baby due? Shall I come to Boston to help?"

"No. I'll manage. I'm due in three months."

"Three months! Are you sure I can't help?"

"Yeah, for now just tell Dad." She cut the connection.

I stared at the receiver trying to comprehend why Sophie had been pregnant for six months without telling either Martin or me. My frustration at being barred from the happy anticipation of my first grandchild was superseded by worry at how she could manage school and an infant.

Martin called Sophie after I gave him the news. I could hear his half of the conversation: "I have a business meeting in D.C. later in the week. I'll fly out tomorrow to help you make arrangements."

He didn't bother to discuss his plans with me, but when he returned a week later, he said he'd fixed everything up: paying all the rent for a larger apartment and household help. He'd stepped up and done the right thing.

I told Tyler and Jenna they would be aunts and uncles. In revealing exchanges both said they'd congratulate their sister but made clear their enthusiasm was muted at best. It made me sad to see how isolated Sophie continued to be. Still, I was sure becoming a grandmother would have its pleasures. I envisioned a teddy bear and tiny cute outfits, size 0-3 months.

Sophie did call me when the baby was born during summer break. She'd named him Jacob and said he was healthy. She would return to school fall term, leaving him with a caregiver during classes and seminars. I couldn't imagine how my daughter could want to leave him when he was so young but it was no use trying to intervene. And who was I to give parenting advice to her?

I sent gifts and she sent photos over the next months but then stopped. Consumed by fear, I called her. After prodding, she admitted Jacob might not be developing normally but it was too soon to know what might be wrong. His pediatrician said it would be twelve to eighteen months before they could be sure of anything. I again offered to help by coming to Boston, but Sophie rejected me—there was no room and she already had someone to help.

Even with the potential problems with the child, Sophie graduated from university with honors and received a full scholarship to law school. Martin and I attended the ceremonies where she graduated summa cum laude. But Jacob didn't talk or look directly at anyone as I held him during the ceremony.

At the celebratory dinner, Martin told Sophie he'd continue to pay for whatever care the child needed until she was awarded a J.D. and found a job. Sophie accepted the offer. I took her positive mood as an opportunity to initiate a conversation, "We are so proud of you, I don't know how you manage with a young child. Have the doctors been able to diagnose the condition and make a plan to help? I do worry."

Sophie lit a cigarette before responding. "They think he might be on the mild end of the autism spectrum. It's hard to diagnose, but he seems to be making some progress with therapy. Don't know about the future."

"Who's helping you? I'd be glad to stay for a while."

Sophie took a couple of puffs before stubbing the cigarette in a saucer. "I'm fine. Just leave it please." She found her phone and began reading.

Shut out again, I couldn't help wondering if Sophie, too, was somewhere on the autism spectrum, unable to relate to others. Not so different from Martin.

****

During one of my weekly phone calls Mom seemed more rattled than usual. In response to my questions, she opened up to say Dad's company changed ownership and he was forced into early retirement shortly before the deal had closed. He refused to engage in any activities beyond watching television and sipping bourbon. To add to my concerns, she said he was diagnosed with heart and liver problems, no doubt exacerbated by drinking.

Mom, helped along with medications, kept going, or at least I thought so. But on my next Seattle visit, I saw Dad struggling to breathe and unsteady on his feet even with a cane.

I took her aside. "You need to talk to me. Dad doesn't look good, and I'm worried about you too."

"Please, Nicki, don't give it a thought. He's got an appointment with a new cardiologist next month. We have great medical care." She started to scrub the kitchen sink even though it didn't need it.

"And how are *you* going to cope? Can't I get you some help through some senior service organization?" I tried to take the sponge but she clutched it tighter.

"I don't like people in the house." She wiped her sniffy nose with a handkerchief she kept tucked in her sleeve until it was needed for such moments.

"But—"

She wadded the handkerchief and interrupted. "You stay where you belong with Martin and Jenna. When she graduates from high school, we'll talk about it again. I've told you before." She turned to look at me as if I was an interloper challenging her autonomy. Like the situation with Sophie, my efforts to help were useless. I was unwanted, unnecessary, except to clients in Rome who loved my tours and cooking stories and recipes. Nevertheless, I flew to Seattle four times a year to ensure they were coping.

I mentioned my parents' situation to my closest American friends back in Rome. Several admitted they worried about their own aging parents. Many were torn between duty to spouses and children in Rome and family left behind. Some planned to quit their jobs to return to the States, but most compromised with phone, Skype, and home leave to resolve the issues or justify remaining abroad for however long the employment contract lasted. I saw those who planned to remain in Rome indefinitely as stateless, neither Italian nor American no matter what their passports declared. A life I refused to accept.

****

Although I'd planned to leave Martin and Rome when Sophie graduated, Jenna was so integrated in her local life I decided to wait until she graduated, another four long years. I counted the months and redoubled my efforts to settle on a plan for a degree in something personally rewarding when my moment arrived. Nursing, teaching, social work?

Once when Maggie and I discussed my struggle to

grasp a meaningful future outside the family bonds, a concept she couldn't fathom, she said, "What about continuing to do what you're doing now? Or start an Italian restaurant?"

"I can't tell you the number of times I've gone over this but it's not feasible. I don't know a soul in Seattle or anything about the local food scene or how I'd get financial backing. The restaurant business is really chancy and I'm not interested in working as a chef for someone else."

"You need to follow your dreams." She looked a tiny bit wistful.

"The question is *where* and *what*? And to be honest, I'm getting tired of thinking up recipes and trying to find new producers to plan outings."

"What about cooking videos?"

I looked at Maggie. She was a genius for sure at least for a short-term solution to what had become routine. I bought a camera and lighting equipment the next day. We'd use her fancy kitchen for the shoots.

CHAPTER NINE

It wasn't solely the children growing up and Martin and my parents aging. I, too, noticed the years, the loss of a time for carefree activities I'd longed for but seldom experienced. To celebrate my fortieth birthday, I asked my stylist for a new cut. When I noticed a slight softening of my jaw line while he snipped, I shut my eyes.

Maggie invited me to lunch to celebrate. Orazio was in the kitchen banging pots and pans. "You can't imagine what it's been like since he's home so much after retiring," she whispered. "He's insisting on helping if you know what I mean—twice as much husband and half as much income. At least he's taken up golf. But it's only once a week." She grimaced.

I couldn't help smiling at this dignified man, recently retired from a senior job at the Bank of Italy, wearing a food-splattered apron.

Maggie served portions of a frittata made with asparagus, olives, sun-dried tomatoes and cubes of pancetta. It was delicious. "Let's try this recipe for my blog."

"Well," Maggie smiled. "Ludo absolutely loves it whenever he needs some special dish from his mamma. He always puts his forefinger to his cheek and twirls it after the first bite."

After a couple of glasses of pinot grigio on her

terrace complimented with small talk, I was feeling good about the birthday after all. And in a surprise, Martin remembered the day and took me out to dinner at a small osteria.

"Happy birthday." He raised a glass of Barbaresco the waiter had decanted. I raised mine.

We ordered and I took the opportunity to attempt an actual conversation for the thousandth time. "Here we are, Martin. Let's go out like this more often."

There was no response. I watched the lines around his mouth tense as he absent-mindedly rolled pieces of bread into balls and shoved them back and forth on the tablecloth. I wished I had a book to read. The food arrived, and he poured the remainder of the carafe into his glass before cutting into his gigantic *Bistecca alla Fiorentina.* A drip from the meat juices landed on his tie. He swore before saying, "What?"

It took me a second to realize he was referring to my remark. I repeated it.

"I'm trying, but I don't like to go out. Too much when I travel. Your cooking is better." He blotted his tie with a corner of the tablecloth.

The compliment was unexpected. It led me to try further. "Can't we try to capture the lost years?"

He looked at me wordlessly. I could see he was distressed, maybe sad. I put my hand on his. He carefully removed it to grasp his wine glass. I knew he'd be up all night with heartburn from the thick and rich steak, big enough for two or more. So would I, but with different symptoms which weren't assuaged when I met Maggie on the stairwell the following day.

After we'd greeted each other, she said, "I hope you didn't mind that I reminded Martin about your birthday the other day when I saw him in the lobby. I remembered you'd mentioned it because you saw it as a major milestone."

****

My business was almost more than I wanted, and I'd neglected my visits to the junk shop. I was a bit ashamed because the few times I'd seen the old count, he was clearly beyond the age to be left alone all day. Over time I'd watched as he'd become as dry and fragile as his books, his glasses dusty, suit spotted with food, the old man smell filling the shop. I wished I knew who I could contact to urge them to do something, but he'd never mentioned anyone except for grandchildren who no longer visited.

One day I had to cancel a tour because the owner of a *caseificio* who planned to give a talk about mozzarella, called to say he was sick. I took the opportunity to visit the shop. I tried to open the door, but it was locked. I pressed my face to the ever-dusty window to look inside. The space was vacant. No desk, our two chairs gone, the shelves and tables empty. I stopped by the bar on one side and then the dry cleaner on the other. The employees from both establishments told me the same story: A van had come by several days earlier and workers loaded the shop's contents, flinging everything into crates without any care. They'd heard breaking glass and crockery. The van driver told them to get out of the way when they'd all left their own shops to see what was happening. He snarled that he had permission. If anyone interfered, he'd call the cops. He'd waved some official-looking papers in their faces. Intimidated, they'd backed off.

"But where is my friend Signor Boncompagni?"

Each told me they'd watched him standing helpless

and distraught while his treasures were looted. Words tumbled from the employees' mouths: "It was a scandal," said the barista while patrons looked at me and back to the barista who jerked his chin in disgust.

"How could this be?" the clerk at the dry cleaners moaned while she slipped plastic over someone's newly cleaned evening gown.

"But what happened to *him* afterward?"

"No idea," was the universal response. No one had ever seen a family member in all the years he'd been in the shop. They didn't know anyone to contact. I searched through the local news outlets for days to see if there was any mention of the incident. There wasn't. I realized I'd never known where he lived. I called all the retirement homes I could find listed, without success. My confidant had vanished as if he'd been a beneficent illusion all along. When I told Jenna, she burst into tears at the loss of her childhood friend, her surrogate grandfather. I joined in, mourning the loss of a person who'd supported me over the years.

Later, I found his engraved visitor's card and tucked it in the biography of Leopardi he'd suggested I buy the first time we'd met. The book rested in the bookcase next to the poetry book given to me by Alessandro.

****

In a second blow, a few months later Franca called to invite me to lunch at a new restaurant in Castel Gandolfo where the Pope had his summer residence. I could tell from the tone of her voice she was tense and uncomfortable.

The reason became clear when a plate of olives and bruschetta arrived along with glasses of local white wine. Instead of the usual toast to health and happiness, she looked at the tablecloth and ran her finger around the rim of her glass several times before raising it to partially obscure her face.

"I've met someone. Someone in the culinary world. We're moving to Sydney to run an Italian restaurant in one of the big hotels."

When I took a sharp breath she added, "So now, I've told you. I haven't wanted to but we're leaving next week. I'm sorry." She gulped half the wine.

"I'll miss you terribly." I carelessly sloshed a bit of my wine on the tablecloth. "I can never thank you enough for what you've done. You gave me a life." Deep down I was demolished.

"I'm sure you would have succeeded on your own. Thanks for all the business you threw my way. I closed up last week. Anyway, I know you too will be leaving. You'll be a success in Seattle so no worries."

No worries? I was besieged with them, but the timing to discuss was wrong now. The remainder of our lunch-time chatter was reduced to inconsequential matters to avoid further emotions. When we left, she stood tall on her toes to give me a bear hug and kisses. I wanted to weep.

****

And then there was the most disturbing incident of all. Martin came home from work to say a man named Trench was coming to dinner the following evening. I'd forgotten all about him and the event when he'd come to Seattle and upset Martin years earlier.

"Why on earth is that disgusting man in Rome now?"

"He's in the defense industry too. I need to work with him on contract issues."

"So, take him to a restaurant where people do business."

"Said he wanted a family meal. Travels so much he wanted home cooking for a change."

"You expect me to believe this story?"

"Believe anything you want, but I invited him." Martin crossed his arms in a defiant gesture almost making me laugh.

"Just don't think I'll welcome him with open arms."

I made a half-hearted attempt to straighten out the living room while listening to Martin in the bathroom repeatedly flushing the toilet.

I lay awake thinking about the first time I'd met Trench. It was in our house in Seattle shortly after Martin got the job with the defense company which led to the job in Italy. He was an ugly little man with hard blue eyes like the gas jets on my kitchen range and a burn scar running down the side of his face.

When Martin had introduced us on the doorstep, he'd grabbed my hand to brush it against his lips instead of a handshake. His whiskey breath was badly disguised with mouthwash. The aggressive gesture made me step back which gave him unwanted room to leer and make a comment about how much younger I was than Martin.

Trench then had turned his attention to Martin, putting his arm around his shoulders while repeatedly exclaiming, "Remember all the good times in 'Nam. It's great to have a buddy to remember the good old days when we could take a break from patrol. Sweet smoke and aces high!" He wagged his head to indicate the times were so fascinating he wished he was still there. Martin hadn't responded.

Later, he and Trench had left together. "Don't wait

up," were Martin's parting words.

I'd waited up anyway. Finally, about midnight I heard a car stop in front of our house. It was Trench's car, a new white Cadillac convertible with red upholstery. Under the streetlight I could see the two men inside, head-to-head, neck and shoulders tensed. Martin slammed the car's door when he got out. Trench was still talking as Martin walked toward our front entrance. I climbed in bed and pretended to sleep. After an hour he fell into bed and snored. The next day I noticed he had bloody knuckles and there was a fist-size hole in the garage drywall. He wouldn't talk to me about either Trench or the hole which was never repaired.

****

When I heard the buzzer on the video *citofono* at the building's street entrance, I busied myself in the kitchen, in the hope my interactions with the man would be limited to serving and sitting at the table for the shortest possible time. I couldn't escape when he trailed into the kitchen with a large bunch of long-stemmed scarlet roses.

"I'm so excited to see you again after all this time. You look as exquisite as ever. I do hope you like roses."

This was a total lie as I'd seen him once on our doorstep in Seattle. "I'll find a vase. Please don't wait. I'm sure Martin wants to get you a drink." I took the bouquet, careful not to touch his hand.

He didn't budge. The sensation of an unblinking stare following me as I found a vase on the top shelf of a cupboard made me want to drop the heavy glass on his head. Instead, I picked up the bouquet from the counter to arrange the unwanted flowers. An overlooked thorn stabbed my thumb. I dropped the rose with an "Ouch."

"Here, let me help." Trench grabbed my hand to inspect the prick as if he was a vampire wanting to lick it. His hand was cold and damp.

I wrenched my hand away, shoving him aside to find a bandage in the bathroom and tamp down my fury. When I returned to place the flowers on the table, I could see the two men deep in conversation. Trench leaned toward Martin to say something. Martin leaned back abruptly.

I placed the bouquet to block Trench's line of sight in my direction at the dinner table and made no effort to keep a conversation going after I'd served. Trench, undeterred, commented on Martin's luck in having such a talented wife, how charming the apartment was, and how fabulous the food tasted. Halfway through one monologue Martin looked up from his plate of veal chops and glared at Trench. The man paused for a few moments before beginning again as if he was a recording. He made my skin crawl.

By the time I'd served the coffee, my face and shoulders ached with the effort to keep anger at bay. I stood to clear the table. Trench popped up as if on a string. He neatly folded his dinner napkin as if he was expecting to return for dinner the following evening.

"Lovely, just lovely."

I knew it was rude, but flicked my chin and turned away. From the kitchen I could hear Martin retrieve Trench's jacket and usher him out the door.

Afterwards, he hovered by the kitchen door, a look of uncertainty crossing his face.

"Martin, what's he to you? You told me you were friends in Vietnam. A long time ago. And don't think I don't remember the incident in Seattle."

"Trust me. I told you, the defense sector is full of people I need to know. And I also told you, I need to work closely with him." He turned away before mumbling, "Do you want help with the dishes?"

"No, I'll clean up." His unlikely offer was worrisome. Something was clearly wrong.

CHAPTER TEN

It was Winter 2013. Now, in her senior year, Jenna was busy deciding where to apply for university. She spent her spare time browsing course offerings, especially those for marine biology. With an International Baccalaureate, high SAT scores, and academic honors, she applied to Harvard and Princeton among others. We flew to the States to tour a few campuses, three on the East Coast, two in California, and the University of Washington. Familiar with Seattle from the annual home leave trips, Jenna liked the school's proximity to mountains and saltwater.

I was delighted at the idea she might attend the UW but said nothing to influence her although I suppose my body language betrayed me. With the other two children so far away, it would be a comfort when Martin and I parted. Letting her know I was leaving Martin needed to wait until she selected a school and was immersed in her new life. There was no point in ruining the end of her high school years with more family discord just to satisfy my needs.

****

The months passed in a flash as graduation approached. Jenna was often out with her friends knowing they'd soon go their separate ways. When she accepted an offer from the University of Washington which came with a partial scholarship, I knew my life in

Rome had arrived at the turning point I desired—one I hoped I could manage in a smooth and civilized manner. All the same, I had insomnia and my gut was unhappy from the stress.

Martin, Jenna and I arrived in Seattle on home leave in June. Jenna wanted to get a running start and had enrolled in summer school. Eager to establish her grown-up status, she threw herself into the search for an apartment and a used car, all smiles and happy talk about the future. She told me emphatically my help wasn't required, a relief because I needed to concentrate on my failing parents before what would perhaps be even more stressful—telling Martin.

I was sick to see the state they were in when I visited my family home the day after we'd arrived from Rome. I'd last seen them four months earlier and mistakenly thought decisions could wait.

My father sat motionless in an armchair, his belly bulging and swollen legs propped on a stool. An oxygen tank was nearby. Mom was so unkempt and worn out, she looked near imminent collapse. Dirty dishes covered the kitchen counter although there were no more bottles. Dad must have given up drinking. But there was little food in the refrigerator. Medical bills and insurance statements were piled haphazardly on the kitchen table. When I asked why she hadn't told me more about the troubles, my mother said she didn't want to bother me.

While Martin was out looking for real estate investments as he'd planned, I took Mom to the family doctor and sat in on the exam. She did not do well on the cognitive test. The doctor took me aside to outline his concerns.

After we returned home, Mom and I sat at the

kitchen table while my father dozed in front of the television, the clicker held in his remaining hand.

"Nicki, I just can't do this anymore." She took the always-available handkerchief from her sleeve to wipe her eyes. "But I don't want to leave my home." She straightened and tried to look determined.

"Oh Mom, let me help."

"No, it's okay. I'll manage. Don't you worry." Her tone wasn't convincing.

I worried, of course. And, after several days of back and forth, Mom agreed it was best to sell the house and move to an assisted living community where they would have appropriate care. No more driving. I felt like a judge and jury condemning them both to incarceration. But there was no way I could imagine handling the situation even if I learned nursing skills. What a terrible daughter I was: first leaving them to marry a man they didn't like, moving to the other side of the world, and now about to leave them in the care of others.

I was strung out between parents, husband, and children not knowing which way to turn. There was nothing to do but get on with it. Useless worries about Sophie had to be put aside; Jenna was grown up enough to manage on her own, Tyler independent for years now. I'd tackle my parents' issues before satisfying my own desires.

I contacted a company specializing in senior issues and talked with a social worker who was knowledgeable about eldercare and its many complexities. She agreed an assisted living facility could provide help for their differing needs was best.

When the business part of our talk ended, I asked if she would have some time to talk with me about a career in social work. We set up a coffee date between her work schedule and my explorations of suitable places for my parents.

****

"I'm looking for a satisfying career when I move back to Seattle. I need to find the right major to finish a degree." I slid into the booth and handed over her coffee and bagel.

The woman, Barbara, said, "I have an MSW, a master's degree in social work; it's pretty much mandatory to get anywhere. Although sometimes it's distressing to see the state people can get into, I do feel gratified if I can provide assistance. It isn't always possible, unfortunately."

I picked up a few crumbs from my Morning Glory muffin before asking about her duties which she said ranged from comforting worried families, referring them to financial and downsizing specialists, to finding hospice care.

We talked for about an hour about the different opportunities with an MSW and I became more certain it would be the right career for me.

She looked at her watch. "I need to get going but one last thing: To be honest, besides the pay not being anything like that from tech, as I've already said, the workload can be killing so you have to learn not to take it home and spoil your own relationships. I admit, though, it sometimes keeps me awake with worry about some of the cases."

She smiled as she handed me a business card from her wallet. "On the other hand, there are times when you know you've really made a difference. Gratifying. So, let me know if you want to discuss further at some other time."

"Yes, I will do so after I settle my parents."

She left and I stopped in the coffee shop toilet after a wave of anxiety merged with the too strong coffee.

****

Barbara had recommended a number of suitable facilities. I visited each, learning there were many business models. I googled local and state resources and narrowed the list before taking Mom to see them. Many were advertised as "gracious." Something about the term must comfort those about to undergo a life-changing event setting them on the path to an inevitable end. Mom liked a place in West Seattle although there wouldn't be availability for several weeks when a new wing in the complex would open. I put down the deposit and helped with the complicated paperwork. Afterwards, I contacted several real estate agents to discuss the sale of their home.

In my new role as caretaker, I hired a helper to come in every day to cook and clean until they could leave. Mom didn't object and I had a brief respite to turn to my other problem.

****

I was about to open my mouth to give Martin the news about my decision to separate when he said, "I think I'll buy a rental house on one of the nearby islands because they're too expensive in town for a good return on investment. And it'll go up in value before I retire. I'm going to look on Vashon Island tomorrow. Do you want to come?"

The prospect of a change of scenery to take my mind off the problems with my parents was attractive even though I felt two-faced for delaying my ultimatum in favor of an excursion.

"Sure. I used to go to summer camp on the island." I thought of old Dolly, my favorite horse. She must have long gone to horse heaven.

The agent, who picked us up at the hotel, was a flamboyant bottle blond with too-white teeth. She looked from Martin to me with poorly-disguised curiosity.

The ferry ride to the island was pleasant, the smell of iodine from the seawater reminding me of childhood summers. The agent's luxury car cocooned me in leather seats as we drove up the hill from the dock past a sign entreating us to KEEP VASHON WEIRD. She spouted a patter about all the "techies" and professionals who lived on the island and commuted to downtown on what she called a foot ferry. It was a great place for rental properties as prices were lower than Seattle or Bainbridge Island.

We looked at a half-dozen houses: some too expensive, some dumps. Actually, Martin looked and I gave them a cursory glance while daydreaming about my new single future. Late in the afternoon we stopped at an older house Martin thought would suffice even though it could use updating. I quickly toured but didn't pay much attention other than to see there were two floors and a good view of Puget Sound from the rooms at the back. I noticed a fig tree on the south side of the property. It made me think of figs and prosciutto on a summer evening in Rome.

Martin made an offer, assuring me it was a great deal. He told the agent to look for more property as soon as the deal was closed and it was rented by a management company. He gave her his business card. She gave him an ingratiating smile. And I thought, *it's time.*

The moment to face my husband arrived after we'd finished lunch and were having coffee in the hotel restaurant the following day. I put my cup down with a bang to get his attention and give me some courage to take the plunge. Martin looked up. "I'm going to remain in Seattle. Things haven't been good for ages and I need a separation now the children are grown."

"What? What do you mean? You're not coming back to Rome with me?" The color drained from his face as he reared back.

I had a brief vision of the start of our marriage and my squashed hopes for partnership and support over the years. No backing out now. "I'm going to remain here for my parents and get started on my own life. I'll stay at their house until it's sold, and use their car. I'll close my business from here and you can ship my clothes."

"What about me?" His voice rose several decibels.

"I'm sorry but I just can't go on. We have no life together. I've tried and tried but—"

"But you're my wife!" He arched his neck then stood, holding his napkin in one hand as if to wave a distress call, his eyes darting around the room as if seeking confirmation. A few patrons glanced our way.

I kept my voice low. "Martin, get a grip. I know your parents died a long time ago so you've never been in this situation, but I know what I have to do. I've been away from my real home for nearly nineteen years and now I'm needed here more than in Rome. So that's the end of it." I could feel tension course through my body. It wasn't the end of it, of course.

"I don't care what you do. And you don't get any money." He threw the napkin down and left the table, knocking over his water glass in the process. The whole scene reminded me of the one years ago when he realized I was pregnant. Then he wanted to get rid of me but I was too useful.

I signed the chit and followed him back to our room. He was watching one of the financial channels. The stock market was up. Without taking his eyeballs off the screen, he said, "I don't care if you ever come back."

I could tell he didn't mean it by the sulky tone of his voice but I needed to get away to avoid a discussion which would soon deteriorate into a shouting match and recriminations if I responded. My turn to flee an argument.

I escaped to a nearby coffee shop where I nursed an iced coffee to help me think how to manage our parting and my future. I was shaking. *Hang on,* I told myself. After some deep breathing I began to focus. The important thing was to ensure a smooth transition with enough financial support to enable me to stand on my own while going to school. If there was a separation the company would continue to help with Jenna's tuition and health care also, so it was the best solution rather than a divorce.

I headed to my parents' home, my mood lightened now I'd taken a first step although underneath there was a tinge of regret and sadness at our failures. Martin didn't reply to my text saying that I would be back late.

With the decision made to move, Mom perked up and busied herself selecting items she wanted to decorate the rooms in the care home. Some of the furniture would remain to stage the house for the sale. When charity workers arrived to take the unwanted items, I checked my former bedroom to see if there was any memento I wanted to save. My room was the same as the day I'd left to marry with its quilted bedspread, Whitney Huston and Heart posters still on the walls. A sense of time rushing by overcame me as I remembered the early days with Martin. He'd seemed so strong as he stood facing the future broad-shouldered, legs apart, ready to stride forward despite the terrible tragedy of losing his first wife. Although I'd had fleeting doubts about the age difference and taking on a small child, the desire for romance and certainty in my life had won.

The marvelous moon of my wedding day had confirmed my decision. It had been a chilly and clear February morning. The moment the sun cast a pink light on the Olympic Mountains, dusted from a snowfall, a full moon crept toward the peaks. As it traveled, it grew ever larger and changed from silver to a blazing red-gold. The brilliance burned into my eyes, beckoning me to follow it into a new life. I was mesmerized, unmoving, until the disk sank below the western horizon. When the last sliver disappeared and sunlight filled the sky, I'd lifted my wedding dress from its hanger and held it to my body with a frisson of anticipation.

How glorious was the time when the red moon lured me on a flight path that unexpectedly arrowed eastward toward Rome.

Now, years later, clouds swept over the Olympics, presaging summer rain. As I watched them obscure the foothills and loom over the waters of Puget Sound, I couldn't stop myself wondering about all the lives I could have lived if I'd not married Martin.

I squatted to look under the bed in case something might have dropped on the floor. A large box was shoved next to the headboard. I squirmed under the mattress slats until I grasped a corner to drag it out. When I lifted the dusty lid, there were gifts I'd sent to my parents from Italy years earlier nestled in tissue paper: ceramics, textiles, a pair of pale blue leather women's gloves, silk scarfs, and several silk ties. Daughterly guilt swept over me like the weather outside the window.

I longed to ask Mom more about her early life, her hopes and aspirations. Did she ever experience true love with Dad or anyone? Did she regret her constrained life? As far as I knew her experience was even more limited than mine. She and Dad had met on a military base where he was enlisted and she worked in the commissary. According to her, it took a year to decide if they wanted a permanent relationship, but they married when she was twenty-eight and he was a year younger. I was born a year later by which time the pattern of their lives was firmly fixed with Dad working for the hardware wholesaler and Mom a "housewife."

I also wanted to ask why my gifts to them remained in a box, unused. I suspected she saw them as guilt offerings and didn't want to be reminded of her missing daughter. But the time had passed when there could be such conversations. I carried the box downstairs and gave it to the worker loading the van.

Mom offered me some of her treasures. I didn't want the figurines but took them anyway while thinking someday I'd be in the same position as she. Like Maggie and Orazio's unwanted antique furniture. I wrapped the little figures with care and took them to the hotel so they didn't get lost when the house was sold.

****

Martin was poking around the mini-bar in our hotel room when I returned. He straightened up with two small bottles of ridiculously expensive so-called champagne in his hand. "You know I've been thinking. When you get back to Rome we'll go on a little holiday. What do you think?"

"I'm *not* coming back."

"I can wait a bit. Maybe the Maldives this winter?"

"Martin, I need to be clear. I'm not going to some resort on a minuscule island in the middle of nowhere. I'm demanding a separation. We don't have to have a lawyer but I want it on paper. I'll go on-line and get a form."

A wave of physical pain passed over his face as my demand soaked into his consciousness. I continued anyway. "Beyond my parents' needs, the children are grown now. I need to do things for myself. I want to have a career. Here in Seattle."

"Career? What career? What's the problem? We're husband and wife. We live in Rome. You have an easy life. You have tours." He spluttered, his shoulders drawn up, his arms tight by his sides. I could see a twitch under his right eye.

"I know we're legally married, but all we have is a piece of paper. And my definition of marriage is a partnership; yours is a hierarchy with you as the boss and me the subordinate. I need some space, some new challenges. Please don't be so obtuse."

"Want, want, want. I have wants too." He paused. "What kind of a career?"

"I'm thinking of social work."

"Social work?" He sneered. "Crazy! What a bunch of useless do-gooders. I'm off to look at real estate. Money matters. Don't know what time I'll be back." He turned to leave but paused again to place his face close to mine. "Remember, you vowed you'd be with me. Me.

You vowed in front of a pastor in a church. My contract isn't finished. If you leave, I won't help you." His face was now purple.

"Wait a minute, Martin. Just once I'm asking you to wait to have a conversation. You've never had time for me in all the years of our marriage. All you care about is work and money."

"Don't forget work is how I've been supporting you and your lover's offspring. Don't you remember standing at the altar and what you promised?"

"Of course, I remember. But what about *your* vows to love and cherish? I've never seen either after the first year or so. You've never supported me personally in anything. I don't even know why you married me." I paused and then added, "It took me a long time to realize it but I did it because I was naïve and insecure."

Martin's mouth dropped open at my heated words.

"Why did you marry me, Martin? Why?"

He looked at the bottles in his hand. "I don't know any more."

So the truth was out and we'd rejected each other. "Martin, can't we sit down and talk about the future? Like adults." I put my hand on his arm but he shrugged it off. The moment passed and he stepped back reverting to his usual tactic of avoidance—not fight but flight.

The door to the room swung shut and locked with a click as he walked out leaving me twisted with tension but determined not to give in.

I stared vacantly at the Seattle skyline from the room on the sixteenth floor. The sun was still high in the summer evening sky, a ferry to Bremerton glided from Coleman Dock, traffic and pedestrians filled the street below. All looked normal, the world outside uninterested in my domestic problems. Would the children care?

Tyler might not be surprised at a separation and he'd left for his own life years ago. He called once in a while from some isolated place and we chatted until the line inevitably dropped. But Sophie? She had plenty of her own problems and might relish more of her father's time without me in the picture. I seldom heard from her, always too busy to talk when I called.

Jenna might be upset at the dramatic change when she was transitioning to adulthood. But watching her, I didn't think she'd pay much attention because her mind was on her immediate future. One day, it was "Mom, I bought an old beetle convertible." Another day it was, "Mom, I've got a place with a roommate. She's a sophomore in pre-med. It'll be so great!" She'd paused before adding, "You know, it's going to be weird to be living in the States after Rome. Hope it goes okay." A small cloud of concern dimmed her excitement.

I assured Jenna she'd adjust, although some of my friends had told me their children were so international in outlook by the time they graduated from high school they never quite fit into life in the States. And Jenna was half-Italian in addition. A complication no doubt.

****

Martin woke me the morning after the argument by saying he'd booked a meeting with someone and would be back later in the day and wanted to talk then. I rolled over hoping to sleep another hour or two. But thoughts of Martin, my parents and everything else invaded my mind like a whirling dust devil. I found the social worker's business card and flipped it back and forth in my fingers thinking of my future.

Later, I wandered through art galleries and whiled

away an hour with lunch at a French restaurant in Pike Place Market. I booked a spa day with massage, haircut, and manicure. Jenna was settling in and my parents would soon be under care. Martin would leave the day after tomorrow. I needed to cancel my own air ticket.

His face was hidden in a financial newspaper when I returned to the hotel. He folded the paper and said in a conciliatory tone, "Look Nicole. I know everything's not always been the best. For me either. But right now, isn't a good time. You can do what you want later. You're still young. But I need you. Please."

"I don't know, Martin. I don't believe you ever loved me. I was sure I loved you at first. But I can't name one single time when you made an effort to please me when we had sex after our first year. It was just sex for you. I don't understand what happened but it did and what we said yesterday confirmed it."

"God, you don't know anything. Please. Just for a year or two. Then things will be settled." He slumped into a chair one leg over the other, jiggling as if he'd developed a tremor.

"Why? Why for a year or so? What will be different? What things?"

He turned to face the window and, after a too-long pause, said, "I just don't want to be alone now." I could see his Adam's apple rise and fall as he swallowed in the struggle to admit he needed me.

Childhood trauma and widower status was surely the driver of his need and it made me sad to realize how damaged he remained. But it was too late to cave in and have him drag me down with him.

I said, "We've been alone for years in spirit, so I can't think a physical separation should be a problem."

Nevertheless, I softened a little at his distress. "Okay, I need to stay here for at least a month to help my parents and then I'll return with you to Rome for three months. No more. I'll help you get organized and arrange for a housekeeper. I want an income covering my living and education costs and the remainder of Jenna's tuition and expenses after the company pays its portion until she graduates from university. I'll find part-time work of course but those are the terms. I'm not trying to bankrupt you."

"What if I don't agree?"

"Martin, let's not end our relationship in acrimony. You needed me to manage your household and I did. I'm grateful for the chance to live in Rome and to have Tyler in my life. I hope he will continue to consider me his second mother. But now it's time for me to do other things. I don't want to talk about this over and over. I'm going down to the bar to have a drink. Alone."

I was so agitated I had trouble finding the correct button in the elevator for the mezzanine where the bar was located.

At the base of my emotional state was the uncomfortable thought: who was being selfish? I'd stayed with him for the children and maybe to have the appearance of a traditional marriage like my parents. Or maybe part of it was inertia. But who had priority with Martin obviously declining no matter what he'd told me about his annual physical a few days earlier, or myself wanting, needing, to pursue my own interests before it was too late to start a career? And I'd never seen such a display of emotions over the last several days. Maybe he did have a smidge of sentiment for me but didn't know how to articulate it.

I slid into a booth in the dimly lit bar and ordered a martini. Ordinarily I hated them but the icy cold gin and vermouth was perfect for the day. I nibbled on the lemon twist and ordered another. After I tipped the second glass for the last few drops, I said aloud, "Whatever, Martin. I'm not giving in."

CHAPTER ELEVEN

Our apartment in Rome was as silent as ever when I returned from Seattle. Martin hadn't made any effort to keep it up. I interviewed applicants for a housekeeper job for him and spent hours looking at websites for apartments and suitable coursework in Seattle. Martin refused to discuss our future; his response to my pleas was, "Not now." He alternated between periods of morose silence and a new problem—heavy drinking making him argumentative. My own mood vacillated between worries about leaving him in such a state and suspicion he was acting out of a need to keep me under his control like some malign creature in a fairy tale. I was continually on edge with insomnia and gut problems. Three weeks had dragged by and the thought of more than two months left was agonizing. That is, until I heard the front door slam one mid-day.

I'd interviewed a couple of promising potential housekeepers earlier and planned to get Martin's preference when he came home from work. It was lunchtime and I was eating a sandwich and reading on the terrace. I marked the page with my finger and returned inside to see what happened. Martin leaned against a table in the entryway with his suit jacket over one arm, his tie loosened, his body sagging. His eyes were glassy and unfocused. He smelled of sweat and alcohol.

"You're early—is something wrong?"

Ignoring the question, he brushed by me, threw his jacket toward a chair as he stumbled to the kitchen to grab a bottle of scotch from a cupboard. He poured a full glass and carried it to the terrace. His hands shook, spilling half the contents. The volatile spirits puddling on the hot red tiles spread fumes to envelop me.

Cursing, Martin slugged the remaining liquor in one long gulp and wiped his mouth with the back of his hand.

"For God's sake, Martin, what's happened?"

"I'm done at the end of the month. No use looking for anything else here because I already know there's nothing at my age. We're leaving. We'll use the house on Vashon."

"I don't understand." I'd rather chew glass than move to Vashon.

"Dante said no more contracts, so cutbacks necessary. Someone in the head office in Milan took my job. Rumors have been flying for months." His words were choked. "Don't know if I'm the only one. The bastard. After all I've done for him."

"What will you, I—"

Ignoring me again, he returned to the kitchen to pour another drink, downed it and walked out.

"—live on?"

I retrieved his jacket from the floor, and returned to the terrace, for once relieved Martin had followed his usual pattern of fleeing conflict. He said he needed peace. So did I. I leaned against the railing to focus on the news that I'd been granted my desire to return to Seattle without further argument. But not in the way I intended.

A few uncaring birds chittered in the potted olive

and lemon trees. Domestic noises from adjacent terraces floated through the humid air along with the smell of simmering *ragù* from a neighboring kitchen. The early afternoon heat radiated off the tiles and a small bright-green lizard dashed along. The sight made me remember Tyler chasing but never quite catching the speedy creatures when he was young.

Unable to avoid the problem, my attention turned from past to future as I saw myself stuck in some silent house in the middle of Puget Sound, a ferry ride from Seattle with its museums and theaters where I wanted to be. "No. Just no," I said aloud, repeating it several times. But what about money for two households; for tuition if he had no income? How much would be necessary? How much was there?

I looked at the suit jacket still in my hand. It needed dry cleaning.

****

"What are you doing?"

"Just getting rid of old stuff. Don't need it anymore." Martin was trying to hold on to a large carton and open the front door at the same time the following evening.

"Need help?"

"I'm good." He grimaced as he balanced a heavy box on his knee to open the door.

When he returned empty-handed, I tried to get his attention. "Martin, I'm begging you. Talk to me. Tell me what's going on. I'm worried about you."

"Down to my last month at work like I said." He focused on the dull-colored still life hanging on the wall. It had belonged to his mother. I'd always hated the painting because it reflected my marriage. Dead Nature was a literal translation of Still Life, *Natura Morta,* in Italian. I wouldn't pack it.

"I know. I'm worried about you with all this stress. You don't need to go to work."

"I'm fine, feel great. We'll be on our way before you know it."

"What about your doctor in Seattle? You told me he gave you some new pills when you had your checkup. What were they for?"

"The old quack said I needed to get more exercise. I'll walk when we get to the house on Vashon."

I didn't say there was no "we" because it was useless. But the phrase "In sickness and in health," from our wedding vows popped into my head. Was I wrong to leave him? No, but I wouldn't cut off contact.

****

A few days later Martin showed up bedraggled after what would normally be work hours. "Gotta clear up a few things with Trench." He had a hangdog face.

"Things?" Why was the odious man back in the picture?

"He's going to be leaving too and we just have to tie up some loose ends. And he wants to thank me for all our years of collaboration by taking us out to a restaurant up the coast as a farewell. He says it was one you wrote about and wants you to come to introduce him to the chef."

The news that Trench read my blog was deeply unsettling. He sounded like a stalker. "You go ahead, I don't care. Like I keep telling you, there's no 'us' and I don't care what he wants."

"You don't understand. I *need* you to come with me."

I could read anxiety on Martin's face. "As I've told you so many times, you're right—I don't understand. And at this point, I don't want to." I turned away when Martin grabbed my arm. Not hard but enough to make me face him.

"Please Nicole. Just this one more time." His eyes were watering.

I caved in out of fear for his well-being.

****

The tension in Martin's shoulders was obvious as he sat in the front passenger seat of Trench's car. I'd climbed into the back, hoping to avoid any interaction between the two men. Trench drove toward the airport before he swung north on the *autostrada* away from Rome. I looked at the sign with its logo of a plane ascending. I'd rebooked my flight and would be on the cutoff road in little more than two weeks, taxi piled with luggage. Martin wanted to remain in Rome until the last day of his contract the following week. If it had been me, I would have walked out the moment the notice landed on my desk but I was happy not to be stuck next to him on the long flight back home.

Despite my determination to stay uninvolved, Trench's gaudy diamond pinky ring drew my attention when it flashed in the sunlight as he waved an arm to emphasize a point in his repetitious reminiscences about Vietnam. I leaned forward, a hand on the headrest behind Martin to catch the conversation. Martin's jaw was tight and I could see a patch of stubble he'd missed while shaving. He said, "Yeah" a couple of times as Trench droned on about the "good old days in the barracks," the same one-sided conversation I'd had to endure earlier. Trench looked at me with a momentary smirk after I'd glanced at the rearview mirror and our eyes met. I held them until he was forced to watch where he was driving.

When he made a remark about the sweet smoke in 'Nam, Martin stiffened as if someone had jammed a rod down his back. "No worries, buddy. No worries at all," Trench added as he clamped Martin's shoulder. Martin flinched but said nothing. Trench continued babbling.

I tuned him and the past out to watch the familiar Italian sights as farmland, blue sea, and billboards with ads for restaurants with rooms for wedding receptions, car dealerships, and signs with distances to the closest Carabinieri station passed by the car window. Scarlet poppies flashed their brilliance along roadside ditches. My favorite flower. Another sight I'd miss. The distant blue hills with thunderheads piled high made me think of the snowy Cascades and Olympics. Maybe I could learn to ski. Snoqualmie Pass wasn't far from Seattle.

Trench turned off the A-1 at the wrong exit. "Hey, this isn't the way to the restaurant." I was alarmed. "Where are we going?"

"Just a quick detour before lunch. Need to stretch my legs and have a chat with your ever-lovin' honey."

Trench turned into the parking lot adjoining an archeological park's gatehouse near Cerveteri. Martin slumped and said, "Sure thing."

I was tempted to wait in the car to avoid further interaction, but I'd always loved the area, a wooded site filled with Etruscan tombs, as had Tyler and Jenna, so I didn't object, not that it would have done any good if I had. Instead, I thought of Tyler barreling around the paths between the round tombs or climbing down into the dark and damp interiors to pretend he was an Etruscan king engaged in some mysterious rite, or Jenna announcing she was a princess leading her warriors against Roman Centurions. Never Sophie who remained impervious to childhood pleasures.

I heard Martin breathing heavily, almost panting, as we walked to the entrance to purchase tickets. The back of his shirt and underarms were soaked with sour-smelling sweat, ankles and feet swollen in sandals. I recalled he'd told me the doctor in Seattle said he was fine. It couldn't be true. Maybe he wanted me to come with him because he wasn't feeling well. But what could I do? I knew first aid but wasn't even remotely an EMT. The thought was one of a cascade unsettling me ever more.

The men walked ahead on the deeply rutted stone path where ancient Etruscan funeral wagons had hauled the dead to family tombs centuries before the Romans obliterated their civilization. Anticipation and trepidation filled my thoughts as the men moved away. Would my new life be stymied with his job loss or need for daily care? In "sickness and in health" rang loud in my consciousness.

My thoughts were interrupted when I heard Martin shouting. "I've paid my dues and I'm done. You hear? *I'm done.* There's no more."

I halted about twenty feet back, my attention now focused on the men who faced each other as if ready to fight. Martin's fists were balled. Trench's response was too low for me to hear. But Martin's answer was loud but with labored breath: "I don't want to ever hear or see you again. Understand? Forget lunch and leave. We'll find our own way home."

No more what? Should I intervene? Martin would tell me to shut up, stay out of his business. *Let it be,* I told myself. They walked again. I could see Trench gesturing, while Martin sped up to put distance between them, shooing him away as if Trench was a yapping dog nipping at his heels.

I followed a few paces onward but the rainwater from the previous night's storm had made the path wet and slippery. My shoes were soaked. The dress I'd retrieved from a suitcase stuck to my back and thighs from the intense heat and humidity. What was the point of tagging along like some girl the boys didn't want around when they were up to no good in their treehouse? This day could not end soon enough.

A nearby rock invited me to perch to wait for the men to return. Tiny wild pink cyclamen flowers poked between the grasses and fallen pine needles carpeting the ground. With petals facing backward like the tail of a comet, I always saw cyclamens as shooting stars. I picked one but it had been partially eaten by some hungry insect. I let the flower fall not wanting to make a wish on an imperfect star.

A local poet, another expatriate American, had recently published his latest work in a slim chapbook. I'd bought a copy when he did a reading at the bookstore Primrose formerly owned. I'd taken time from packing my things to attend and still had the chapbook in my shoulder bag. Uncertain what to do while I waited for the men, I read to pass the time. The first page I turned to held the perfect poem to suit my mood.

We could have shared a glass today
but now you're gone.
I wonder what the day will bring
with its gray and lowering clouds.

On the opposite page was a woodcut of a wild

cyclamen, the flower I'd picked moments ago. The words raised bittersweet memories. I could feel Alessandro's tender touch on my body again, emotions I didn't want to deal with. Not now; maybe in Seattle where it would be easier so far from Rome. I closed the book and headed for the shop where there might be some historical fiction to read on the plane. Or better, in front of a cozy fire. The apartment in Rome didn't have a fireplace. It would be a non-negotiable amenity when I looked for my own place in Seattle.

The shop had a good selection of books along with the usual fridge magnets and postcards. A novel set in Etruscan times looked interesting. I purchased it then lingered in the shop to look at souvenirs. An American entered with his family. He shouted about some financial deal on his cellphone while his wife corralled toddler twins who wanted lunch. I remembered the times when my children were small and wanted their meals, their toys, my attention. Tyler called me "Nicole," Sophie "Mother," and Jenna "Mom." Such unique personalities.

I was about to buy a terracotta model of a Roman child as a last addition to my collection when my stomach growled as if in response to the twins' demand for hamburgers. My phone told me nearly an hour had slipped by since we'd arrived. The two men were probably waiting impatiently, their argument at an end. I put the head back on the shelf and returned to the spot where they'd walked away from me. Neither were in sight.

I looked around the archeological complex—it was after one o'clock, time to get the lunch over and end the dismal outing. I returned to the half-domed tombs made of stone blocks to duck into the dark underground but could see little beyond steps leading downward. As I threaded the puddles between the tombs, I listened for the men's voices. A distant baby's cry momentarily filled the air while a tour leader droned on to a nearby group of elderly Brits clutching guidebooks. Several looked furtively at their watches. I interrupted the group leader to ask if he'd seen the two men. He and his charges all shook their heads.

Back to the ticket office. "*Mi scusi signore*, but have you seen two men who might be looking for me? One, my husband, is wearing a striped blue shirt and khaki pants."

The ticket taker looked up from his *Corriere dello Sport*, filled with the latest soccer and cycling news. "Signora?" He put his finger on the line he'd been reading and said, "Sorry but no. I've been busy."

I called Martin. But the phone switched to the message mode after a few rings. I left a voicemail. "Where are you? Call me now. Please." Ten minutes later the phone was still silent. I texted the same message though Martin seldom responded to them—at least those I sent. Still no response.

Phone in hand, I rushed to circle the tombs again, forgetting my worry about slipping. The afternoon sunlight now penetrated the entrances. I could see the rock floors, but many were flooded with murky water. I called Martin's name tentatively. With no response I shouted. My unanswered cries hung heavy in the humid air. I ran back to the gatehouse.

"I can't find him!" After a breath, "My husband, I mean." I could feel sweat coursing down my face.

The ticket seller removed his glasses and said, "Once in a while we do have a child who runs around and gets too far but—"

"We somehow got separated. It's lunchtime."

The man smiled at the thought of lunch. "When you see him, I can make a good recommendation for a restaurant."

Frightening thoughts rushed through my mind—he wasn't lost but was sick or injured. My steps matched my heartbeat, pulse pounding as I ran to the parking lot. And sure enough there they were.

I could see Martin was white-faced and leaning against the open car door while Trench had his arm around Martin's waist to support him.

"What's wrong? What's happening?' I shouted as I neared.

"Hubby doesn't feel good." Trench didn't have his usual smirk.

"Martin, let me help you into the car. We'll find a doctor." I shoved Trench aside and substituted my own arm. His body was heavy against mine, too heavy for me to support.

"Ohhhh," he moaned as he struggled unsuccessfully to stand straight. Then he clutched his chest. His knees folded and he dropped to the ground face down at my feet.

"Call 118 for an ambulance," I screamed at Trench. He punched in the numbers on his phone as I knelt on the sharp gravel by Martin's still body. I rolled him over and looked into his unseeing eyes. I knew he was dead but tried CPR anyway.

CHAPTER TWELVE

A few minutes later I heard the distinctive ambulance wail *ee-oo-ee-oo* before the vehicle came to an abrupt stop in the parking lot. The crew jumped out with their equipment to administer CPR and defibrillation. Nothing. They continued to work in relays until accepting the truth and standing up to face me.

I heard one say they weren't allowed to transport a deceased person but would call a local mortuary service to collect Martin and do an autopsy. I turned to ask Trench what had happened earlier. He and his car were gone. Instead, a clump of tourists hovered nearby taking photos to tell the folks back home about their exciting visit to the tombs. At this point spots were swimming in my eyes and I was dizzy. One of the EMTs helped me to sit in the front seat of the ambulance.

By the time I got a few wits back, the local police arrived along with the Carabinieri and the mortuary representative. He and his helper loaded Martin's body into his van before I could even touch his face in a goodbye.

I was in shock when the questions began. Uncertain about what Martin and Trench had really been doing, I stuck to the facts about Martin's health and his collapse while I inwardly wondered if I'd intervened earlier events would have turned out differently. The Carabinieri also wanted to know why we were without a car. I said Trench had gone to get help and I didn't know where he was. I was sure he was on the run. After giving them his name and the type of car, the Carabinieri said they'd follow up. I didn't expect to hear more.

I accepted the offer to drive me home. I forced my eyes to remain open to avoid the picture of dead Martin imprinted on my eyelids as I sat in the back seat of the Carabinieri's car. My fingernails dug sharp crescents into my palms as I watched the brooding clouds blot the sun, turning the sea to mercury, shiny and viscous.

I must have dozed because, next thing I knew, we parked by my apartment building. I let the officer hold my arm as we entered the building and took the elevator to our, now my apartment. Italian lunch hour noises filtered through the shutters in other apartments—pots and pans, plates and cutlery. The smell of a meaty sauce, normally mouthwatering, made my sour stomach turn.

"Shall I come in to sit with you for a while? Make some coffee?" the officer asked.

"I'm fine. Please thank everyone for their help, but I prefer to be alone." I let myself in. Suffering vertigo, I leaned against the inside of the door until the sensation passed and I could stagger to the sofa where I wrapped up in an old cotton throw despite the oppressive heat. The apartment was deathly quiet, stifling.

I turned on the television to quell my racing thoughts. It didn't help. I tried the radio, tuning in to the classical station, but the program was all Bach. The relentless progression of notes in a fugue played with insistent mathematical precision heightened my obsessive mental images of Martin lying on the sharp gravel. I switched the radio off. The apartment was filled with silence. I wept for Tyler and Sophies' father and for my sudden change of circumstances where the straight trajectory upward was now veering in a pattern like an exploding rocket.

The threatened storm arrived with violent thunder and lightning. The power went out. I woke from a fitful sleep on the sofa and felt my way to a window to watch forked bolts split the sky. Deafening thunderclaps assaulted my ears. Sheets of rain fell, drains overflowed. Trash containers crashed against parked cars and lampposts. Lightning struck a plane tree across the street from the apartment. The trunk split in two, the top half falling onto a parked car, crushing it. I crept into bed, pillows around my ears to mute the flashes, the rumbling booms, and the day's events.

****

The Rome weather had cleared but my own internal storm still raged with competing thoughts jostling for dominance. "What if—, What now—, How shall I—?" I gave up at dawn to stand on the terrace with a mug of coffee to watch the sky slowly turn from the pale blue color of an antique porcelain cup I'd inherited from my grandmother, to citron and then apricot and gold as the sun rose to illuminate another brilliant Roman day. The thoughts returned. How was I to mourn a man who was only a husband on paper, and how was I to move forward with my plans? I remembered the cup had been smashed to bits when I'd dropped the box of china on moving day years ago.

I needed to tell the children but was so exhausted I fell asleep the moment I sat down on the sofa. It was several hours later before I scrolled the contacts on my phone to find Sophie's number. There was no answer. The ringing stopped, replaced by a voice message. I waited until the beep. "Sophie? Please call me right away. Something's happened. Please call."

It was too early to call Jenna in Seattle, so I tried Tyler where it was afternoon.

A crackly voice answered, "Nicole?"

The connection broke. I tried again and managed to say, "It's an emergency," before I was cut off again. I stared at the useless phone. A few minutes later it rang with my familiar marimba tone.

"I'm on a satellite phone," Tyler's crackling voice said. "I'm in South Sudan out in the field."

"Something has happened. To your father."

"To Dad? What's happened?"

"He had a heart attack and couldn't be resuscitated."

"What? Surely not!"

I stuttered, "It was out where the Etruscan tombs are, where you liked to play." My shaky composure wavered further. "We were about to leave to go back to Seattle. Did you know he lost his job?"

"No, I didn't know. What can I do? This is terrible. I'll come to Rome as soon as I can. I might be able to hitch a ride on one of our supply planes back to Kampala to get a connecting flight."

I wanted his steady presence but couldn't insist. "I know it's hard for you to get away and there's nothing you can do here, but I wish you'd come to Seattle when I get there. Unless something changes, I'm leaving here in two weeks. I'll keep you posted." It hurt to say it, but I couldn't ask him to leave others in desperate conditions facing starvation, rape, or murder. And what really was there for him to do?

"Are you sure? Please tell me if you need me to come. And why were you out at Cerveteri?"

"Your dad hadn't been well lately, quite anxious, and I think he was mixed up in some way with the guy we were with yesterday. He's called Karl Trench. I don't know if you ever saw him. He was involved with your father's work in some way. I didn't want to go but your dad insisted. I think going out of town was some ruse to get him alone. At one point I thought they were arguing when they walked away from me. Then when I found them, it was clear he was in terrible distress."

"I can't imagine Dad being involved in something bad, but I guess I never knew much about his job. Are you sure I shouldn't come to Rome? I can be there in a few days."

"I'll call if I need you here. I don't think I'll have a memorial but will let you know." I wiped my nose before I added, "The important thing is you take care of yourself. Love you."

South Sudan? He never found a home, not with Martin and me nor anyone or anyplace else. As Tyler grew from child to teen to adult, Martin's relationship with him developed from indifference to one of disagreements as if he'd seen Tyler as a challenge to his authority. Tyler responded by finding ever more ways to stay away from home. Now he was thirty-one, a rootless wanderer always searching but never finding stability.

I tried Jenna next, even though it was five in Seattle.

"Mom?" Her question was followed by a crash. "Sorry. I dropped my phone." Her voice was thick with sleep. "It's really early here."

No use avoiding the news. "It's your dad."

"What's happened? Tell me!"

I told at least some of it.

Jenna said, "I'll be on the first flight to Rome I can

book. I'll let you know the schedule. Get Maggie to help and call me whenever you need. Please, Mom."

I said I would and put the phone on a table near the sofa waiting for Sophie's call. I must have fallen asleep. The chapter from the *Aeneid* my book club recently studied invaded my dream. I was on a raft slowly floating down the River Styx on the way to Hell. The sluggish brown water was like the Tiber. The raft was swept into an eddy and turned in a circle before it tipped over. I was dumped into the filthy water with Trench mocking me. The mournful tolling of a bell filled my ears. I raised my head to look around the room. The ringing continued. It was my phone. It wasn't Jenna with her flight schedule, but Sophie.

"Did you want something?"

"Sophie, I have terrible news."

"What? What's going on? I've been in a meeting. I'm busy."

"Your father. He's…gone." I choked.

"What do you mean, gone? Where'd he go?"

"I'm sorry to tell you he passed away."

"No! No, no, no!" She howled.

When she quieted, I summarized what happened.

"I always hated the place. Why you wanted to go there is beyond me. And, see, I was right." She paused to catch her breath before saying, "You said he was with a man? What man?"

I repeated the same words as I had used with Jenna.

"Wait a minute—I have a call on the other line. A client who needs a restraining order. She needs me even on Sunday. I'm in my office now and I'm slammed by work." Her voice was shaky.

I wanted to reach through the ether to grab her to get

her attention. What was the matter with her to pretend she was hardened and emotionless? How like Martin she was with her reluctance to engage when she must be devastated.

When Sophie came back on the line after five minutes, she said, "I'm coming."

"I know you'd have to make plans for Jacob. Do what's best for you. I could stop in Boston on the way home to Seattle." I regretted discouraging Tyler from coming to help balance Sophie.

"Listen, I'll call you later, okay?" Sophie cut the connection although not before I heard a muffled cry of pain.

I mouthed a prayer someone would come along to break through the barrier cutting off my oldest daughter from happiness.

Jenna called an hour later to say she'd booked a seat for Monday and would arrive Tuesday morning.

Shortly after, Sophie called again. "A friend in my office will help with Jacob. But I'm a bit short now and need help with the fare."

I could tell by the tone of her voice she was reluctant to come, still pretending to be unemotional after the one outburst. "Jenna will arrive on Tuesday. I'll be here another couple of weeks, so you don't need to hurry. Don't worry about money."

****

The horror of Martin's death and the tenor of my conversation with Sophie so agitated me I couldn't sit still. I needed to call the consulate but couldn't face it. To buy time, I opened the door to the terrace to be near my beloved lemon tree. Several lemons were ripe and the profuse flowers were fragrant in the soft air. How I'd miss this little tree in its terracotta pot. I dragged the chaise lounge near it, lay down and told myself to breathe slowly and deeply. The command was useless. Past, present, and future insistently coiled around my brain like a python squeezing the life from me.

The need for practicalities brought me back to today. Was there anyone else to notify? From what Martin had said years ago, the aunt who took him in as an orphan was already elderly and surely must be long dead. He'd said he had no brothers or sisters and had never mentioned any cousins either. Maybe at some point I'd put an obituary in the Seattle paper to see if anyone turned up from a family or his past work life. But not now.

Sophie's mention of her office during our telephone conversation reminded me of Martin's office. I left a voicemail for Antonella, the office manager, asking her to call because of Martin's unexpected death and the paperwork required to get my benefits. She wouldn't be in until the following day, a relief because I dreaded talking to the woman. I'd met her a few times at recent Christmas parties where she was underdressed and over made up even for Italy. She flaunted her curves, constantly leaning over to show her ample cleavage. The men loved it; the women, including me, rolled their eyes. And now with Martin losing his job, I wondered what the company management's reaction would be since Martin was still on the payroll until the end of the month. Or so he'd said.

I called the consulate's weekend duty officer next to tell her about the death and make an appointment to meet with an official to go over what had to be done when an American citizen dies in Italy. Then I changed the sheets on our double bed where Martin had slept. And Jenna's where I'd slept since my return from Seattle. She would expect her own room as would Sophie. Neither of them needed to know about my sleeping arrangements anyway.

The remainder of the day passed as if some malignant power held the clock's hands back, so each minute took an hour. Confused thoughts continued to claw and scratch my brain and heart. I poured a large glass of Martin's scotch to sip on the terrace. Instead, I swilled it as bells for an evening service at a nearby church reverberated in the warm air.

CHAPTER THIRTEEN

Antonella called first thing Monday. Her histrionic lamentations shocked me.

"Oh my god, O *dio*," Antonella said again and again. "Martin, Martin."

I held the phone away from my ear while the unseemly outburst assaulted me. It seemed like an act, making me sure she already knew.

After the crazed words, Antonella collected herself to ask about the circumstances of Martin's death, but, now wary, I told her I didn't know anything specific other than the heart attack. She said she'd tell Martin's boss, and would come to the apartment to comfort me. Repelled by the thought of such an intrusion, I said I'd visit the office as soon as possible. Afterward, I sat in a daze, unable to capture the random thoughts about Martin and Antonella flitting by.

When I'd emailed Maggie from Seattle about returning to Rome after home leave, I'd looked forward to telling her about my plans, but she'd responded she'd be in Parma for an extended visit with her daughter. Her return date was several days from now. What a rock she'd been during the time when I tried to get settled and when Jenna was on the way. And we'd had such good times with our food blog and tours. Dear Maggie with her Irish brogue. I thought of our beginning conversation when she mentioned a first husband who "didn't work out." How lucky she'd been with Orazio.

Contessa Franca had dropped out of sight, living the life in Australia. She too would have been such a help as I struggled to manage the immediate future. She'd tell me not to go down without a fight. I would tell her I wouldn't.

My thoughts were finally annulled by sleep but I awoke to silence at two in the morning as rumpled as if I was a pile of laundry carelessly tossed in a hamper with Martin's dirty clothes. Sunrise was hours away but I made coffee anyway. With my head propped against the armrest, mug cradled in my hands as the warmth seeped through, I willed myself to think rationally. Would there be life insurance to help me begin again? A pension? After all, he'd worked for the company for nearly twenty years. What if there was nothing? That couldn't be the case, could it?

I hauled myself up to find the Italian and U.S. checkbooks along with the key to the safe deposit box in Seattle. The Italian account held enough to tide me over for a couple of weeks but death could come with more than an emotional cost.

The U.S. checkbook with money we used when we returned to Seattle on home leave, showed a balance of $2,156.39. I could convert them to euros but what other ready money was available? Where was the key to Martin's desk? He must have some investment records stored there along with his employment contract unless they were all online. And where were our tax returns? I'd signed them every year without anything more than a cursory review showing Martin's six-figure income.

I looked for the key in his office and saw his laptop was gone. The desk surface was clean except for a framed photo of the two of us placed face down, and his reading glasses. I picked them up. One lens was broken. He must have stepped on them. Or he fell. Or had he been involved in an altercation? My stomach lurched as I thought of Trench. I put the glasses on the windowsill and resumed my search for the key: nothing. Back to the dresser to search every drawer: no key. No key where we'd kept the others for the cars and a spare for the apartment for guests. It must be on his key ring. I found a screwdriver in a kitchen drawer, but it wouldn't work in the lock. A hammer didn't make the slightest dent on the desk's steel lock.

I opened my laptop and scrolled until I found the document containing my passwords. I logged in to the joint savings account. The balance was $19,568.06. I'd been so busy with my culinary tours I hadn't looked at it for ages, and now it was plain it had dropped rapidly over the last year. Martin must have invested the money elsewhere. I attempted to log into our investment account but received a message I wasn't recognized. My effort to set up a new password resulted in a notice that I was locked out. Martin had always boasted about how much money he made on his investments. I'd trusted him.

****

Jenna called when she arrived at the Rome airport on Tuesday morning to say she'd take a cab. When the *citofono* at the building's entry buzzed, I ran downstairs to hold my red-eyed daughter before we took the steps to the apartment. Jenna's tears salted her tea as we two sat on the terrace while I told her the story again. Later in the afternoon we entered the American consulate on the Via Veneto.

A security officer pointed us to a room where we

stood in front of a heavy glass window with a hole in it. A young man in a dark blue suit, a U.S. flag pin in his lapel, and conservative tie appeared on the other side.

I showed him my passport and Martin's before telling him about the incident. After he asked a few questions and finished taking notes he offered brief condolences. Then, abruptly, he said, "You will have to decide what to do with the remains when they are released. Do you want them shipped back to Seattle or…?" He fiddled with a pen, studying it as if he'd never seen one before.

"What are the choices?" I hadn't thought about the steps necessary to deal with the body still in the morgue in Cerveteri.

"It's complicated. Normally it takes about a week to get the autopsy completed and certificates signed. The procedure in Italy is you need to get a lawyer who would find a doctor to be present at the autopsy on your behalf. We are not allowed to become involved. We can give you a list of lawyers. Also, we will issue an official death certificate after we receive the Italian one. You must take it to a funeral home. I can also give you a list of some in Rome who deal with this sort of thing."

He thumbed through a file I could see was labeled "What to do when a US Citizen Dies," holding a list of lawyers, and another of funeral directors who worked with expatriates. He said whomever I chose would take care of contacting the crematorium or local cemetery, or manage all necessary formalities for shipment of Martin's remains including the paperwork and the return of his personal effects.

Without looking up, he riffled the papers into some order apparently pleasing him and, using his forefinger, shoved them through a slot at the bottom of the glass.

Jenna stuffed them into her bag before she took my hand.

"I don't see any point in legal help but I'll look into it. The autopsy can proceed without one for now." How much would a lawyer cost? How much for handling Martin's dead body? And what would Martin have wanted done with his remains after the autopsy? He'd never said what he'd done with his first wife's. We'd never talked about the possibility of either of us dying in Italy, or anywhere else.

The young man droned on about the complicated rules for shipping bodies: the preservation steps to prevent decomposition, the hermetically-sealed zinc container enclosed in hardwood, and the problems next of kin sometimes faced with shipping documents and heavy costs. If I wanted Martin cremated in Italy, there were different rules on transporting the ashes if I wanted to take them home.

I looked at Jenna who grasped my hand more tightly after the onslaught of ghoulish information. I'd zoned out.

"Ma'am?"

I turned back to the young man. He was perspiring.

"As I was saying, when the body is released, you could have the remains interred in Italy in a cemetery. If your husband wasn't Catholic, there might be the possibility of burial in the Protestant Cemetery if there's room."

Martin never had time for the spiritual side of life. One of many things he never wanted to deal with. I sometimes wondered if it had to do with the loss of his parents or his wife, like the poverty of our relationship.

"Ma'am, please let me convey my condolences again on behalf of our staff. I am personally sorry for your loss." He paused before adding, "It's the first death case I've had to deal with."

It was my first death case too. How could it be so complicated?

As Jenna and I walked down the Via Vittorio Veneto toward a Metro stop a few blocks away, I turned my thoughts to the 1960s when starlets in cafes and paparazzi filled the area every night. Now it was filled with upscale tourist hotels and American-style bars.

I made sure to turn away when we passed Santa Maria della Concezione, the church with a macabre crypt held the bones of four thousand monks, some whole skeletons, others whose bones were arranged in patterns or made into chandeliers. Once I read how the living let the dead rot in upright stone seats to retrieve the bones. Tyler had reveled in the scene when he was a teenager, but Sophie and Jenna had agreed for once it was revolting. I tried not to think of Martin's body and the autopsy. Jenna clasped my hand again as if she could read my thoughts.

Later, Jenna made one of my favorite pasta dishes, *cacio e pepe*, tonnarelli pasta with grated Pecorino Romano and lots of ground pepper, but I was unable to eat more than a few bites. I retreated to bed, too tired to think about the coming days filled with problems, known and unforeseen.

****

Sophie showed up Wednesday afternoon without calling from the airport. She let herself in and surprised both Jenna and me while we were eating lunch on the terrace.

I could feel her tense when I embraced her. "I'm relieved you're here. How is Jacob?"

She stepped back. "Same as usual, but I want to know all about this. I want to know what happened to *my* father." She stepped to the railing, her muscles tensed, like a boxer waiting for the bell to signal the start of a fight. "So?"

The aggressive posture made me fear Sophie was about to blame me for Martin's death. I repeated the bare facts but didn't mention my concerns about the relationship between Martin and Trench as I had with Tyler. Nor did I give details about the argument I'd overheard. When Sophie persisted, I said they'd had a business relationship which I guess was true. I didn't offer an opinion, afraid it would make Martin look devious. Sophie wouldn't like that at all.

Sophie didn't like any of it anyway. "I don't understand. You must know more."

"He died of a heart attack. I tried CPR as did the EMTs. He wasn't in good health and he wasn't young. I don't know anything more. And please stop calling him '*my* father' as if you were his only child." I regretted my sharp response, but Sophie knew how to get to me and she'd succeeded again.

Sophie grumbled something under her breath.

"I'll make some tea. You must be tired."

Jenna, who hadn't said a word, left for a walk. I rummaged through the kitchen cupboard for teabags, leaving Sophie on the terrace. While the water heated, I concentrated on what to do while waiting for the autopsy report. My flights were booked, but instead of filling a few suitcases of my own things, now I needed to empty out the apartment.

I'd need to call a moving company. But even if I could get them to come right away, where would all the furniture go? I didn't have an apartment in Seattle, and now no assurance money to rent or buy would be readily available. My parents' house had already been sold; the proceeds set aside for their care. I'd learned then that commercial storage was hideously expensive. The best option was to park the goods at the old house on Vashon Island until I got my finances settled. I couldn't remember what the house looked like. Whatever, it was a stroke of good fortune the agent had never been able to rent it.

I made tea, found a tray and carried it out to the terrace to talk to Sophie about the most immediate problem.

"I'm not sure what to do with your father's remains. Perhaps have him cremated here. We could scatter the ashes somewhere or put them in a columbarium. Or in Seattle."

"What are you talking about? Slow down. I want to know a lot more about his death before any decisions are made. He was *my* father, after all. *I* loved him." Sophie's tired face turned fluorescent.

"I've told you what I know. We understand you loved him, Sophie. We all loved him." It wasn't true but what else could I say? I'd tried to take his place by offering extra love to the children but with little success when it came to her.

Sophie looked unconvinced. "You never loved him. What if I want him buried near my home?"

"Stop it! Do you think this is a pleasant, happy time for any of us? If you want him buried near you, you can make the arrangements after we talk to Tyler and Jenna.

This needs to be a family agreement, not just your wants. If the other children agree, fine. I won't stand in your way."

Sophie's eyes narrowed and her mouth pinched with suspicion but she didn't say more.

As I began to pour I knocked the pot onto the tiles where it shattered. The hot liquid splashed both of us. Sophie wiped her slacks and said she needed to do some work on a case coming up for trial. I picked up the shards and watched the liquid evaporate like my efforts to keep the conversation at a low pitch.

Jenna picked up Sophie's favorite, Pizza Capricciosa, loaded with black olives, artichoke hearts and sliced ham, at the pizzeria down the street, but the leaden atmosphere squashed any dinnertime conversational initiatives. Sophie returned to her bedroom. Jenna and I cleaned up. As I passed by Sophie's room later, I could hear her crying, the sound faint as if she had her head face down on a pillow.

CHAPTER FOURTEEN

The following morning, I opened my door and there was Maggie. She embraced me and said, "My dear, the neighbors told me they'd seen Jenna and Sophie arrive, both looking very unhappy. Tell me what's happened."

"Martin…he's dead. A heart attack while we were out at the tombs at Cerveteri. We were with some man he worked with." I was breathless with relief that she'd showed up.

"What can I do?"

"Just be here for me. It's awful. He got fired, and the more I think about it, I'm sure he was involved in something. And I think he might have lost our money but I don't know because I'm locked out of our investment accounts."

"Jesus, Mary, and Joseph!"

I wanted to invite her in to talk but the phone rang. I mouthed a "see you later" and Maggie waved a response.

The voice on the phone was Antonella calling to demand I come to the office as soon as possible to discuss payments. She added I could collect the personal items Martin had left in the office. I imagined pictures of the children, maybe some tokens for outstanding work or the pen and pencil set I'd given him. A diary? I was about to hang up when she said, "The branch manager would like to personally offer his condolences. He was so sorry to hear of Martin's death. We all valued his work."

"I'll come this afternoon." I didn't believe a word about anybody's sorrow.

Martin had already returned his company car after he received notice that he'd be fired. That left my dented and sputtering old junker to drive along the Cristoforo Colombo toward EUR, the area of Rome where his office was located. My mind was on the meeting, not on driving. I jerked to attention when I narrowly missed a produce delivery truck. The driver cut me off as we careened around the obelisk honoring the inventor Marconi erected in the center of a six-lane road. A crate of tomatoes teetered before it fell off the truck, followed by several loaded with eggplants. Nearby drivers honked and gestured when I swerved sharply to avoid them. The truck driver, wearing a sleeveless undershirt, leaned out his window to spout the usual Roman obscenities while making a slashing gesture as if to cut my throat though he was at fault. I raised my hand to my chin and then flicked fingers forward as if sweeping him away before I turned on Viale Europa.

As usual in Rome, there was no place to park. I left the car by the curb where a crosswalk was marked with faded paint. I'd plead I didn't see the stripes if the traffic police came around. For the first time in days, I found myself smiling when I thought about trying to get away with such whining in Seattle.

I found the entrance to the office building. The guard looked at me on his video screen when I asked for the company offices. After a pause while he consulted a directory and used his phone, he unlocked the entry. I took the elevator to the top floor where Antonella waited at a thick glass door etched with the company's logo—a missile soaring into space. She looked composed; the hysteria gone from her voice. When she caught me in an unwelcome embrace, I kept my arms at my sides, suffocating in the odor of her heady perfume.

After that, she grasped my elbow to lead me into a meeting room saying the president would soon finish a conference call and would I like a coffee. A few minutes later, a young woman brought a tiny cup and a sugar wafer. She precisely placed them on the table directly in front of me before leaving silently.

I was lost in thought when the door latch's soft click announced the arrival of Federico Dante, the *pezzo grosso*, big shot, as Martin had called him. He reminded me of a modern-day version of an ancient Roman senator with silver hair, a perfectly-tailored suit made of some shiny blue material, silk tie, tailored dress shirt embroidered with his initials on the cuff, and heavy gold cufflinks. The outfit must have cost as much as Martin's monthly salary. A signet ring circled a little finger. Even with all the fancy clothes he looked shifty, his aluminum-colored eyes moving from me to a picture of some middle-eastern-looking location on the far wall, then back again as if appraising the likelihood of me causing trouble.

I stood. Dante took both my hands and leaned back. "You are beautiful in spite of everything, my dear." He released me and waved toward the chair where I'd been sitting. "Let's have a chat and you can tell me what happened. We were all greatly shocked." He sat next to me, moving his chair close so we were knee to knee. I held my ground.

I seethed at his insincere remarks and the invasion of my space. How dare he put a move on me? I barely overcame my desire to walk out.

"I'm not sure what happened beyond what you already know. It was a heart attack. He'd been under much stress since you fired him."

Dante's hard eyes widened for an instant at my remark but didn't respond.

"Why *was* Martin let go?" No need to be polite.

"It was unfortunate we had to cut back. We've lost some of our contracts with the U.S. military and others in NATO. Budget considerations. Also, this branch office will be consolidated with Milan to be closer to the financial center. I am sure you understand we needed to make business decisions. This includes selling the apartment we have maintained for you all these years." His gaze turned to the painting before he looked back at me as if I would be sympathetic.

"As you no doubt know, we offered your husband a cash payment in compensation for breaking the contract. And, of course, there is the life insurance. A policy was part of his employment benefits."

Martin had never mentioned the compensation, but the news was a relief, as was the confirmation there would be money to help me start again.

"My executive assistant will go over the details." He looked at his diamond-studded watch before he stood to look down on me. I rose and he extended his hand. I hesitated before briefly touching his icy fingers.

"Signora, please accept my deepest regrets for your loss." He bowed. The overhead light caught the glitter of gold links as he opened the conference room door to let himself out.

I took a closer look at the picture as I prepared to leave. It wasn't just desert, but a picture of a mud-brick town with some men in camouflage holding weapons and more in the background. A place ruined by war. I shuddered involuntarily.

Antonella was lurking when I stepped into the hallway. I held onto my handbag with both hands to avoid further contact. The woman, looking not all offended, asked me to follow her to an office where there was a low, hard chair in front of an enormous desk furnished with a gold pen and pencil set and a leather folder embossed with the company's logo. She seated herself in a high-backed executive chair. I wanted to snigger at the display of power, but I was a supplicant and couldn't afford to take the risk.

"We'll miss Martin. Mr. Carlisle, I mean. He was such a doll, always bringing flowers to the office and so generous at Christmas or when anyone needed a little help even if he had to dig deep into his wallet. So sweet." She beamed a solicitous smile in my general direction.

A doll? Until our recent return from home leave in Seattle, Martin bought me the occasional bunch of blooms home if he remembered my birthday. Helping others? I'd never heard of him donating a dime to charity. I looked at Antonella's left hand with its substantial diamond and sapphire ring. I tried to ignore an unpleasant notion, but there it was again. Exactly how generous *was* Martin? We'd lived well, but while he mentioned promotions, getting the first two children through university was a stretch even with the company's help.

I took a close look at her. At least five years younger than me. She looked back, unblinking, compelling me to break the impasse.

"Tell me about the compensation you offered to my

husband. What about his state pension? And the life insurance."

Antonella said there would be six months' severance pay and confirmed my air ticket to Seattle and shipment of our goods would still be paid.

"When will this payment be made?" Surely Martin wouldn't have hidden this money from me.

"We will pay after you give us a copy of the death certificate and your banking instructions."

"I don't have the death certificate yet. What about the pension and life insurance?"

She focused on the door to her office. "I don't know about the state pension system or if it applies to your late husband. You should get a lawyer to deal with the government. It's complex, especially since he was a foreigner. For a payout from the company's insurance, we will need banking instructions from the beneficiaries before any money can be dispersed. I'm sure you understand."

"What do you mean beneficiaries?"

She turned to look at me evenly. "Actually, I will tell you there are several. I am not at liberty to reveal their names. We will begin the payment process after we contact them and they supply the proper documents."

"But *I* am the widow."

"I understand, Signora Carlisle, but I must follow your late husband's wishes."

Seized with a need to get away from this witch, I grabbed my handbag to leave but then remembered. "One more thing; I'd like to collect the personal items from my husband's desk. And his briefcase."

"Oh, sorry. I was wrong. He took everything with him several weeks ago. I forgot." Her voice was creamy, eyes cold. "And if you find anything your husband may have mistakenly taken which might belong to the company, please return them at your earliest convenience."

What did he do with the family photos I'd framed? And the expensive red-enamel pen and pencil set I'd secretly bought for the Christmas right before we left for Rome? The seed of doubt about Martin's private life grew again.

"I'll return with banking information when I have the death certificate. And I don't have any papers from your firm."

"Do contact me if you need anything more." Antonella stood to end the audience. She clutched my elbow to steer me out. She even pressed the down button on the elevator as if I was too weak, or more likely, to make sure I left the building. The door silently slid shut as I had a last glimpse of her wearing a brilliant and false smile.

I leaned against the mirrored wall on the way down. Dante surely knew more about Martin's death than he'd said. His name reminded me of the poet's circles of Hell. I wasn't sure which he should be assigned to although the one for liars and flatterers would be about right. Circle Eight, near the lowest.

As I stepped from the elevator, I noticed the smear of lipstick on the mirrored glass where I'd leaned against it. "Tough," I said aloud. I should have written the company's name in the scarlet color along with an Italian obscenity shouted during the incident on the Cristoforo Colombo.

I couldn't remember where I'd parked the car. It was somewhere near the complex of government buildings built in the 1930s I always found menacing with gigantic square pillars and dark porticoes. They were remnants of a difficult time in Italy when ordinary people were made to feel like unwanted insects by the all-powerful bureaucracy. Like I felt with the triumvirate of Trench, Antonella, and Dante trying to control my life. I squinted as the merciless sun cast knife-edged shadows off the graffitied white marble as I searched.

CHAPTER FIFTEEN

I made an appointment with an attorney on the list from the consulate after all. As I ended the call, I overheard Sophie on her own cellphone. She took it away from her ear for a moment to say to me, "Jacob's caregiver tells me he's not doing well, and I need to get back. I have some court dates on Friday and have to get ready anyway. I changed my reservations to fly out tomorrow. I'm sure Jenna can take over. Not much I can do anyway."

"I understand, honey. Give Jacob a big kiss from me." I turned to prepare a salad for dinner and to hide my face I knew expressed torment. What good was Sophie's academic and legal success compared to her troubles? Her troubles never ended.

She excused herself immediately after dinner, saying she needed to pack. I knew she hadn't unpacked since she arrived but didn't argue.

"What's with Sophie?" Jenna asked as she cleared the table. "She's acting so weird. I hardly ever see her, but I wish we could be like sisters. I think she hates me."

"She's terribly unhappy. She loved your dad in her own way, I know, but she and I always have had a hard time of it. She's a champion when it comes to anything intellectual, but I don't know how to make her happy. I'm sure she doesn't dislike you." I gave Jenna a pat on her arm hoping I'd diffused the situation. "Would you reserve a cab for her?"

****

"Mom, I heard you moaning late last night, but I didn't want to wake you."

I blinked in the morning sunlight. "I had a nightmare, but I can't remember it now." I did remember vaguely, a scene with Sophie and me boxing.

"I'm sorry I said anything about Sophie. I know she's got problems with Jacob. I remember when the dear old man in the junk shop vanished along with his treasures. I cried and cried. But losing my father is way worse. I guess it hasn't sunk in yet."

"I don't have time to grieve yet either. Problems weighed on your dad, but he would never talk to me. And I could see his health was declining. Maybe because of the man Trench I told you about about. Sometimes I thought your dad was almost pleading for me to do something, but he wouldn't or couldn't explain."

"I didn't know about all the problems. I wish I could have helped. This is all so sad." Tears rolled down her cheeks. I wrapped my arms around her, and she put her head on my shoulder before moving away to pour a coffee and snuffle. "I'm sure tomorrow will be better, I promise."

I looked out the window to avoid her seeing my doubt.

****

Sophie dragged her wheelie bag into the hallway near the door. I asked, "Want some breakfast? There's toast and eggs. I doubt the taxi will be here for another half hour."

"The airport's good for me." Sophie thumbed through her cell messages, already mentally back in

Boston.

She ignored me as I stood near the door, arms outstretched. Her father's child always. The smell of burnt toast filled the apartment. I ran to check the toaster, unplugged it to pry the smoking blackened bread out of the slots. The front door slammed as Sophie left with her baggage of unhappiness.

How would I ever repair the gulf between the two of us? Maybe we could go to some kind of therapy together although it was hard to imagine after I'd made the suggestion to Martin years ago about marital counseling and been rejected. It was as if both Martin and Sophie savored their grievances. The Sophie problem added to everything else made my mind feel like it had been shoved through a pasta strainer. I found some aspirin before pouring a mug of coffee and opening the door to the terrace where I distracted myself by looking at the people in the apartments across the street. A woman hung laundry on a rack set up on her balcony, another watered pots of geraniums, yet another was on her cellphone waving the other arm in agitation. I turned back to the kitchen to begin filling packing boxes the moving company had brought.

Tyler called to say he didn't have any preference about his father's remains. He repeated he would try to come to Rome if I needed him there. I said there was little for him to do because I'd decided not to have a service given the short time before I left. I didn't tell him I was sure, except for Maggie and Orazio, the attendees would be curiosity seekers whispering about Martin's firing and picturing the circumstances of his death.

After the call I looked at the waiting boxes and said to Jenna, "Hon, I don't know about you, but I need some time to think before I continue packing. Do you mind if I go for a walk?"

"Sure, we can pack later today. I got a message from Tricia, my roommate. A water pipe burst in the apartment building but our stuff's okay. And she got us tickets to the next Husky game."

Everyday life. I would try for a taste of the positives in my Roman life and be a casual observer of the passing scene to fix it in my mind before I departed forever. I set out to put financial worries along with Martin and Sophie out of my mind by turning my attention to old streets, artisan's shops, and *palazzi* turned into museums when the powerful families who'd owned them died out.

I walked along the old streets in the *centro storico*, the desiccated leaves of the plane trees crunching underfoot. The sound made me think of stepping on dead beetles. When I came to Sant'Ignazio, I followed the stream of visitors filing up a ramp to enter the church without thinking. I opened the battered wooden side door marked *INGRESSO*. Huddles of nuns and knots of tour guides talked to their charges as all craned necks upward to gawk at ecstatic images of saints, angels, and plump naked little boys with rosy bottoms painted to spill over the ceiling's edges as they floated effortlessly in the heavens. As I passed a row of confessionals where the faithful waited their turn to relieve their burdens of sin, I remembered I'd read the naked boys represented life force and sex. No doubt the subject of most confessions. It would have been mine too if I'd ever dared speak through the screen to the confessor.

I entered a side chapel to evade the crowds and massage my neck. But here too there was no peace. Swirling gold leaf-covered carvings like wild vines climbed the wall above the small altar. The Baroque frenzy of tendrils captured ornate glass containers holding bits of long-dead holy people. I leaned closer to peer into the vials. Were they truly relics? Guilty for my lack of piety, I deposited a euro in the offering box below a glass case with a finger bone resting on a silk pillow with a yellowed piece of paper pinned below. The Latin was written in tiny faded copperplate script identifying some saint whose name I couldn't decipher because a blot, like a tear stain, obscured half the inscription.

Dozens of silver hearts on the walls surrounded the altar, but the combination of bone fragments with disembodied hearts gave no comfort. I remembered a quote from medieval times: "Rome is the city of echoes, the city of illusions, and the city of yearning." The overwrought atmosphere made me eager to leave Rome—enough of constant echoes of the past with its illusions, although yearning for a lost love would continue.

****

Jenna leafed through my books in the living room. Books about Rome and Italy, histories ancient and modern, dictionaries, and historical fiction filled the shelves. I felt a tug in my heart as I remembered the old man in the junk shop who became my mentor on history and parental obligations so long ago.

She found the book of poetry by Leopardi. I held my breath, willing her to put it away. But she didn't. As she turned the pages the old photo spiraled to the floor. She bent down to retrieve it.

"Who's this guy with the cute baby? He's so good looking."

It was as if a noose tightened around my neck as I

held out my hand to take the picture, the one I kept in the book after I'd met Alessandro the last time. I looked at the photo because I knew my face would betray me if I looked at Jenna. "It's a picture of a man I used to know. He was so proud of his baby he sent a photo. Haven't heard from him for years."

I studied the picture as I had so many times. One corner was bent and another torn but the figure of a tall well-built man with dark curly hair holding an infant in a dress and matching frilled pantie over her diaper wasn't faded at all.

Jenna had kicked one plump leg into the air, turning it into a blur in the snapshot. The other foot wore a minuscule patent leather Mary Jane. Alessandro looked proud, with his crooked grin, Jenna looked like she was cooing or maybe was about to burp.

I put the photo back in the book and placed it on a table away from the packing boxes. "I haven't looked at these poems in a while. I think I'll read them on the flight. Let's begin with this shelf, shall we?"

We removed the other books from the shelves one by one. I looked briefly at each to determine its fate. I saved the poetry, some in Italian, and some by American or English poets, a few histories of Rome and the biography of Leopardi I'd bought from the old man.

"Let's save the rest for tomorrow. We'll have a glass of wine on the terrace instead. Can you pour? The white's in the fridge and it's such a gorgeous day."

We moved to the sunny terrace with our drinks, but instead of relaxation in the leafy ambience, I was filled with fear for what would happen when I upended Jenna's life and revealed what I'd done.

****

The next morning, I stood in the shower until the water turned cold. Forced to face the day, I toweled off and found an old pair of jeans and a T-shirt, and combed my hair without looking in the fogged cabinet mirror. The door was partly open with Martin's personal items on the top shelf. No use for them now. I swept all—shaver, aftershave, pills, deodorant—into the can under the sink and turned to the bedroom closets.

Jenna appeared. "Let me help, Mom. Is there anything you want to save as we go along?"

"You can work in your old bedroom and Sophie's too to see if there's some things we might throw out."

I sorted my clothing into two piles, one for charity and the other to pack. It didn't take long. Everything of Martin's would go. I turned to his side of the closet: business suits and casual outfits, shoes arranged side by side below the clothes.

Two jackets retained a faint odor of strong perfume when I put my face close. I recognized it as the same heavy scent Antonella favored. A torn ticket to a theatrical production I'd never attended along with a piece of paper folded into a tiny square was at the bottom of an inside pocket. The paper was soiled and heavily creased as if it was folded many times. I opened it to see an unfamiliar address written by someone other than Martin. I stuffed the items into my jeans. His dresser drawers were next on my mental list.

I'd washed shorts and undershirts for years but now it was too intimate to handle his underwear after so many years lacking any real closeness. I tossed them into a garbage bag. When I pawed through the dusty contents of the drawer of his bedside table the shock at first made me withdraw my hand and knock the lamp to the floor.

There were a few old coins, a card with the dates of yellow fever and other inoculations, expired passports, and a pen knife. But what grabbed my heart was a religious medallion on a chain, a small tin windup toy fire engine, and a photo of a man and women with a small boy between them in what looked like clothes from the 1950s. They must have had deep meaning. Why had he never opened up to me, oh why?

I turned back to look at his shoes, not as emotional as underwear or dusty mementoes. He'd owned about a dozen pairs. I picked up an old pair to throw in the bag. A tissue-wrapped bundle fell out of the left one. I opened it to find a pair of gold cufflinks with Martin's initials. Martin never wore French cuffs. But Dante did and this pair reminded me of him. Combined with the odor of Antonella's perfume on the jackets I doubted it was a coincidence. And why would he hide the links if they weren't a memento of something he didn't want me to know about?

What had Martin had wanted in life? "Peace," he'd said. If true, he'd been thwarted: the loss of parents at a tender age, the early death of his first wife, a child who wasn't his, and whatever mess he was in between his company and Trench. And me, I suppose.

I jammed the cufflinks into the same pocket where I'd put the tickets and folded paper and found Jenna who must have finished in the other rooms because she was busy with her laptop.

"I put my clothes to be packed on the bed. If you could fold up all the rest and all Martin's for the charity, I'll take the garbage out."

Jenna said, "Sure thing." I dragged the bulging bag to the garbage container on the street. No more reminders in the form of pills, toiletries, or underwear. Things closer to Martin than I'd been.

When I returned, Jenna said, "I'm done. What's next?"

"You can take a break. I'll work on a list of stuff to do first thing in Seattle." I didn't say it, but the top of the list was money.

Jenna must have read my mind. "Will you be okay? I mean about money."

"I'm going to get some from Martin's company. And I know we have the U.S. checking and savings accounts. We have a brokerage account too, but he took care of it. I haven't checked it in a while."

"Can't you look up the information?"

"No, it isn't working.

"Don't you have passwords written down somewhere or are they on your laptop? Mine are in the cloud."

"Something's gone wrong with their website, and I can't access the information."

"Weird! Maybe Dad had a paper copy with the phone number so you can call."

Poor Jenna and her ever-bright outlook. I looked at Martin's desk with its locked drawers. The photo of us taken not long after we'd met remained on the desk's surface. I remembered buying the silver-plated frame in honor of our first anniversary. I'd put it on his desk in Seattle and again when we moved to Rome.

I picked it up. The color had faded as if it reflected our marital life. I'd leaned my head on Martin's shoulder, my face full of happiness. He had his arm around my shoulders, but his mind appeared to be focused elsewhere. Could he have been envisioning a future of continuing unhappiness, of a life headed in the wrong direction? Or simple regret at our marriage? The sensation of rejection of me and the children flowed from my brain to the pit of my gut and outward to every muscle, tendon, and nerve. I hurled the picture at the wall. It missed and sailed out the open window, taking Martin's broken glasses from the windowsill with it. I heard a shattering noise as they hit the travertine curb below.

I stuck my head out. No one was hit but a woman holding a baby in her arms looked up with a frightened face. I ducked back in hopes I hadn't been seen. Jenna stood still for a few seconds before blurting, "Mommmm! What are you doing?" She hurtled down the stairs to retrieve the remains.

"I couldn't find Dad's glasses, but I want to know what's going on here. I know you're upset but you could've killed somebody." She put the photo and broken frame in the garbage can and led the way to the terrace. I followed, keeping my gaze on the tiled pavement to watch ever-busy ants hurrying in a line across the space. They knew where they were going but nothing about how their lives would play out. Neither did I.

"So, tell me." Jenna sounded apprehensive.

I recounted an edited version of my marriage: after the first year or so, it had never been what I expected or dreamed about except for the children who meant the world to me. Now that all were grown, I'd planned to separate, remain in Seattle, then as soon as my situation was stabilized, I'd file for divorce.

Jenna was silent, but the look in her eyes told me she hadn't wanted the life lesson even though I was sure she'd picked up on my unhappiness earlier despite my effort at disguise.

"I'm sorry. I shouldn't have burdened you with all this. Stuff happens in everyone's life, but I didn't think mine would work out the way it did, some of it a bit hard, so much wonderful with you, Tyler and Sophie, and the experience of Rome. I'll start over. Now's my big chance." I managed a semi-sincere smile.

"Sometimes it's good to just say it aloud."

"No more about this now. I remembered a long time ago your dad said we needed to keep cash around and had this odd idea. I think he might have some stashed away in an electrical outlet in his office. I'll get the screwdriver."

I knelt on the floor to remove the cover from an unused wall outlet. A tightly rolled wad of bills was inside. It added up to a thousand euros. A relief from the most immediate financial worries.

I spent the rest of the day sorting the accumulated detritus of our lives. How little of it I wanted now. Jenna was busy with a biology assignment before she'd have dinner with a friend from high school. My meal was a package of stale crackers and a piece of cheese I found in the refrigerator behind a tub of expired yogurt. I had to pare off the mold before it was edible. It seemed an analogy for my future unless I could atone for hiding the truth and keeping Jenna from her true father.

CHAPTER SIXTEEN

The consulate called early in the morning. The death certificate was ready. The lawyer called a few minutes later. She had the autopsy report, and the coroner would release the body to a funeral home which specialized in international issues if I wanted Martin or his ashes shipped. To stall, I told the lawyer I'd come to her office tomorrow. The same day, I'd pick up the death certificate. I picked an establishment from the list the consulate had given me and made an appointment to meet with the funeral director. A trifecta of unpleasantness but I might as well get it over at one miserable time.

Sophie had never replied to my question about what to do with Martin after our disagreement. The young man at the consulate had suggested the English Cemetery might be an option.

Bright sunshine illuminated the small cemetery crammed with tombstones marking the remains of both the forgotten and those still honored. A gardener swept dried brown umbrella pine needles from the graveled paths edged with neatly-trimmed boxwood. Bright red cyclamens bloomed between the graves.

I walked slowly around the crowded monuments to look at the hodgepodge of styles bereaved relatives chose to help them remember loved ones. A young woman, neck encased in camera straps, lay on the ground to get an original shot of a life-size angel drooped over the tomb of a nineteenth-century sculptor's deceased wife. An old woman in black sat on a bench daubing at streaming eyes.

Nearby was a monument to a young man who rested peacefully, his head propped up by his bent arm, his dog and a book by his side. The poignant monument to an eighteenth-century youth who met his end in Rome while on a Grand Tour made me wonder what happened to the dog. Maybe I should I get one for company in Seattle.

A few people stared at the Keats monument. He'd died of fever in a house near the Spanish Steps in 1821. A woman in flowing layers of clothing dramatically draped herself over the memorial to Shelley, waiting as a friend focused her camera. Shelly's monument memorialized the poet who drowned at age twenty-nine, a year after Keats' death. Mary Shelley supposedly kept his heart as a memento when the body was placed on a funeral pyre on the beach. The few remains were deposited in this cemetery.

What would happen to my heart? An imaginary piece would be left in Rome, but the remainder? Martin's? Either buried or burned.

A shiver ran down my spine at the thought of hearts and burnings. It was impossible to imagine Martin in this cemetery full of tourists. He'd never expressed any particular interest or love for Rome, of its antiquities and beauty. He certainly wouldn't care if poets rested nearby. I'd have him cremated like Shelley but without the drama. The container would go into my luggage. But then what? Keeping him in my new home was unthinkable. He'd be watching me, judging my every act, preventing me from finding someone else if I ever wanted to. Would I be alone now for the rest of my life? Another unhappy thought plaguing me.

****

Jenna had made lemonade with fruit from the potted tree on the terrace when I returned. She stared at me in a silent question while handing me a glass. I knew she wanted to know more about my marriage. But what more was there to say? I wasn't yet ready to share the one secret she needed to know. *As soon as I get back to Seattle,* I tried to convince myself. I glanced at my left hand with the engagement and wedding rings still on my third finger. I'd remove them in Seattle too. A new life.

"What I can't figure out is why you two got married. Why would anyone marry someone they didn't love? And stick with him too. Dad was so much older than you. Lots of women have kids alone now and they do okay."

I swirled ice cubes in my glass to make a chinking sound while I thought of what to say.

"Jenna, you're young. Raising a child alone is hard work. I had three. And look at Sophie coping with Jacob. I cried when she told me about a possible diagnosis of autism. She always wanted her own way and now I'm worried there will never be anyone to share her life with." I took a sip of sour lemonade before continuing.

"I was so naïve. I was sure I loved Martin. He changed so much, and I changed too. It might have been easy to divorce when we were still in Seattle and could make parenting arrangements, but after the move to Rome, it was clear to me I needed to honor the commitment to remain in the marriage until you three were grown. I know it sounds terribly old-fashioned now but it was the decision I made. It was the right one."

"It's okay, Mom. I loved Dad, though sometimes it

was like we didn't know each other or he didn't like me. Maybe he didn't want me. And I'm smart enough not to get stuck."

The barb found its mark. "You're right. I wasn't smart when I married too quickly. I was way too young to understand how it would affect my life. It was my good fortune to have Tyler, Sophie, and you, so in the end I'm blessed. Anyway, I'll take it slower next time." I hoped my forced smile eased the situation, but I thought to myself, why would there ever be anyone to think about marrying either slowly or quickly? And even if there was, why would I give up my freedom when it took such a long time to gain?

Jenna put her hand over her mouth before saying, "Sorry, I didn't mean to imply anything. I want to help you with all I can. I'm sure you'll be fine and I'm happy you'll go back to school. So what major are you thinking about?" She grasped my left hand. The rings dug into my fingers. "Hey, I can help you do your homework, like you used to do with me."

I remembered how Jenna used to stick the tip of her tongue out of the corner of her mouth when she concentrated on algebra homework. "I'll go back to school if I can afford it. I'm thinking about social work, maybe concentrating on senior care after what I've seen with your grandparents. If there isn't enough money, I'll get a job. Both school and a job because I've wanted to be in the working world and independent for such a long time."

"Gosh, Mom, I thought you'd want something more exciting like going to culinary arts school or marketing with all your experience here."

"I've thought about it a lot over the last year or so as

I watch your grandparents struggle. Maybe if social work turns out not to be the right career, I'll try something culinary again. But I'm really ready to take a break now."

To avoid further discussion leading to guilty feelings for my long absence from Seattle and them, I walked out to the terrace to look at all the garden furniture accumulated over the years. It would be too much in case I ended up in an apartment without a balcony. "Hon, will you go up to Maggie's to ask if she wants the outdoor furniture when she takes the lemon tree and the other plants?"

Jenna returned with an invitation to dinner and added, "Since it's my last day, let's go out to lunch someplace too."

"How about a restaurant at Fiumicino? I haven't been there for ages and I'd like some seafood. Let me do a little more work before we go."

I sorted kitchen odds and ends—this pan goes with the shipment, that one goes to charity. All of them made me think of Franca, whom I hadn't heard from for months.

The small appliances would be donated, because they ran on different voltages than in the U.S. The range, refrigerator and washing machine belonged to the apartment. I wouldn't miss them. Would there be money to rent while I sold the house on Vashon without moving in? Martin had mentioned it had been on the market for a couple of years before he'd bought it.

I changed clothes, tied my hair back with a ribbon, and put on a pair of sandals when I finished the kitchen. My reflection in the bedroom mirror told me the new widow looked tired. One day at a time.

Lunch conversation lingered on light subjects:

Jenna's schedule, the possibility of a boyfriend named Dave, the annoyances and virtues of Tricia, Jenna's roommate. I added a few anecdotes about some Roman scenes I'd witnessed since returning, like the woman trying to park her tiny car and getting stuck crosswise blocking an alley until a crowd, who were following a priest in a religious procession, hoisted it and placed it against a wall without stopping. All the shouting and arm waving. I'd miss it. Thoughts of death and its consequences were momentarily chased from my mind in favor of laughter, local white wine and *Insalata di Mare* composed of shrimp, mussels, baby octopus, and squid bathed in a soul-soothing sauce of olive oil, lemon juice, and garlic and topped with a sprinkling of parsley.

****

I always loved watching Maggie and Orazio in action together, the way they smiled and sat close to one another in affectionate companionship. I even had a soft spot for the modest bragging about their successful children and bright grandchildren. This evening they proudly announced another was on the way, and that their youngest son, Ludo, was an honors student.

Silver-framed family photos lined a console table in the entryway. I admired them before following Jenna and our hosts to the terrace. What was the line in *Anna Karenina* about how all happy families are alike? I didn't remember the exact quote, but I did recall Tolstoy wrote that all unhappy families were alone in their misery. It was true in my case.

Maggie gestured for us to move to the roomy pillowed chairs around a low table set under the umbrella on the terrace. I held on to the arms in an effort not to slouch, Jenna slipped off her sandals and folded her legs

The Measure of Life

sideways, Maggie eased down with an exhale of relief and put her feet on a stool, while her thin and erect husband sat upright. I noticed Maggie's hair had turned completely gray and Orazio appeared to be losing weight, maybe from all the golf he said he was enjoying.

He opened a bottle of Frascati and filled the four glasses. Maggie passed bowls of toasted almonds, olives, and crackers. I took a small portion and put on a smile when she asked, "How are you, my dear?"

"Thank you so much for the invitation. A much-needed break from packing. And to congratulate Ludo, I'd like to offer him my old car. It's not much, but it should do for a while."

"You are very kind. He needs a car and I'm sure he'd be delighted with yours. I meant to add, he's hoping to graduate with a medical degree. Years from now of course. But is there anything at all we can do for you? Do you need a ride to the airport?"

A doctor like Alessandro. I came back to the present after a moment and assured Maggie all was taken care of. Maggie asked Jenna about her university work and how the American educational system compared with the Italian. As the two talked, a new moon lying slightly on its side as if it was a crooked smile rose to cast a faint misty light over the city, changing the daytime vibrant colors into shades of soft gray as if the city had turned into a photographic negative.

The bats performed their acrobatic stunts as they searched for dinner. An owl hooted in the darkness. I didn't hear them often, but when I did, it made me think of ancient Greek and Roman mysteries, auguries and portents. The still night air stirred for a moment as the bird ghosted off toward the Colosseum on silent wings.

Maggie broke into my thoughts by suggesting we move to the dining room table. She served a platter of prosciutto and figs followed by a perfect *vitello tonnato*—cold veal slices in a mayonnaise-like sauce flavored with tuna, anchovy, and capers—and grilled vegetables. The conversation centered on Rome's many problems. Maggie bemoaned the transport system collapsing with constant strikes and poor infrastructure. Orazio talked about the corruption. The banal conversation comforted me as it would have been no different two thousand years ago.

We shared a chocolate *semifreddo* for dessert and espresso after. I yawned despite my efforts to look alert. Jenna suggested it was time to go. I thanked both my hosts and said I'd get the car transfer arranged by the end of the week. I gave Maggie a tight hug and said, "Stay well my dear."

Jenna's flight left early the following morning. I walked with her to the taxi. She waved out the rear window but was lost to view in the thick traffic a moment later. Afterwards, I returned to the apartment to stand on the terrace wishing the rising sun would illuminate my future life.

CHAPTER SEVENTEEN

I checked my watch every few minutes to mentally calculate Jenna's flight path while I waited at the U.S. Consulate to retrieve the death certificate. Jenna's plane would soon cross the Alps before turning west over France and the English Channel to London Heathrow for the transfer to Seattle. The same route I'd take.

The tissue in my damp hand was reduced to mush as I waited. Finally, someone called my name and I approached the glass. This time, an officious-looking woman held an envelope.

"Mrs. Carlisle?"

"Yes." I showed my passport.

"I have the death certificate." She slid the envelope toward me. "Please accept our sincere condolences on your loss. You need to take this to the funeral director and give him your instructions immediately. We do not wish to let the matter remain unsettled."

I almost retorted that a death certificate wouldn't settle much of anything but took the sealed envelope and stood outside the building to open it. There was no mystery. Martin had officially died of a heart attack no matter what other problems dogged him—burdens I couldn't understand.

Next was the law office. The *avvocato* offered sympathy after I entered her office.

I acknowledged her condolences before I said,

"First, I'd like to ask if you could check on my late husband's Italian pension."

"I'll let you know, signora. It will require research, but it seems unlikely he'd be covered as he was an expat. But here is the autopsy report. Would you like some time alone to review it before you leave?"

I said yes while picturing bills for legal fees rolling in indefinitely if the answer to his pension wasn't clear. She ushered me into a small office. Again, a sealed envelope confronted me like at an awards ceremony.

I hesitated, first moving the envelope away then back to me. I stuck my finger under the flap, cutting myself in the process. A droplet of blood smeared the document as I slid it out.

The report was full of technical terms, but the conclusion was the same: heart attack.

There was more: Martin's heart was abnormally enlarged, and his prostate was cancerous. He had liver problems too. He must have known with all the prescriptions. But why would he have insisted on buying the property on Vashon if he knew his problems were serious? Prostate cancer often was slow growing, and he'd lived long already with the heart problems so maybe he didn't believe anything would happen. A hideaway? Maybe an inkling the company was in trouble. He'd mentioned rumors. Or maybe it was just an investment. Another mystery I'd never solve. I shoved the autopsy report back in its envelope, not wanting to know more of his failing body.

An elderly man dressed in sober black with a matching demeanor greeted me when I arrived at the funeral home, the last leg of an agonizing day. I told him Martin was to be cremated and I'd take the ashes in my luggage. He said it was impossible to schedule a cremation so quickly.

"But I do have Signor Martin's keys, wallet, watch, and ring for you." He placed them on the desk. I stared at the objects. What to do with them? Maybe Tyler or Sophie would like the watch. But the ring? What do you do with a symbol of devotion which never lived up to its promise? I dropped it in my handbag along with the other remnants of his life.

"Do you have his cellphone?"

"No signora. No *telefonino.*"

Martin had bought a new high-end phone a few months ago. Someone must have stolen it after he died. Trench? But he'd never answered my desperate calls the day at the ancient tombs so maybe it was gone earlier. No laptop, no phone. It was as if he'd been electronically erased.

I turned my attention back to the funeral director as he described the bureaucracy surrounding death. I learned death was expensive, more expensive than I ever imagined. It would clean out the Italian bank accounts and the euros I'd found. What an irony: the little profits I'd made from food tours, food Martin hated, were to be eaten up trying to settle the issue of his body.

****

Too rattled to return to the apartment, I meandered through cobbled streets. I nearly tripped over an old woman shelling green peas while perched on a stool outside a dark doorway. My "*mi scusi signora,*" resulted in a curt acknowledgement. I would have liked to chat but the woman abruptly took her basket and apron filled with the peas into her apartment. A moment later shutters opening above the entrance drew my attention. A younger woman stuck her head out briefly before withdrawing. Next to the window I spotted what appeared to be a red-rimmed eye affixed to the building wall.

I stepped back to get a better look at the bizarre object. Large letters on the white face said "OCULARIUM," and around the upper part of the dial were the Italian words for heavy rain, rain, variable, beautiful, and stable. A pointer connected to a mechanism showed today's weather was *variable*. In fact, damp clouds floated above the city. The more I stared, the more it became a forecaster of my future. *Stabile* would be a welcome state, *tutto bello* so desirable, but there'd been too much *pioggia*—rain. Maybe *variable* was all I would ever get.

Curious about the object, I found a definition later. It meant a domain where the eye can see into imagination's far reaches, a useful faculty to possess when I'd first met Martin.

****

The apartment was as quiet as a tomb when I opened the door. The heavy atmosphere made me want to nap, but when I booted up my laptop, a happy surprise appeared.

My dear Nicki.

My Rome grapevine extended its tendrils all the way to Sydney. I was shocked to hear about the loss of your husband. I never knew him of course but all the same I can fully understand the harrowing experience. I know you will be able to surmount this setback to your plans. You are as strong as I was or maybe even stronger.

So make yourself a big bowl of your favorite pasta, pour a glass of wine, and put your plans into action!

The Measure of Life

We love Australia and the restaurant is a big hit. Do come for a visit when you can. We have a guest room overlooking the bridge and Opera House.
Keep in touch!
Fondly, Franca
P.S. I married him!

Dreams of kangaroos had to be put aside the following morning. As I considered what to wear to Martin's former office to present the death certificate, I saw the jeans I'd worn the day I'd sorted clothing were still draped over a chair.

I felt the cufflinks and the folded paper with the address. I tossed the links in a packing box but opened the folded paper again to look at it more closely. My *Tutto Città* map and street index showed the address was in Parioli, one of Rome's most expensive quarters. Why was Martin there, if he'd actually gone? Some love affair like one with Antonella? On the other hand, after what I'd done, why should I be surprised? He never asked me if there were any more men in my life, nor did I suggest he had another woman, or women. Still, it was a surprise because of the location. She must have been wealthy.

The young woman who had served me coffee when I met with pompous Dante sat in Antonella's place when I arrived at the office. She introduced herself as Valeria, her replacement, and said her predecessor had resigned to return to her home in Sicily.

I handed over the death certificate and the savings account information.

Valeria said, "We all liked Martin. He was such a nice person. I'm sorry he passed away so unexpectedly. I'd been worried about him, he appeared preoccupied lately. Didn't look good either."

"Yes, I was worried too. Did he say anything to you?"

Her eyes widened. "Oh, no. He never talked about himself or his family."

"I'm glad he was liked." No photos, no talk of family. It was as though we never existed for him outside our home. Or inside. It reminded me of an actor who could play any part behind a mask of comedy and tragedy.

"We'll wire the separation payment as soon as we finish the calculations."

"How much will it and the insurance add up to?"

"We're working on it, but I'm sorry to say the separation amount won't be for six-months' salary, but two. Money issues."

"I need the money now and I was told it would be six. You can't do this to me!" I could feel my face tense in anger and my voice become harsh.

"As I said, we must make the computations. There seems to be some issues with the life insurance. You will have to wait, I'm afraid. Things don't move fast here, I'm sure you know. And we have to follow international regulations to wire money."

I backed off in case I upset her and slowed the process even further. The insurance? Could he have left some of it to Antonella or some woman who lived in Parioli? I took a chance and asked Valeria why Antonella really left the company.

The young woman looked uncomfortable as she whispered even though we were in a private office, "There were rumors. I don't know and shouldn't be talking to you, but I think there might be an investigation by the authorities, even the *Guardia di Finanza*, I don't know who else. It's bad when they come marching in."

My God, I'm going to be stiffed. Beset with worries I left quietly.

****

Later in the afternoon, I plotted the complicated bus route to the stop nearest the address on the paper. It was in a quiet neighborhood, wide streets lined with trees and grand apartment buildings, many built before World War II. They were well maintained and looked solid, the kind the wealthy would inhabit. I lingered on the far side, debating whether to cross. Uncertain why I wanted to know, I found a nearby bar to defer a decision by ordering sparkling water. I concluded that since I'd bothered to come this far, I should check the names on the polished brass plaques near the video camera and speakerphone.

The shining plaques told me the building was filled with professional studios or consulting rooms occupied by accountants, lawyers, and doctors. Among them was the name Dottore Alessandro Antonio Lombardi. A string of abbreviations followed along with *cardiologo, professore,* and *primario.*

I was startled and backed away, bumping into a woman waiting to use the call system. Was it possible there was another person with the same name, also a doctor? Impossible. Alessandro was a department head and professor at Rome's University, La Sapienza, and a specialist in coronary disease. From all the initials after his name he must be one of the leading doctors in Rome. Why would Martin have had his address? Did Martin's doctor in Rome refer him? Or had he somehow learned the name of Jenna's father and had wanted something from him. Maybe child support. Martin had managed to entangle himself into my memories of Alessandro from beyond the grave.

****

I was too busy sorting final items to be shipped and cleaning the apartment to think about the ocularium or Alessandro's office in the following days. Pressured by the company to get out, I was continually interrupted by real estate agents showing clients the apartment, forcing me to stand outside the door or to visit Maggie when she was busy.

Finally, I watched as the movers loaded the last shipping crates and boxes into a van double parked on the street below. When it lumbered off, I walked up the stairs to Maggie's apartment to give her the keys and documents for my car.

"Come on in—I've got just the thing for us." She opened the door to the drinks cabinet to take out a bottle of 18-year-old Irish whiskey. "I've been saving it since the last time I went to Ireland a couple of years ago." She put it on the coffee table and found two crystal tumblers. "You say when."

"Keep going."

Maggie poured a half glass for each of us and raised it. "To your future. I know it will be beautiful. Everything will be *tutto bello*."

"And yours." I raised my glass in salute to our friendship.

After the glasses were empty and I rose to leave, she said, "Mind yourself, my dear," as she stood in her doorway a few moments before gently latching it.

I returned to my barren rooms woozy after whiskey talk. I detached my apartment keys and those from Martin's key ring and placed them on a windowsill. The key to his desk never turned up.

The key to the house on Vashon I'd found in the kitchen junk drawer was already in a zipped pocket in my handbag. I tossed the remaining keys into a last sack of garbage to drop off on the street when the taxi arrived. I sat on a suitcase to wait, and when I saw it outside the building entrance, I disturbed a few leftover dust balls as I shut the door to my former home for the last time.

The cab driver popped the trunk and loaded up. He accelerated, speeding toward a Leonardo da Vinci airport hotel where I'd stay before the early morning flight. The city disappeared behind me. The hotel bar was noisy as night overtook day. With no appetite, I toyed with a glass of Tuscan red and a plate of olives before a return to my sterile room. Unable to sleep, I repacked my suitcases before watching the planes as they arrived and departed on the moonless night, landing lights blurred by ground fog. Where were the passengers going? My own ticket said FCO – LHR – SEA but it didn't answer the real question: How would my flights lead toward a fulfilling life?

PART III

CHAPTER EIGHTEEN

The immigration agent in Seattle swiped my passport. "Welcome home, Mrs. Carlisle." I gave him a bleary smile. *If you only knew. If only I'd known.*

After I'd dragged through customs and collected my baggage, I stopped in the restroom on the way to freshen up before meeting Jenna in the airport arrivals hall. The harsh light on the mirror reflected my appearance and mood: disheveled and apprehensive. My eyes were circled darkly with messed up mascara and insomnia. My hair needed a shampoo and cut. I rubbed on a small crease between my eyebrows.

Jenna ran toward me to help with the luggage. "I'm so happy you're back. Want to go somewhere for dinner?"

"Let's hold off for a day or so. I'm rather disoriented right now. Maybe we could just stop at a store to get some food. Even a frozen pizza would be great."

We stopped at a grocery store to load a cart with cleaning supplies, coffee, tea, two bottles of wine, one red and the other an already-chilled white, along with a couple of frozen Pizza Margaritas. Jenna offered to heat them up when we got to the little place I'd rented but I declined, too tired to eat. I gave her one to take to her own apartment.

She promised to stop by the next afternoon to help. I looked around the silent apartment I'd rented until I could move to Vashon when the furniture arrived. The rent was high, the rooms dark, the kitchen faucet dripped, the furniture worn. It reminded me of my apartment in Rome before our furniture had arrived.

I unlocked a suitcase to retrieve nightclothes and shampoo and then found a glass in the kitchen cupboard. I opened the white wine, poured a glass and downed it in three swallows. Cold and cleanly astringent, it spread comfort, so much so, I poured another glass. I set it on the counter before turning on the shower full force to luxuriate the stream of hot water. After that, I closed the drain and turned the water back on, and added some of my favorite thyme-eucalyptus scented bath salts. I padded, naked and dripping, to the kitchen to pick up the glass while the tub filled. Holding the glass, I climbed in to soak in the soft water, so different from Rome's with its perpetual scum around the tub.

The wine blotted out the challenges on the horizon as the shampoo and soap had cleansed my body when I showered. When the bathwater cooled to lukewarm, I threw on my robe and opened the bedroom window for fresh air. I stood before a full-length mirror in the bedroom, letting the robe fall to my ankles to inspect the new single Nicole. "Not too bad for forty-four, I guess," I heard myself say as I surveyed my body while avoiding my face. Breasts and bottom not yet sagging, waist nearly as small as it had been when I was a teenager. No sign of menopause. Yet. "I guess I'll do for a while." Then I blubbered, "Damn, damn, damn men."

The last thing I remember was falling into bed drowning in a sea of doubt. At midnight I woke up gasping from a dark dream where I was underwater in the bathtub unable to breathe. The towel had loosened, my uncombed hair a tangled mess. My robe remained in a heap on the floor, the last glass of wine untouched on the bedside table. I dragged myself out of bed to get water to quench a raging thirst and find my nightgown. I returned to bed, fearful the jet lag I often suffered would prevent a return to sleep.

****

Something was shaking my shoulder.

"Mom, what's the matter with you? Wake up, wake up. Are you sick?"

"Where am I?" I croaked. My eyes were glued shut, my throat burning with inflammation.

"I'll get coffee. I've called and called but you never answered. It's Sunday afternoon in Seattle. I got worried. It's lucky you gave me a key."

I pried my sticky eyes open to see Jenna's face close to mine. The face disappeared. Coffee came into focus. I couldn't smell it but saw steam rising. I propped myself up while Jenna stuffed the other bed pillow behind my back and handed over a cup of strong brew. If it was Sunday where was the melodic peal of church bells? I'd heard bells ring all the years we'd been in Rome. Now there was silence. I looked around the bedroom. It was unfamiliar, but there were my suitcases open on the floor.

A second cup of coffee jerked my brains into gear. "What's happened?"

"I think you've got a terrible cold. Must have picked it up on the plane."

Now I remembered I was back in Seattle. For good or at least forever. The fulcrum of my life had tilted irrevocably from the years of sun and color of Rome to the cool and gray Pacific Northwest. Raindrops pattered against the bedroom window as if the weather gods confirmed my new life.

"I'll make some breakfast." Jenna scrambled a couple of eggs and made toast.

It hurt to swallow.

Jenna stopped by each evening until I could convince her I was fine. I wanted to be alone to plan my future and forget my embarrassing launch to life in Seattle—half drunk and admiring myself in the mirror.

I'd intended to visit Mom and Dad and begin to get my finances in order first thing but the cold accompanied with a cough and laryngitis stopped me. Me, the one who was never sick, who nursed children through sniffles, scraped knees, and hurt feelings.

I called the care facility to ask about my parents although the duty nurse had difficulty understanding me. She said my dad sat in a recliner in front of a television all day as he had at home. I pictured his blank stare as an oxygen feed softly swooshed and hissed. There was no measurable change in Mom's physical health. At least she'd calmed with no worries about caring for home and husband. I asked the nurse to tell her I was home and would call as soon as I could talk and visit when was I sure I wouldn't spread germs.

By Friday my voice returned sufficiently to call. The phone rang ten times until an uncertain voice said hello.

"Hi Mom. I'm back in Seattle. Got a bit of a cold so I'll wait to stop by 'till I'm all better." I put on my most cheerful voice.

"It's time for breakfast. We always have good food on Sunday. I need to get dressed. Bye-bye."

"Okay, Mom. See you soon. Love you."

****

Despite my concerns about Mom's fading mind, the gorgeous morning lifted my spirits as Seattle showed off its best late summer colors. A good day to explore Vashon, my home-to-be for at least a short period, and a respite from financial and parental issues. My appointment with the banker was on Monday and there was no point stewing for the intervening days.

A bus took me to the Fauntleroy dock, southwest of downtown Seattle. An unfamiliar sense of exhilaration filled me as I boarded the ferry and climbed to the observation deck. The boat's engine throbbed, sending the pulses through me as it propelled the vessel through the bright blue water toward the island. I looked back at the receding Seattle skyline; so many new skyscrapers and so many cranes dancing above the skeletons of yet more new buildings. There were no skyscrapers in Rome; nothing higher than the dome of St. Peter's. I turned to face the island where a few houses lined the water's edge and thick forest covered the hills, not with the blue cypresses and umbrella pines of Italy, but the dark firs, cedars, and maples of the Pacific Northwest.

The wind made a mess of my hair. My lips tasted of salt from the spray. Gulls circled and screamed as if they were lost souls. Small boats hastened out of the ferry's way. A cargo ship glided silently past, orange and red containers glowing in the sun. The white bow wave rose high on the black hull. I looked for orcas. None were around, but a harbor seal with round eyes watched as the ferry slowed to nose into the dock. A few lazy cormorants rested on the pilings, stretching wings and sinuous necks to dry in the warm air.

Foot passengers walked off; cyclists in tight shorts and shirts mounted bikes ready for the uphill slog.

Helmeted motorcyclists gunned their motors and roared away. I'd learned the local bus ran a circular route and didn't go near my house on this leg. I struggled up the steep road, winded from the cough, until I arrived at the short side street leading to my house.

The front door was stuck. A musty smell poured out when I shoved it open. Dust and cobwebs greeted me as I crossed the threshold. The odor of emptiness was compounded by the absence of furniture. I opened the windows to let fresh air circulate and returned to the front door to walk around the exterior to take a good look.

The yellow two-story house had been built in the late 1950s with an added wraparound deck, an ideal spot for lunch on a sunny day. I found the now-squashed homemade sandwich in my handbag and opened a can of over-sweetened lukewarm ice tea bought from a vending machine at the ferry dock. The sandwich was tasteless, nothing like the panini I'd so often eaten in Rome. I choked on a soggy crust, coughing so hard my eyes watered.

I blinked a few times before opening my drippy eyes to see a small boy with a finger in his mouth wearing blackberry-stained overalls in front of me.

"Hi sweetie pie, where did you come from?"

He didn't respond. His brown eyes were round with curiosity, like the harbor seal.

"Sammy, *Sammee!* Where the heck *are* you?"

A dark-haired woman in jeans and a Seahawks T-shirt loped up the short driveway. "There you are, you little devil." She scooped the boy into her arms before she spotted me. "Oh dear. I'm sorry I didn't know anyone was here." She hesitated. When I smiled the woman said, "Are you going to live here?"

I got to my feet. "I'm Nicole. And yes, the home belongs to me, but I can't move in until my furniture arrives next month."

"Where are you from?"

"Rome. A container is coming by sea."

"I'm Deirdre," the woman said. "I'm Sammy's mom. Great to finally have a neighbor. I can't wait to hear all about Rome. I'd love to visit someday. I felt sorry for the old house. It's been empty for a long time after…" She frowned as if reliving the story.

"So, what happened here?"

"It's sad. An old man lived here alone. When he died no one found out for a week. Poor old guy. I think he was terribly lonely."

I felt an icicle pierce my heart. My emotion must have shown because Deirdre said, "Oh, I shouldn't have said anything. I assumed you knew. Please forgive me. I didn't mean to upset you."

"Don't worry. It's nothing."

"Please come to my house for some coffee. We live over there." Deirdre pointed at the second story of a large house; the lower portion hidden by shrubs.

"Love to, but I can't stay long."

Deirdre said, "It's this way. And it is a great place to live despite what I said."

I found a smile.

Sammy hopped and skipped alongside his mother as we walked along the path overgrown with white Everlasting, Queen Anne's Lace, and green bracken ferns. Late summer wild blackberries hung in clusters on the sharp-thorned canes; sprays of salal berries gleamed dark blue against leathery green foliage.

"Sorry, I used to keep the walkway clear, but with

no one in your house and this little guy here, I gave up. Maybe we can both hack away at it when you get organized."

I caught a lilt in the woman's speech for the first time. "Are you Irish? You remind me of someone. A dear friend in Rome."

Deirdre chuckled. "Easy to tell, isn't it, even if I missed out on the red hair and green eyes. Originally from Dublin where I met my husband, Josh. I used to own a restaurant. Gave it up when he got transferred back to Microsoft's home office. When Sammie is in kindergarten I might see if there's a good spot on the island for another bistro. People like to eat out here."

"I have a daughter in Seattle, she's at the U. One of my grandmothers was Irish but from Boston. My best friend in Rome is named Maggie. From Cork. And I used to do food tours and cooking videos in Rome."

"We've common ground for sure and it will be fun to talk. Have you ever visited Ireland?"

"It's on my list." When there had been time between children and pasta I'd traveled to London, Paris, Florence and other cities to enjoy art, food, and design but there were so many places still waiting. How my life played out here would determine if I'd ever see them.

I followed Deirdre through her kitchen door and found myself in a dream world with granite countertops, a built-in espresso maker, gigantic refrigerator, and a six-burner gas range. Cookbooks filled a glass-fronted cupboard.

"How I'd love a kitchen like this." From my brief tour when Martin and I looked at what was now my house several months ago, I remembered the appliances were old. But at least they were full size, not like Rome where I contended with a half-size fridge and a stove with a drop-down top to use as counter space when I wasn't cooking. I'd give myself credit for managing a business using them.

"Josh is always working. I guess this is my compensation. But, yes, I do love it. And our Sam of course." She picked him up and mussed his hair. "Back in a sec. It's nap time."

I stood in the middle of her tiled floor wishing Maggie could fly out for a week to help me get organized when the furniture arrived.

Deirdre returned to say, "Now, let's sit and talk. Do you want coffee or tea? I can tell you all about Vashon if you want. As much as I know I mean."

"Coffee, please. I don't know anything about Vashon except I came here to summer camp as a kid. We, my late husband and I, bought the house as a rental. But here I am."

Deirdre poured two large mugs. She asked if I wanted milk. "Sugar is over there. No cream, sorry to say." She paused, waiting for me to continue.

I looked at my host over the rim as I raised the mug to my mouth. She had an open face, a person who would be easy to talk to.

"My husband died recently so my plans were changed. Heart attack out in the countryside." I stirred a teaspoon of sugar into the coffee although I normally drank it black.

Deirdre's face fell. "I did get my foot in my mouth, didn't I? I'm so sorry to hear of your loss. It must have been heartbreaking."

"You couldn't have known. Tell me about living on an island."

Deirdre talked about the many virtues of the village a few miles from her home: bookstore, art galleries, and a new arts center under construction. With the low crime rate, good schools, beaches and space to walk, and quiet atmosphere, the island was ideal. Lots of people wrote or painted. Everyone gardened if they could keep the deer at bay.

"You have trouble with deer? They're so beautiful."

"Yes, but the beasts absolutely adore roses. Look outside." Deirdre used the hand holding the mug to point toward her kitchen window. The large garden was enclosed by a high wire fence, presumably too high for deer to jump.

Overwhelmed with all the information, I said, "It's getting a bit late and I need to take a closer look at the house before I get back to my place in Seattle. You've been so helpful. Thank you so much. Give Sammy a kiss for me when he wakes. He's such a darling."

I followed the path back to my own house. It looked modest and in need of care, but cheered with coffee and conversation, I made a quick tour to look at each room trying to picture where the furniture would go.

Sunlight filled the rooms despite the dirty windows. The hardwood floors were much warmer than the terrazzo of Rome—no need for slippers. Two bedrooms were on the second floor. The smallest would be a good place for an office. It faced the water; to the side was a field where Deirdre's home was visible between trees. The second bedroom also had a saltwater view and would be mine. The downstairs bedroom would be for Tyler or Sophie when they visited. Jenna would probably want to stay over once in a while, too. And for guests. But who? I doubted any of my former clients, even though many were friends, would come unless they happened to be visiting Seattle before taking a cruise to Alaska. Maggie would be wonderful, but Seattle is a long way from Rome.

When I tried to decide where to place my bed, the same bed Martin and I had unhappily shared for far too long, the room seemed cavernous, too big for one person. I mentally changed the layout. The small office would be my bedroom with the bigger room for the office. At least a new mattress would cancel some of the memories.

So much house for one person after all the years in a Roman apartment filled with a family. I'd been surrounded by other apartments, occupants with their own lives of happiness or not. Now when I had space and quiet, there might be too much of both.

I made sure the house was closed up and walked back down the hill, enjoying the warm afternoon and hoping for the best. That night I dreamed of deer leaping over a scooter parked in an Italian piazza.

CHAPTER NINETEEN

I dug the key to the safe deposit box from the bottom of my handbag and followed a clerk into the vault to open my box, the first stop on a fraught day devoted to money. The deed to the Vashon house was on top along with an agreement with a financial management firm. Martin's will, prepared immediately after our marriage, was next. He'd left everything to me. I murmured a short prayer of relief. But what had he actually left besides two children and bitterness? I'd soon find out.

I continued to sort through documents: his birth certificate, Social Security number, honorable discharge from the military, our marriage certificate, and the one from his first marriage and Yvette's death certificate. The children's certificates were there along with my own.

I returned to the present reality and added Martin's autopsy and death certificate to the records of beginnings and endings. Then, I looked at the other birth certificates one by one, mine with married parents still living; Sophie's certificate. Nothing to indicate my fraught relationship with her father or Sophie's difficulties. Next in the stack was Martin's. What hopes had his parents had for their child? Probably the same as I had for Sophie and Jenna. His certificate couldn't give even a hint of the dark pools of his life, orphan, widower, maybe his Vietnam experience. Maybe his job. Me. What would have happened if Yvette hadn't died? For sure I wouldn't be sitting here tormented about whether Martin left me enough money to live on.

Tyler's certificate showed Yvette as his mother. How hard it must have been for a four-year-old to lose her. He'd appeared happy when Martin and I took him to a movie, a pizza, or a park before our marriage, often making sure he was near me. But he hadn't adjusted to my constant presence in the house. Martin assured me he'd talked to the boy about having a stepmother, but whatever he'd said hadn't worked. Tyler spent most of his free time in his bedroom with his adventure stories after I moved in.

I was about three months along with Sophie when I was cleaning his room. A small photo album lay on top of his bookcase. I'd picked it up to dust underneath just as he burst into his room after school. He saw me with the album. "Don't you dare touch! It's mine. Mine. It's got pictures of my mom and me."

"Oh, Tyler, I was dusting not prying. Someday maybe you can show me the photos. I'd love to see them because I know you loved your mom very much."

Tyler grabbed the album and threw himself on his bed, silent, with his face hidden by the album. I'd left quietly but in pain. The incident was never mentioned by either of us again, but he gradually warmed to me. A decisive moment in our relationship arrived a year later when Tyler was eight. I'd taken him and his team to a Saturday soccer game. I cheered loudly even though they lost. He ran to me after the final whistle and put his arms around my waist. His teammates snickered but he ignored them. I recognized he'd accepted me, not as his mother, but as a person who he could depend on for support. My heart had soared with happiness.

The last certificate, issued by the US Embassy in Rome, was for Jenna. I thought of the bureaucratic nightmare of trying to get it. First the hospital handed me a form attesting to her birth. It had to be taken to the *anagrafe* to be officially registered, a process done by entering the information by hand in one of the large volumes stacked on shelves lining the office walls. Martin managed to be out of town so Maggie accompanied me as a witness and to help. Next, I returned twice, first to pay and then pick up the document to take to the embassy. Martin, forced to attend, looked so sour the clerk cut the happy small talk and hurried to prepare the form. Even though I was the mother, Martin was the one whose signature was required. Jenna's official birth certificate and passport were ready for collection a few days later.

What would happen when I confessed to Jenna? She might want the birth certificate reissued to reflect the truth if it could be changed. I put the thought aside and continued to sort through the box.

A small leather pouch rested under the papers at the bottom. I put it in my handbag to look at later.

My anxiety soared into the stratosphere as I walked from the bank, where I received confirmation our savings account had rapidly declined, to the brokerage firm a block away. The receptionist led me to a woman about Sophie's age. The woman, whose desk plaque identified her as a senior executive, reviewed the account details. "Hmmm. This is interesting," she said as she scrolled back and forth though the account record.

She turned from her screen to face me. "Your late husband changed the account profile two years earlier from quite aggressive to totally self-managed. I see he bought speculative tech stocks on margin, and was heavily involved in the futures market. Something we don't usually recommend unless the client is very knowledgeable. It doesn't appear he was."

She added there was note specifying he'd withdrawn nearly a half million to invest in a start-up. The woman said she didn't know the details but remembered reading in a business journal it had failed.

She explained at its highest point about two years ago, the account held over two million dollars. As a result of Martin's lack of acumen, the balance was currently $32,430. "I do see a note he'd told my predecessor he needed to be more aggressive because he expected to leave his company and retire early. Wanted to be sure there was enough money."

"What kind of responsibility did you have to let this go on?" My stomach dropped to my feet.

"I'm sorry you didn't know about this but as he self-managed the account we had no obligation or right to make him be more conservative in his choices."

"This is outrageous!" I couldn't keep my voice down. The account executive looked alarmed, as if she might call security.

"I'm sorry, but as you might guess, this news when I've just lost my husband is upsetting. He wasn't investing; he was gambling."

"I wasn't your late husband's broker. He left the company several months ago. But as I said, we followed Mr. Carlisle's instructions." She had an apologetic smile. I wanted to smack her.

"I want to close the account entirely. I can't afford a financial manager, especially one from your company."

The Measure of Life

"I'll prepare a form to transfer the balance to your bank. One more thing: there was also an annuity. Your late husband had over a quarter million in it but cashed in at a loss. He said it was to buy a house. The notes about his actions are in the account record. Do you want to see them?"

"No."

****

Martin's former office in Rome was closed when I called to inquire about the separation compensation. I'd already forgotten the nine-hour time difference. When I tried again the next morning, a clerk said they'd received the forms from my bank and the money would be wired to my savings account in a day or so. What about the life insurance? The woman said she didn't know the status.

I checked my bank account obsessively in hopes the money from Italy would arrive. On the following Wednesday, the deposit for two months of his pay was there, slightly over $31,300. It wouldn't begin to cover room and board plus tuition and fees for Jenna after this year let alone mine, especially after I found out how much the property tax and home insurance would be. Health insurance was out of the question.

For sure I'd have to find a job immediately. And, I'd have to apply for a loan if I could attend school at all. The thought of student loans was terrifying with the news full of stories about people burdened with the payments years after they graduated. At least there would be insurance money to help.

The phone rang to interrupt my muddled thoughts.

"Guess what? I can't believe it. It's fabulous." Sophie's voice was loud.

"Hi Sophie, I'm glad you called. How are you both?

What's so exciting?" It was the first time I'd heard from her since the visit to Rome after Martin's death.

"We're fine, especially since I just got nearly $250,000 dollars from Dad's life insurance! I'm going to buy myself a shiny new Italian sports car for openers. A red one. Isn't it great?"

I wanted to ask what she'd do with the remainder if there was one, but Sophie continued regaling me with details about the car. The dealer must have welcomed her with open arms.

"I'm so happy your dad did that for you."

"I'll send a photo of the car."

In fact, I was shocked. Why would Sophie use the money for a luxury car? Maybe she didn't have any more money sense than Martin. I'd chosen her name because it meant wisdom but the word apparently had no influence. And where was my portion? Jenna's and Tyler's? A deepening suspicion spiraled from the top of my head to my toes as I leaned against the worn kitchen counter surrounded by financial papers the account executive had printed out. I threw them on the floor.

Jenna called several days later. "Hey Mom. Just wanted to tell you I got a thousand dollars from Dad's life insurance. Not sure what I'll do with it yet, maybe help buy a new laptop. Nice, huh?"

Not wanting to upset her, I managed to agree it was a good use for the money. After the call, I looked at my account. The same amount had been added to the balance.

A thousand dollars. All I'd been worth to him over the years. What to do with the tainted payment, Martin's way of saying I wasn't important or his revenge for the separation? I needed all I could get, but the token amount was too humiliating. I wrote a check for a thousand dollars to a non-profit organization helping seniors. The moment the envelope disappeared through the slot at the post office, I knew I'd made a stupid financial decision, but felt liberated anyway.

What to do? The furniture was on the way to the house and storage costs would be astronomical if I didn't move in. I didn't want to have to pay first and last months' rent and a security deposit for an apartment. The house, owned free and clear, was my single substantial asset. If I sold, I'd be stuck paying rent with nothing to show for it, and who knew how long it would take to sell anyway. It had been on the market for two years before Martin bought it.

I needed a car to live on the island. I'd parked my parents' old clunker at the care home where there was a charge to use the garage. It would save money and relieve me of buying anything for a while if I used it.

My emotions turned dark with anger at Martin's recklessness with money and his revenge by cutting me and Jenna out of his insurance proceeds. Who knew what he'd done to Tyler? I'd Googled "grief" and skimmed a few relevant websites to see if that's what plagued me. Advice ranged from get over it to you must go through five, or more, or less, stages. After I passed one stage, would a door simply open to the next? Or was it more like a pregnancy, but instead of giving birth to a baby, presumably I would produce my own pristine new life when the ordeal was over. But the more I read, I knew I wasn't grieving. Instead, I was in limbo, untethered to Rome, to Seattle, or to Vashon, unsure how to progress toward my goal of successful independence.

I did manage to take a tiny step when I twisted off

my engagement and wedding rings after my shower the next morning. The skin was a white band in contrast to my summer tan. The bone looked shrunken from the years of pressure. The round rings could represent a zero. The sentiment wasn't accurate because of the children, but the rings didn't represent circles of eternity either. I stuffed them in the back of the rickety dresser drawer where I kept my sweaters and T-shirts. My finger was raw.

CHAPTER TWENTY

My bank account was sinking. I hadn't heard from the Italian lawyer about a pension from the Italian social security system. A clerk at the Social Security Administration said the sole record of payments was for Martin's work in the U.S. years ago. I'd be eligible to receive minimal benefits at sixty, more than fifteen years from now. On top of everything, the car needed new all-weather tires and a brake job, and generous voters had approved new parks and school levies, raising property taxes. I was on a merry-go-round always chasing the brass ring of financial stability.

While I was fishing for the car key one morning, I touched the leather bag I'd found in the safe deposit box. I sat in the car to look at the contents: diamonds and a wedding band. It had an engraving inside, "To Y with all my love forever. M."

I needed to contact Tyler before selling them.

Hi Tyler. I hope you are well. I need to tell you when I opened your dad's and my safe deposit box, I found an old leather bag containing some jewelry – I believe they are your mother's diamond engagement and wedding ring, and a diamond pendant. Your dad's ring, if he had one, wasn't there. I think the jewelry is valuable given the size of the stones and I'm attaching some photos so you can see if you want them. Maybe if you get married or for your children? Anyway, I'll keep them until you find time to visit Vashon. With Much Love, Nicole.

Tyler replied several days later.

Thanks so much for asking. I've been away from my office (such as it is) for a couple of days. Unless Dad specifically left them to me, they're yours. I still have the old book of photos of me and my mother which is enough, and I have no use for jewelry nor would want something so ostentatious for anyone I might marry. Dad did leave me a lot of money from his life insurance. I didn't need it either and donated it to my organization. Can't get away now but hope to see you next year. With love, Tyler.

I reread the email while wondering how Martin could have produced such a selfless soul. Tyler must have inherited his generous instincts from his mother.

The manager at a jewelry store got out his loupe and said the gold was 18 karat and the diamond in the ring was good quality and weighed two carats. The pendant, of French manufacture, was smaller but also of high quality, the diamonds set in platinum and probably made in the 1930s. I assumed it had belonged to Yvette's mother.

"So how much are you offering?"

He talked down the value.

"If you're not interested, I'll go elsewhere."

The dealer looked alarmed. "I'll give you fifteen for the lot."

"Twenty or I'm leaving."

He pretended to take another look at the pieces. After a minute, he said, "Seventeen. Take it or leave it."

I held my ground. "Nineteen." I slid my hand over the counter to retrieve the jewelry.

"You're going to ruin me but I'll take them." He fumbled under the counter for his checkbook, found it and scribbled a check to me for $18,500.

I should have argued harder but drove to the bank to make the deposit to my wounded account. I couldn't help but wonder how Martin got money for the wedding set when he'd been recently demobilized from the Army and was a junior real estate agent? I tried not to think of drugs or some other criminal behavior but couldn't subdue the suspicion. Sweet smoke?

****

Mom and Dad settled into their ever more restrictive lives. I talked to a social worker about moving them to Vashon where there was a small group home, but the woman said my mother had already made friends, and new programs in art and music for the memory impaired were being formulated. I put my idea aside, though I continued to be concerned whether there would be enough money from the sale of their home to pay their fees even if invested conservatively. The care home's social worker assured me, at least "statistically," the money should last. Statistically—what a cruel term to describe end of life care.

One afternoon on the way for a visit, I took a detour to drive by my childhood home. I slowed down to coast by the house. The shabby entrance was already remodeled and the formerly unkempt landscaping was now immaculately groomed. Several new Japanese maples replaced dark firs. A woman in a sun hat was on her knees pulling petunias to replace them with waiting flats of chrysanthemums, those flowers Italians placed on tombs on All Souls Day.

The home's color scheme was different, the soft gray more pleasing than the dead white Dad slapped on one summer years ago long before his accident. I could see my parents' bedroom but my old room was in the back and out of view. I accelerated, not wanting to think about the past or seeming to be a voyeur.

Dad smiled when I entered their rooms at the care home and held out his hand for me to hold. I looked at the row of medications sitting on a nearby table. Mom, who was on some new drug which might delay cognitive decline, was bright. It was time to ask about buying their car, and to tell her about Martin.

"Heavens, Nicki, take the car. You didn't even need to ask. It's yours."

I kissed her on the cheek. "There's something else."

Her attention had begun to wander but I needed to get this chore finished. "Martin passed away last month in Rome. I'll soon move to Vashon Island and you can visit. Remember, I told you Martin and I bought a house there when we were here last summer?"

A questioning look passed over her face. "Who is Martin? Do I know him?"

Was her memory rapidly worsening or was this a glimmer of brilliance, verbalizing the same thing about Martin I'd wondered? Either way, it was deeply unsettling.

****

I'd enrolled at Tacoma Community College for fall quarter, beginning in a month. Happily, my credits from the first year at University of Washington and some of those I earned in Rome were accepted. I'd decided to pursue a degree in social work despite the time it would take to get a BS and then an MSW. I'd specialize in eldercare.

The commute to the college would be easy and inexpensive because I would drive to the nearby dock and walk on the Tahlequah ferry to the north end of Tacoma and then take a bus. If everything worked out, next winter I'd transfer to the U to complete the course work. I'd take classes year-round to make up for lost time. Finding part-time work to fit my planned school schedule and give me relevant experience would be imperative.

Deirdre raised her eyebrows when I told her my plans. "Not cooking?"

"I need a change and want to be in the helping profession since I've dealt, am dealing, with my parents' problems. There's a real need. Anyway, I don't know anyone, don't have any "ins" with the restaurant industry here and don't have the funds to get set up."

"Maybe if your plans don't work out, we could investigate opening a bistro here when Sammy gets older."

"I'll pencil that in." We both laughed.

****

Although it felt good to have made the decision, there were many tasks waiting before I'd have a semblance of being settled. The furniture would arrive as soon as it cleared customs and I had to finish cleaning. Spiders had taken up residence. Husks of flies caught in webs still needed to be swept away, along with other insects all perished in futile efforts to escape from the closed house. I found a tiny lifeless bushtit on the floor of a closet. It must have become separated from the others in the flock and flown in when an agent showed the place. Its feathers were faded, the eyes dulled, the feet clenched in defiance of fate, the little beak half open in a last cry for help. I scooped it up with care and buried it in the garden, remembering the flocks nervously twittering and flitting around the shrubbery in my parents' garden. After the burial, I sat on the front steps bawling like a baby.

****

The furniture delivery van appeared through a foggy morning with its intimations of fall. I stood on the front deck to welcome the driver and laborer as they unlatched the cargo hold, set up ramps and wheeled hand trucks heavy with packing boxes. Acting as semaphore, I pointed the workers to the correct locations. I told them I'd open the boxes myself but asked if they'd wrestle the new mattress I'd bought the previous week onto my bed.

Martin's old desk was lugged to my office. I asked the movers if they had something to open it. One found a hammer and chisel and, after a few blows, pried the lock off. It was empty.

The van disappeared down my driveway as the sun burned off the gloom, raising my spirits at the same time. I found the box labeled "Master Bedroom." Master wasn't the right word for the situation but I felt a moment of satisfaction when I gave the sheets a shake and watched each billow over the bed.

****

I opened boxes labeled "kitchen." Silverware, dishes, utensils, pots and pans emerged. My stovetop espresso maker appeared. I filled the filter from a can of Italian coffee I'd bought in anticipation and added water. When the hiss of steam and the smell of coffee curled into the air, I mentally returned to Rome. Memories of Martin and Alessandro flared vividly in my mind, one who cared for nothing but domestic services, the other wanting to share love.

I poured the coffee into a tiny cup and sat on the

kitchen floor, my back against a box. What if I'd never met Alessandro? Perhaps there would have been someone else. Maybe it wouldn't have happened if Martin had been more considerate, had truly loved and cherished me. How I'd longed for him to say "I love you" and mean it.

However I tried, I couldn't deny my role in the further deterioration of our relationship when I fell in love with Alessandro. And I was the one who'd failed to let Jenna learn about her father. He'd said to let him know. But how could I have when the repercussions with the rest of the family would have been a nightmare, especially with Sophie? Deep down, I wondered if Sophie had an inkling. Tyler accepted Jenna without question. There was no doubt Martin knew the truth.

My worries were interrupted by the sensation of someone staring in the kitchen window. Three deer, a doe and two yearlings, had black noses close to the glass. I couldn't help laughing, thinking if they had hands, they'd cup them around their long-lashed eyes to see me better. The sound startled the animals. They leaped back and trotted away across the field, leaving a trio of nose prints on the glass.

****

By late afternoon, the kitchen was in semi-order. I climbed the stairs again to look for boxes labeled towels when I heard a knock on the door. Surely not the deer. I returned to the first floor to answer, stair treads creaking.

"Lights were on as I drove by and figured you must be moving in. I'll bet you don't have anything for dinner." Deirdre stood at my door; her hand outstretched to knock once more. "Would you like to eat with us?"

"I'd absolutely love it. Sure I'm not imposing?"

"No problem. Get your jacket and come on."

The chance to relax with someone else taking the initiative was too welcome to refuse even though I was tired and rumpled. I washed up, put on a bit of makeup before finding a rain jacket and jumped into the passenger seat for the short drive. A man who looked to be in his late thirties opened the kitchen door. He held Sammy, who stretched out his arms to me. I took him and kissed his sticky cheek decorated with a dab of ice cream near his ear.

"Wine?"

I turned to the man who, relieved of Sammy, raised a glass in my direction.

"I'd love some. Whatever's handy. Sorry I'm a bit of a mess."

"Actually, you look very Vashon. Deirdre says you moved here from Rome. Lucky you to have the chance to live there. We'll travel overseas again when Sammy's a bit older. He acts up on airplanes now. You can't imagine the looks we get."

"Did you introduce yourself?" Deirdre called from the dining room where she was setting the table.

"Sorry, I'm Josh. Welcome, we're glad to have a new neighbor." He tilted his head toward Deirdre, motioning her to join. "Let's sit by the fire for a bit if dinner can wait."

Deirdre took Sammy from me to put him on a rug in front of the fireplace. He happily played with blocks, building a fort for toy cars. She said, "We're not getting him anything electronic for a while. Way too early."

"It's one issue I never had to think about with mine."

We adults sat by the fire keeping watch over Sammy. I glanced at the couple. The firelight reflected on their contented faces.

Deirdre asked me how they might help and I mentioned a place called Costco. I said I'd like to get a membership to buy a few things like a TV and a food processor. Josh said, "You'll find everyone around here has one. Would you like to go? I'm making a run this Saturday."

"Thanks so much." One more step forward.

Deirdre put Sammy to bed before serving bowls of beef stew, rich with vegetables, accompanied by a tossed salad and cornbread. Talk centered on Sammy's day, and plans for the weekend interspersed with mundane remarks about island life. Nothing fraught, all routine. Family talk like Maggie and Orazio, although I recalled Deirdre's remark about the elaborate kitchen was compensation for Josh's long hours. Was their marriage as happy as it appeared? I dearly hoped so. Many women in Rome I'd talked to at parties or lunches changed stories of marriage from portrayals of love to more honest acrimony after too much wine loosened their tongues. I'd kept mine still.

CHAPTER TWENTY-ONE

Jenna showed up Sunday morning. I poured coffee and served Danish pastries I'd bought in the town center. She eyed at a 20-pound bag of cat food propped in the kitchen as she licked a sticky finger.

"I got carried away at Costco."

"You're not the first person who ends up with extras there. Anyway, it would be nice if you got a cat for company. I can't have pets in the apartment, and we never had any in Rome. Dad said he was allergic." She turned her attention to the unopened boxes.

"Shall I help with the rest of this stuff?"

My idea was to sort slowly through the remains of my previous life, to consider each item before either keeping or tossing it after I'd packed without much thought. But Jenna was enthusiastic, so I gave in.

She tore into boxes as if on a treasure hunt. The third one contained napkins and tablecloths along with items I'd dumped in without sorting just to fill the box in the press to finish packing. Nestled inside was my Venetian red glass goblet. I put it in the kitchen window where the light cast a ruby shadow when the sun appeared between scudding clouds. The glass made me remember the old count in his junk shop. It was eons ago when we talked about life, love, the pursuit of happiness, and duty to children. One of three adults who gave me courage and comfort during my Roman time. The memory of our relationship remained vivid, as was the true sadness of losing him.

Jenna's raised voice interrupted my thoughts. "Hey, Mom, here's part of your collection." It was a terracotta head, perfect as its namesake Alessandro. Like the ancient Romans, I would have my own household god, one of the *Lares* who guarded the home.

"I love my collection of portrait heads. It took ages to put it together. I'll finish digging out this stuff later today." I sensed danger even though I wasn't sure what else was in the box.

Jenna wasn't to be deterred. "I'll just go through this stuff before we quit."

"I'd rather you'd help with the living room boxes."

"It will just take a few minutes. You need to get this unpacking finished." She turned back to the box.

I couldn't think of a reason to disagree. Jenna lifted out a layer of her old baby clothes I'd kept for sentimental reasons and hadn't remembered I'd packed. Underneath little dresses and some hand-me-downs from Sophie was the pair of infant-sized patent-leather shoes, as shiny as when they were new and Alessandro had held her.

Jenna took them out. "Mom, are these mine?"

"Yes, honey. Aren't they sweet?" *Oh, God, no. Just no. I'm not ready.*

"I think Mary Janes are perfect for little girls. If I ever have a girl, I'm going to get her some." She paused, a tiny frown marring her face as she looked at me then back at the shoes. "Weird, they're like the baby was wearing in the old photo I found back in Rome a couple of months ago when we were packing. The one stuck in the book you've got over there on the end table. The photo where the baby kicked one off." I watched in agony as she inspected the shoes more carefully. The frown deepened.

I almost said all baby shoes looked alike, but it was the moment I'd dreaded for years and I needed to face it without sugar coating. The moment when everything could change between us. I couldn't find the words before Jenna interjected the question I knew would come someday.

"Mom? Why *did* you save that photo? What kind of a friend was this guy? It's kind of weird you'd save it in a poetry book. Who's the baby?" I could read the beginnings of fear in her eyes. Her voice was full of trepidation as if she too sensed a turning point.

"Jenna, dear, come and sit beside me."

Jenna, who kneeled by the box, looked up, head cocked to one side like a bird who'd found some curiosity and was trying to determine if it was edible. "So, what is it I need to know?" She remained on the floor holding the shoes in her outstretched hand as if they were possibly poisonous.

I wanted to look at her directly but failed. Instead, I looked at my terracotta god to give me courage as I choked out the dreaded revelation.

"I was terribly lonely when we got to Rome. Martin was busy at work or away, Tyler and Sophie were in school. The city was overwhelming. After I got the apartment organized, I found an ad for someone who wanted to exchange Italian lessons for English. I needed to learn the language to manage and it was a practical way to do it. It turned out he was young, a medical student named Alessandro. It progressed in a way I didn't expect. Didn't intend at all. We had a brief affair.

I got pregnant with you." I forced myself to look into her face.

She whipped back, eyes wide, mouth agape before dropping the shoes as if they were on fire. I tried to grab her hand but she'd scrambled to her feet to run to the kitchen.

I followed but she screamed, "How could you? You're a liar. All these years and…" She choked and pushed me aside on her way to the bathroom and turned on the taps. Despite the noise of rushing water, I could hear cries of anguish.

Devastated, I waited for her to take the next step. She emerged from the bathroom, face blotchy and swollen, nose dripping, eyes watery. "I've always wanted to know why Dad didn't ever act like he even liked me. Did he know? And Sophie, too. I'll bet she knew all along. Dumb me, so dumb I couldn't figure it out." She was near breathless.

"Please, honey."

"Don't call me honey! I never had a chance to know my own father because of you. Maybe he doesn't even know I'm alive. If he's alive. It's grotesque. I'm just a mistake." The last few words spilled from her open mouth in a stream of misery.

"I've wanted to tell you for years, but it was never the right time. Please, please forgive me. You were never, ever a mistake. I'd always wanted another child and I wanted you from the day I knew I was pregnant." I tried to put my arms around her again but she stepped back as if I was infected with smallpox.

"Okay, maybe sometime I'll accept your story but I wonder if you planned to go to your own grave without telling me." She stood by the fireplace opposite from me, conflicting emotions passing like wind-driven clouds over her distraught face.

I stammered as I recounted the story of a few months of great happiness followed by a long period of misery. I added, "Jenna, honey, I was lost in a big and unknown city. And Martin did act as your parent because he supported you as he did Tyler and Sophie even though he knew. I did violate my marriage vows but I wouldn't have had you if I hadn't. I will never, ever regret the relationship. Alessandro and I did truly love each other. And we met once after you were born. He held you in his arms with the most tender adoration and I took the photo."

I waited for a response. After an eternity, she said, "So what happened to him? Reject me too, did he?"

"No, he wanted to be kept informed but I just couldn't handle the complication. I even tried not to go to areas of Rome where he might be. At first, I was afraid I couldn't control my emotions and would have to leave Tyler and Sophie to return here with you. Then so much time passed I was afraid you'd leave me and go with him if he wanted. I'm so sorry. I don't know how to make things right." I couldn't look at her. My heart pounded so fast I worried it would never beat normally again.

"I want to meet him, this Alessandro guy. Your secret lover. My father. You can introduce us." Her voice quivered.

The thought of returning to Rome to dig up the past was terrifying. How could I manage a meeting with Alessandro whom I hadn't seen in over eighteen years? What if he'd forgotten, or remembered but rejected her after such a long time?

"I don't know if it's a good idea for me. I don't have

money to travel anyway. Right after Martin died, I learned by chance he's a prominent doctor in Rome. His name is Alessandro Lombardi. I imagine you could find out more information on how to contact him. I've never tried and I'm not sure I want to after all this time." Somehow this didn't sound true. I realized I was clutching the chair arms as if there was an earthquake.

Jenna stood over me. "Well then, I'll find him. If you won't go with me, I'll travel alone. Maybe I won't come back. I'm half Italian thanks to you."

Before I could say I'd try to arrange the meeting after all, Jenna grabbed her car keys and rushed out the door, leaving it open to bang in a cold wind.

I'd failed both my daughters.

CHAPTER TWENTY-TWO

I don't know how long I sat as if brain dead before pacing around the house to replay the disastrous scene with Jenna and how I could have handled it better. I must have been in shock because in an effort to keep unpacking, I tripped on the stairs, falling halfway down the flight with the box I'd been carrying. It landed on top of me.

After scrambling to my feet, I climbed up the stairs on all fours and dragged myself into bed where I stayed staring at the ceiling watching a fly as it wiped its face with its legs. The next day was equally painful as I made an effort to calm myself—breathe in, breathe out, focus on the future, focus on a beautiful Roman scene. I tried to ignore my mental and physical bruises. It didn't work, so I showered and crept down to the car to shop for food, hoping not to have an accident on the way.

I'd often seen the sign LABYRINTH OPEN TODAY near a small Episcopal Church when I drove into the town center to shop. I knew people walked these circular paths for religious reasons, but I was never interested enough to visit. Now I needed to learn if it might provide solace. I steered my old car into the parking lot and followed an arrow.

A clearing below the church was surrounded by old-growth fir, cedar trees, and a mix of evergreen salal and huckleberry bushes. A circular path divided into two connecting halves like a brain had been laid out in the center of the grass.

I sat on a bench near the entrance contemplating my wet shoes and my failure to measure up to my family's expectations when a slow swish of footsteps in the damp grass caught my attention. I looked up to see a woman in an anorak following the path, lips moving as if in prayer. She placed one foot in front of the other until she arrived at the center to mark the completion of half her journey. After pausing for a minute with her eyes closed, the woman stepped on the path leading back to the beginning. When she completed the cycle, she stopped at the bench where I sat.

"This walk gives me peace. If you are also troubled you will find help here." She briefly placed a hand on my head as if in blessing before she walked toward the parking lot.

I remained on the bench for several more minutes wondering if I'd really heard the woman. Wasn't it silly to walk in circles when my mind was already running on the same endless path? But it couldn't hurt either. Soft rain descended over the scene. I zipped my jacket, pulled up the hood and turned toward the path. I stepped forward slowly, deliberately, then on another and another. The sole sounds were the relentless drip of rain falling from tree branches and the distant cawing of crows.

My mind filled to the brim with thoughts of my past, of loneliness, failures, and death as I paced the left half of the path. I stood for several minutes in the center to cleanse the troubles before facing the right half to find a future filled with promise. Quietude seeped into my soul for the first time. I knew I'd survive.

****

I looked for a text or email from Jenna. There was none, but I received a request for a video interview for a half-time job as an assistant to the manager of a retirement facility in Tacoma where I'd applied. The pay wasn't much, nor were there any benefits, but it would give me experience to decide if the work was what I wanted and slow the hemorrhaging of my bank account. The thought of having to borrow money from my parents' account was something I vowed not to do.

At the interview's conclusion the next day, I was offered the job to begin in two weeks when the current staff member left. I wanted to share my news with Jenna but was afraid to initiate a call.

I waited one more day then sent a text. *"Can we talk?"* There was no response. Unable to wait, I called two days later. Still no answer. By this time, I'd reverted to my childhood habit of chewing my fingernails. I let it go for a week. I tried once more and she answered with a guarded, "Hi."

The conversation was strained at first, but Jenna's voice resumed its normal tone when she congratulated me on my job. I took a chance and invited her to the island for Sunday brunch. A new restaurant had recently opened and there were already good reviews.

****

Silence enveloped our booth while we each studied the menu longer than necessary. Then she looked up at the same time I did. After what seemed an eternity, she said, "Look, Mom, I'm sorry I acted up, but it was such a shock. I've been thinking though. I don't look like Tyler or Sophie. Tyler was great when I was a kid, but Sophie, it's pretty obvious we've never been real sisters.

I'll get over it, but I do wish you had told me earlier. Like I said, it makes me feel dumb. I mean, my gosh, Mom, did everyone else know and I, was like, just fat, dumb and happy?"

I assured her neither Sophie nor Tyler were aware. Possibly another lie, especially with Sophie, but her semi-forgiveness was a balm.

The two of us were finishing the last bites of our Eggs Benedict when Jenna said, "Did you give him a copy of the photo? The one where he's holding me?" I could read the hope in her eyes.

"The situation was impossible for both of us. There was nothing to work out but I arranged the meeting because I wanted him to see how lovely you were."

Jenna smiled at the compliment. I added, "It was to be a memory for him and me too. The shadow on the grass in the photo was me behind the camera. And, yes, I gave a copy to his landlady to give to him."

"I need to meet him. Alessandro, my father. But I still can't wrap my head around this. I know it happens in lots of marriages but…" The thought hung in the air, though she flashed a tentative smile.

We reverted to mindless talk. Jenna glanced at me between bites as if she was trying to imagine the love affair, and what life would have been like if she'd been raised in Italy with a father who was a doctor. I wondered the same thing.

A drizzle dampened us when we left the restaurant, but I asked if she'd like to visit a labyrinth where I'd found respite.

"Sure. I've heard about them but never seen one."

Sunday service was over. A few people remained in the parking lot talking and shaking hands before they parted.

"Let's go to the church first. I haven't seen the inside yet."

Jenna followed me. A woman placed prayer books and hymnals in the racks on the pews. I approached the altar. Instead of stained glass with a religious scene in the apse, an enormous pane of clear glass looked out on the labyrinth and the surrounding trees. When the woman stopped her duties to welcome us, I asked about the unusual window. She said it was given in memory of a Vietnam veteran because the family loved the peaceful view.

Had he died in the mud, or from an overdose, or suicide? Or had he been one of the ragged men who'd hung around underpasses in Seattle after they returned home waiting to die? Or had he been like Martin, damaged but functioning for a time?

What happened to him there? The war had been over for over fifteen years when we married. I never considered him a wounded veteran, but I'd read about PTSD and he had some of the symptoms. And I'd read of terrible things during the war: of drugs, of troops murdering their lieutenants, of napalm and Agent Orange, massacres of innocent villagers, of death in Vietcong tunnels. The poor kids fighting a war they didn't understand, had no stake in but to survive. The ghastly photos, worst of all the screaming naked child.

It was unbearable to contemplate so I turned to Jenna. "Come on, honey, let's do the labyrinth."

We walked in silence. I didn't know Jenna's thoughts, but my own burden of a secret kept too long finally lifted from my shoulders.

When we returned to the car, Jenna said, "Really

neat. Thanks Mom. And have a happy birthday. Sorry I won't be able to be with you, but I've got a big test coming up. I'll give you a call."

Alone again, I flipped the switch for the gas fireplace to watch the leaping flames. The fire made me think of Martin's cold body sliding inexorably into the super-heated crematory fire to be reduced to a handful of ashes—ashes on a shelf in the bedroom closet waiting for me. But meeting Jenna's need to know her father was far more important. Would he want to see his daughter? Would she really want me to go back to Rome with her? If I did, I'd have to find a cheap fare, probably borrow the money. But family was more important than money.

Maybe Alessandro had forgotten about both of us and, anyway, it was too soon to make a firm decision when I'd returned to the States just a couple of months ago. A return to Rome would be an emotional rollercoaster for both of us. And my burgeoning fear Jenna might reject me and choose to remain with Alessandro if he wanted her added to my disquiet.

There was no longer a need to hide the photograph of Alessandro and baby Jenna. I propped it on my desk among others of my three children and Jacob before I found a scrap of tissue paper to wrap the baby shoes to put away in a drawer.

Determined to continue unpacking, I opened more boxes. The top one contained an old album with photos of the children. Sophie never smiled. Underneath were more old baby clothes and Sophie's childhood books. And the tattered stuffed toy, Threadbear. "Oh, Sophie, help me, help us connect," I prayed as I held the old teddy bear as tight as she had as a child.

CHAPTER TWENTY-THREE

On the morning of my forty-fifth birthday, I stared out the rain-splattered kitchen window, my forehead against the cool glass. An occasional burst of sun turned the raindrops into balls of liquid mercury as they slid downward. The weather filled me with melancholy. Maybe a condo in some busy part of Seattle would be a better place to live after all. A place where there were people, ambient sounds of neighborly chatter, children playing, music, an aroma of coffee brewing, or baking from someone else's kitchen.

My thoughts were interrupted by a knock on the door. I looked down at my old robe. It needed a wash and I hadn't yet combed my hair. It was nine o'clock. I opened the door a crack to see who it was. Deirdre held out a plate of blueberry muffins. Sammy stood behind her, peeking out from under a yellow southwester hat.

"I took these from my oven a few minutes ago and they're still hot. Would you like some?"

"I don't think I'm ready for company as you can see."

Deirdre's face fell. "Oh, sorry. I didn't mean to interrupt you." She turned toward her car with Sammy close behind.

"Wait. Wait, please. I'm a mess. I'm sorry if I was rude. The weather has gotten to me. I'm not used to it yet. Come in and give me a minute or two."

Deirdre took off Sammy's raingear while I rushed upstairs to improve my shameful appearance.

"Hey, your house looks great." Deirdre's voice floated up the staircase from the entry.

"Thanks. Go on to the kitchen where it's warm." I found my jeans and sweatshirt and took a swipe at my face and hair.

In the kitchen I started a fresh pot of coffee, got out another mug and asked if Sammy wanted some orange juice. "Juice please." He held out his arms. I poured a small glass for him and set out the butter dish and plates.

Deirdre took the cling wrap off the muffins. My mouth watered as I put one on a plate and handed it to her. She passed it to Sammy who stuck his fingers in to break it into crumbs. I served the two of us and took a bite. "These are divine. I'm so ashamed but I've never baked since I moved back."

"I'll bake for you until you have time. Anyway, the reason I came by is to invite you to an opening at an art gallery in town tomorrow night. It's a photographer friend's new work, time-lapse pictures of airplane lights from Sea-Tac airport. I suppose you've seen them at night. Anyway, it's not a big deal, but a chance to meet some people. No pressure."

"I don't know. I'm really busy. I...well...yes, I'd love to." I heard myself waffle again. I couldn't even make up my mind about a visit to an art gallery.

"I'll pick you up in about five minutes to seven. It's another great thing about Vashon—it just takes a minute to get anywhere." She added, "You know, I'm really happy you're here. Come on over to my place any time and we can talk. Sometimes I need somebody to talk to."

"Thank you so much. I'll do it. I do need someone

too." I looked into my mug instead of Deirdre. A warped version of myself appeared before the rising steam made my eyes moist. I almost mentioned it was my birthday but let it pass. The less said about a date I saw as presenting a personal challenge, the better. The cards from Jenna and Tyler were enough.

After Deirdre and Sammy left, I drove into town to find a salon and arrange for a haircut and mani-pedi. Back home, I found my old desk calendar and wrote in it "Haircut, etc. 11:00; gallery opening 7:00 with Deirdre." I flipped back through the pages. The last entry for Rome was for the taxi I'd taken to the airport. The few "dates" for my new life related to financial matters or visits to my parents. I didn't need to enter the times Jenna was here; they were always in my memory and she'd cheered me with a birthday phone call after I'd returned from town.

Deirdre knocked on the front door right on time. No one in Rome ever showed up on the appointed minute for a social occasion. I opened the door in my violet silk dress and bare feet. "Hang on, I can't find my shoes and I need to finish my makeup."

"Oh my gosh—I should have said it's casual. Are you sure about the dress? Remember it's Vashon."

"I'm dressed now. I haven't had a chance to go out for months." I ran upstairs to finish.

Deirdre said, "Uh, a bit much for here," when I returned wearing open-toed platform heels complementing the purple dress. After a pause, she added, "Oh, don't worry, it's fine and we're late anyway." I could tell she was flustered about something.

When we parked in front of the gallery, I could see people holding glasses of wine while they looked at the photos. All looked comfortable in jeans and sweaters like Deirdre. I could feel my face was beginning to match my dress. Why hadn't I settled in for the latest episode of a British mystery on the TV instead of making such a fool of myself?

People paused conversations to welcome Deirdre and her unknown and strangely dressed guest: me. Some stared briefly. Not unkind looks, but more of astonishment their friend had found such an alien.

A woman rescued me by saying, "Hi. I'm Meg. Don't think we've met." Like Sammy, she wore overalls. I looked to Deirdre for help.

"Hey, everyone, I want you to meet my new neighbor, Nicole Carlisle. She's recently arrived from Rome, Italy. She's in Harry's old house. You know."

All the eyes which hadn't yet focused on me did so. I put on my best smile, and said, "It's great to be here but guess I didn't quite understand the Vashon dress code despite Deirdre trying to tell me." There were smiles and words like "nice change" and "no problem," but I couldn't help wondering what I was doing here. Surely, they dressed up in Seattle for openings and concerts. I wished the floor would open up.

Deirdre saved the day. "Nicole is interested in local art and wants to meet the artist."

"Hey, Zo', come on over," Meg said. "Someone wants to meet you."

Deirdre said to me, "You'll be surprised when you meet her. You have a lot in common."

The photographer, Zoe, introduced herself. She held out her hand and I took it. "So pleased to meet you. I studied in Rome for a year. At the American Academy. It was heaven. And you look so Roman in the beautiful dress."

Zoe was young, tall, with cropped hair and long tapered fingers with perfect manicured nails. She wore a black turtleneck cashmere sweater, tight black jeans, and ballerina flats. We briefly chatted about Rome, places we liked, the food, the sunshine, even the fashions, before she began to mingle with other guests. Deirdre brought two glasses of wine. I took a large swig of mine before holding the chilled glass to my still burning face.

The wine was good and the photographer's short presentation about her concept resonated with all my flights to and from Seattle, always accompanied by worries about my parents, the children, or Martin. All the time-lapse photos were of night flights with streaks or dots from the plane's lights set against the moon or stars. Some had the Seattle skyline with the Space Needle and a full moon as the plane flew low. The lights called to mind the rush of time marked by my birthday the previous day. Time fleeting, ever accelerating.

After Zoe's presentation, I approached her again and said I often watched the flight from my window though I didn't know if I'd ever return to Rome.

"I can't imagine anyone not wanting to return to Rome. I'd go in a nanosecond. You're so lucky to have lived there."

"It can be tough. Anyway, it was time to come home after so many years."

Zoe leaned toward me with a questioning look. I hesitated before saying, "I was recently widowed. I grew up in Seattle."

"Oh. I'm so sorry. And to have your husband pass away when he must have been so young."

"Yes, it was a shock." I let the misunderstanding

about age pass but the image of Martin's body lying on the gravel appeared in my mind.

"What will you do now you're back?" Zoe asked. I said I wanted to become a social worker. "Good! We need more people in the caring profession. And one was such a help when my mom was sick back in Pittsburgh and I was stuck here for a while."

I warmed to her even more at the validation of my choice. When several others clustered around the photographer to ask questions or convey compliments, I backed away to look more closely at the photos displayed on the gallery's white walls. There were already a number of red dots placed by the captions on the placards next to the expensive pictures. I wanted one but kept my credit card safely stashed.

When I found the table where the wine and snacks were set out, the woman whom I'd first met, Meg, refilled my glass and said she was Zoe's partner. I told her how enraptured I was by the photographs.

"Yeah, she's good, isn't she? Is the sauvignon okay? It's local. Nice people own the winery."

I praised the wine. Meg invited me to visit the studio during the annual artist's open house event in early December.

"I'd love to. I'm so pleased to meet such a talented photographer."

Meg smiled, basking in the glow of her partner's accomplishments. I circled the room to introduce myself though my store of small talk of local interest was limited. I was relieved when Deirdre said she needed to return home. The effort to be sociable while dressing like a fool resulted in my shoulders knotted like macramé.

Home again, I relived the conversation with Zoe.

Her comment about Martin passing away wasn't correct. He'd passed from me early in our marriage. I put the thought aside. Tomorrow I'd start work.

****

The coffee at the snack bar in the assisted living community wasn't half bad. I'd arrived nearly an hour early and sat on a bench near the entrance looking at the pastel colors, seasonal silk flowers in vases on every table, reproductions of kitschy rural scenes on the walls, and noise-canceling carpets in the main reception room. The coffee bar and dining room filled a nearby windowed area. It was similar to where my parents resided and, I supposed, to every other institution for the elderly and infirm.

A woman with a walker with old-fashioned red, white and blue bicycle streamers attached to the handles asked if she might sit with me. Happy to meet a resident, I introduced myself as a new staff member.

The woman smiled and said, "I'm Sally. Just to clue you in, it might take a while to get used to all of us tottering around and the EMTs coming and going day and night. Kind of depressing, but the staff are nice here."

"Have you lived here long?"

"About two years." I could see she wanted to cry but suppressed the feeling. "After Ervin passed away, I didn't want to be alone in the old house. The children all moved away, and you know…"

"Yes, I do know." I patted Sally's fleshless blue-veined hand still wearing wedding rings.

The executive who'd interviewed me beckoned. I excused myself, telling Sally I'd have a coffee with her soon.

The Measure of Life

I signed the employment contract and pinned a name badge to my blouse, jubilant with this new step forward in the process of my reinvention. After a discussion of my duties and a detailed tour of the building, I was assigned to help welcome a new resident, a man.

He kept his gaze on the carpet and spoke in monosyllables during introductions. His daughter and son-in-law looked both harried and relieved, as if they'd finally conquered the old man's resistance to the change engulfing his life as he left a home filled with mementoes to live in a one-room apartment. It was a replica of the experience I'd had with my own parents.

I led the man and his daughter to his room. He said, "But I don't understand why." His daughter replied, "Oh Dad, we've gone over and over this. It's done."

I said, "Why don't we take a walk around the terrace and then it will be time for lunch." I held out my arm for him to grasp.

The daughter said, "I'll see you next week, Dad." She gave the man a quick kiss on his stubbled cheek and hurriedly left to meet her waiting husband. A family now split apart.

By day's end, I was worn out. Sally was correct—it would take a while to adjust. The bland atmosphere was anything but and I needed to quell doubts I was up to the challenge.

****

Whatever my doubts, I found satisfaction helping the frail residents yet sadness at the inevitable changes they faced with dignity. Now, in late September, I became a student. Although it was sometimes difficult to juggle school and work schedules, I found the rhythm of attending lectures and studying to my liking, even peaceful. I often sat in the cafeteria with my laptop, earbuds and cappuccino to work on a paper along with other students. Their presence gave me a sense of belonging and common purpose, similar to work.

I remembered my year at the U when I didn't have any goals. I was intimidated by the other ambitious students who all knew what they wanted. Now, no longer reticent, I developed friendships with a number of my classmates, some my age, many younger. It was enlightening to listen to them share their hopes and dreams, and to hear their perspective on current events. I avoided older students who I found cynical, a trait I tried not to emulate.

The days ran together as the cycles of school and work repeated themselves. The weather was changing, and I liked to curl up with a novel on my rare time to relax. I thought of a quilt I'd inherited from my mother's mother. I'd always been comforted by it as a child. Its cozy warmth would cut the fall chill and also be a nice addition to the guest bedroom décor. Maybe Mom would recognize it if she could come for a visit.

One Sunday, when homework was done and I had a day off, I opened a closet to haul out several boxes where I thought the quilt might be. I rummaged through the first box and touched a flat rectangular object at the bottom. Curious, I grasped an old composition book like the ones the children used in high school. I opened it. The first page said, "For my eyes only." The handwriting was Sophie's.

What to do with it? The right thing to do was ask if she wanted it. But I was tempted to learn what was in Sophie's mind at the time, maybe gain some insight to help us come together. She'd never confided in me when she was a child, and in her high school years it was as if she'd divorced me while continuing to seek her father's attention.

I placed the book back in the box. Learning her deepest thoughts could risk sending me into a tailspin after the near disaster with Jenna. It could wait until I was more settled.

CHAPTER TWENTY-FOUR

Jenna made Thanksgiving dinner reservations at a restaurant with reasonable prices and suggested I stay over at her apartment so we could shop the sales on Black Friday.

I sat in the ferry line on Thanksgiving morning with others on the way to the mainland watching as the walk-ons lugged pie carriers, wine totes, and grocery bags. Most were in rain jackets over sweaters and jeans. Small children, bundled and blanketed, sat in strollers. Infants were cradled in carriers strapped to fathers' backs or mothers' fronts, while older ones cavorted around their parents in excitement.

Jenna and I met in the restaurant lobby before being escorted to a table overlooking the cold gray water lapping at the bulkhead in front of a picture window. Relentless rain, the drops reminding me of tadpoles, wiggled down the glass. I didn't suggest a prayer before the meal, but silently gave thanks that I had a home and a family—however far away three of them were.

Jenna raised her glass. "Mom, I keep thinking about, well, you know. It's still a shock, I told my roomie and she said I was a love child! So in a way it's kinda cool."

I raised my own glass. The rims touched with a soft clink. "You are a wonderful daughter and I have much to be thankful for this and every day." I prayed silently that my resilient and sunny child would be able to maintain her outlook on life as it unfolded—life with its unexpected moments of bliss and inescapable sorrows.

The next day, we set off for our bargain-hunting expedition. It was pouring with rain again and I watched the Seattleites hunched in rain jackets holding paper coffee cups as they maneuvered without umbrellas along the crowded streets. Christmas music I hadn't heard for years blared through loudspeakers in shops. Sucked into the frenzied atmosphere and beguiled by the low prices, I soon filled a couple of bags with three sweaters, a down-filled jacket, a pair of walking shoes, and several pants and blouses in casual Seattle style. Not as sophisticated as Zoe's but clothes suitable for working and university classes. The women who wrote about the hedonism of shopping were right, even with my sensible choices. I hummed along with the canned music.

During our lunch we overheard two women chatting in the next booth. "If someone had told me I be going through menopause with two teenagers I'd have slit my wrists." The other woman said, "Bah! They'll be out of the nest soon and you know you'll miss them." Jenna and I looked at each other, both of us with a small smile and shrug. How easy it would be to talk to her if she ever was in such a position. I couldn't picture such a conversation with Sophie.

The moment passed and I told her about my fashion mistake at the gallery opening. She giggled. After more chit-chat, I asked if we would be together on Christmas and what presents Tyler, Sophie and Jacob might like. She suggested a book for Tyler and gift cards for Sophie and Jacob. She'd love a small one too. The card was enough, and of course they would make a day of it.

How different this holiday was from the past.

Although Sophie hadn't returned to Rome for Christmas once she left, Tyler had visited occasionally when he could get away from work. When Jenna became a teenager, she often arranged to go with friends to their family vacation homes in the Dolomites to ski over the school break but was always home for Christmas Day and the twenty-sixth, St. Stephen's Day. She and I loved to go out after dark to view the colorful lights strung high across the streets in complicated designs. We'd listened to the bagpipers down from the hills, snacked on roasted chestnuts, and checked out the stalls in Piazza Navona filled with children's toys and figures of *la befana*, the witch on a broomstick who gave good children presents and lumps of coal to the naughty ones on Epiphany, January 6. Christmas on Vashon would be very different for sure.

We parted after lunch and I drove to the car ferry line at Fauntleroy for a long wait. By the time the ferry docked in Vashon, the weather had changed from occasional sunbreaks back to another fierce rainstorm. I was drenched when I hopped out to raise the garage door. Another improvement to add to my list if I ever had any disposable money: an automatic door opener.

I hauled my bags into the house and brewed coffee. My mood sank with the heavy weather. I carried the cup to sit on the bed surrounded by evidence of my spree. Ashamed of wasting money, I shoved the bags off where they lay in disarray, contents spilling on the carpet. It would have to be consignment shops from now on. I found my car keys and drove to the labyrinth to repent for my extravagance.

Raindrops fell from my umbrella as I watched two squirrels, undeterred by the weather, chase each other around a tree trunk. Cheered by their antics, I headed home to make an Italian dinner. Rummaging through the cupboards, I found a package of linguini, a tin of anchovies and one of plum tomatoes. The black olives and capers came from the refrigerator, the garlic from the bowl on the counter. Even though I halved the recipe, the *Pasta alla Puttanesca* was too much for one person. I put the remainder in the refrigerator to nuke up for tomorrow's lunch even though it would be a gluey mess.

The following day I dressed in one of my new Pacific Northwest outfits before I walked to Deirdre's house in search of some companionship and maybe a compliment on my new look. The path was soaked and the moisture on the bare shrubs reflected the weak late fall sunlight. In a few weeks, the days would begin lengthening again.

Deirdre opened the door. "Hey, you look great. Come on in. Sammy's asleep, Josh's in his office, and we can talk."

I stepped into the warm kitchen, where Deirdre had been chopping vegetables for soup. She shoved onions into a pot, wiped her stinging eyes, and poured two mugs of coffee. Mine said "Kiss me, I'm Irish" in gold letters.

"Italians are coffee drinkers, but they're amateurs compared to everyone here. Coffee with meals, coffee all day long. No wonder I can't sleep." I took a swallow. "I have a question. I want to get to know more people here, but I don't know how, especially after the dress disaster. Should I host a coffee party some morning if that's what you do here? Or would something else be better?"

"I was thinking the same thing but I want to host it so I can introduce you to my friends. How about a holiday coffee?"

"A wonderful idea. I'm so grateful to you for everything you've done to make me feel at home."

"Believe me, it's nothing." She found a calendar and asked me about my schedule to fix a date.

****

The recipe for oatmeal cookies in my old *Joy of Cooking* lay open on the counter as I scooped a taste of leftover dough from the mixing bowl. The cookies destined for the party were in the oven. The raw dough reminded me of earlier days when Tyler and Jenna both "helped" when they were young. Sophie refused to participate, saying it was gross to stick your fingers in the bowl and then lick them.

Christmas was just over three weeks away and I would have the day off. After my Thanksgiving conversation with Jenna, I'd been too busy to give the holiday serious thought until red and green decorations at the retirement home reminded me. Tyler had mentioned he might be in the States on business sometime in January in his last email. To my disappointment, he'd not been able to come earlier. I'd ask him if he could bump it up to December. But Sophie? Was it too late to ask? The fear of rejection stalled me. How to even ask when Sophie hadn't participated for years?

The kitchen timer interrupted my thoughts. I opened the oven door to check the progress. The sweet aroma filled the kitchen. One more minute should do it.

The timer buzzed again, and I took the cookie sheet out of the oven. They looked perfect. Gratified at my culinary success, I climbed the creaky stairs to my office to contact Tyler first, less fraught than starting with Sophie. A message told me I needed to download some important security updates. I returned to the kitchen where the cookies cooled on a rack. I tried one. It was good. I wouldn't disgrace myself at the gathering.

The download was complete when I returned to my office to contact the children.

Hi Tyler. I remember you said in your last email you might be in the States in the near future. If you will be traveling and if it's not too late, can you add a trip out here around Christmas? I'd be so happy to see you – it's been way too long. I'll send you info on how to get here from the airport as soon as you have your flight schedule. With much love, Nicole." I added, *"P.S. If you can't make Christmas, anytime would be wonderful.*

A message easily written. But Sophie? A phone call would be efficient but could put her on the spot. The last time we'd talked it was the one-way conversation with Sophie crowing about the insurance payment. Email was best. After several false starts, I sent a message:

Dear Sophie. If you and Jacob haven't made Christmas plans yet I would love to have you visit. I know flights get booked early but am hoping there's still one available. I'm mostly settled now and the house has plenty of room for you both. I have invited Tyler and Jenna too so you are aware. Please do come. Your loving mother.

I put aside my fear Sophie wouldn't bother to respond since I didn't mention paying. Surely, she still had money from the insurance settlement.

The cookie fragrance found its way up the stairs to remind me to get going. I followed the aroma back to the kitchen where I found one of my gaily-painted Italian plates in the cupboard. I dressed in one of my inexpensive new blouses and a pair of designer Italian wool slacks. At the last minute I tied an Italian silk scarf around my neck. Sort of a combination Vashon – Rome axis.

****

Deirdre welcomed me to the gathering, a group of women diverse in age and profession: a couple of young mothers staying at home at least until their children were in school, several attorneys, some in high tech, the others in the art world like Zoe. Their conversation turned to the challenge of finding the right work-life balances: particularly children's needs versus careers.

"I had to put off a deposition because of Jon Junior's track and field event."

"Marisa came down with a tummy bug just when I was scheduled to hang my latest paintings at a gallery in Seattle."

"Jim had to be out of town when the kids' play was produced and they were so disappointed. I don't think they really understood."

I told them a few cooking stories and about Jenna's nursery school and they asked questions and smiled in the convivial atmosphere where the fire glowed and the decorations added warmth. Several suggested I might give them a cooking lesson. With the ego boost I pictured some of these women becoming close friends. Women with whom I could share unguarded talk, seek and give support, like Maggie and Franca. How different they were from many expat women in Rome trapped in velvet cages: careers on hold, waiting for their husbands' next assignments, or to return home after the blip in their domestic landscape. I recalled one woman who told me at her goodbye coffee she'd run around her Roman kitchen whooping and waving her arms in glee when her husband said they were returning to the States.

When Deirdre invited everyone to the laden dining room table, I stood next to a woman who introduced herself as Betty Jo. She was older than the other guests and used two canes. She had a mop of unruly white hair and wore a sweater with cat hair clinging to the wool.

"I'm pretty busy and stay in my office most days but came today because I wanted to meet my new neighbor." She raised one of her canes. "Arthritis acting up. Usually don't need these unless it's damp and cold. Unfortunately, pretty often around here in the winter."

When I offered sympathy and helped by carrying her cup and plate, she thanked me and said, "Doesn't stop me from writing. Vashon's ideal, enough solitude to get some work done, but not so much as to be isolated. I'm doing a reading at the bookshop in town next weekend. Can you come?"

"I'd be delighted to attend if I don't have to work. What do you write?"

"Cozy mysteries. Do you read them?"

"I don't know what they are." I smiled at Betty Jo while thinking the last thing I needed was more mysteries in my life, cozy or not.

Betty Jo explained the genre where the sleuth is an amateur and the gore quotient is low. "My settings are in cottages and the sleuth is a cat."

"A cat?"

"Yes, she's a clever black cat with green eyes. Her name is Marple."

"I haven't had time to do much reading lately. Are your stories set on Vashon?" I looked at her hair-covered sweater.

"Yes, but I use a different name for the island. If

people aren't nice, I put them in the book. As a victim." Betty Jo looked at me with a mischievous glint in her eye.

"Oh dear, I shall be extra pleasant. What about my house—was it in a book?"

"Yes. I couldn't resist after old Harry died. He had a wife, but she disappeared a few years after they moved in. I always thought there was a body in the yard or somewhere because I heard them shouting all the time on summer nights when I got here in the eighties."

I drew back involuntarily but Betty Jo, full of enthusiasm for the subject continued without noticing: "Anyway, I read a few years ago she turned up in San Diego, wife of an admiral of all things. I guess Harry was in the clear. Poor guy, so old and all alone, worked on the house, added the deck and whatever else I don't remember. So there you are. You're living in a house in a novel."

"Did you name it after the cat?"

"Nope, I called it *Board to Death*." She spelled it out. "Get it?"

I laughed at her cleverness.

"I hope we can get together again. I'll attend your event if possible." I'd put it on my calendar but hoped my work schedule would allow an escape. What would Betty Jo think if she knew about Martin? Maybe she or her cat could figure it out. I couldn't.

When the food and small talk ran out, the guests began to offer their thanks and goodbyes. Many said they looked forward to seeing me again and wanted to hear more about my life in Rome, especially the food adventures, and repeated their interest in lessons. I put my arms around Deirdre and told her how happy I was

The Measure of Life

for the introductions before taking my jacket from the closet and finding the satisfyingly-empty cookie plate. She said she'd make sure I was on everyone's contact list.

I was filled with contentment hoping for more coffee dates as I walked the wet path home. But as I neared the house, my thoughts were irresistibly turned toward the old man who'd died there. Had he been as lonely as the old count I'd treasured in Rome? And the woman, Betty Jo. Was she lonely too?

I'd briefly toyed with the idea of attending the local loss support meetings but feared it would rake up negative feelings I didn't have time for. My anger at Martin's meanness had already turned to resignation when I recognized it was useless to dwell on the past. I became more involved in island life, even though I'd have to back off as soon as school started again after the holidays. I checked *The Beachcomber* for news and found far more activities than I'd expected: sheep dog trials, new films at the local theater, gallery exhibitions.

One day I found an article about the Vashon Opera's production of "The Elixir of Love." It would be a perfect choice for someone who needed an elixir. I opened my desk calendar to pencil in the date with a question mark while picturing people in flannel shirts and jeans instead of gowns and tuxes always worn for opening nights in Rome. I called Betty Jo to see if she would join me. The writer said, "Sure thing. I was looking for a good setting for my next book." I erased the calendar's question mark and entered the date in ink. I planned to wear the same neutral outfit I'd worn to the coffee just to be careful.

Though I'd been skeptical, I loved the production with its colorful costumes and high-quality singing, better than some in Rome. Betty Jo scribbled notes in the dim light. She planned to call the new novel *The Elixir of Murder.*

****

Tyler called the day after the opera to say he'd arranged to be in Seattle near the end of December for consultations with his employer, an international aid organization headquartered there. A friend would come along but they would stay in Seattle because he had so many meetings in town. He didn't identify the friend. I was both elated and curious.

Although I checked my phone several times a day for emails, texts or missed messages, there was no response from Sophie. I debated calling but didn't want to nag lest she back out.

The next concern was my parents. Dad was too weak to leave the facility for any reason except medical care. I called the nurse most familiar with Mom's situation to discuss a stay on Vashon for two nights. The woman said it would be a nice change, but someone would need to prevent her from wandering and ensure she didn't get overtired. The next time I visited, I asked mom if she would like to come for Christmas.

"Oh, I always make fruitcake and mince pie. I need to get the ingredients for this year. I'll talk to your father about when we can cut the tree. Maybe there will be snow."

"Sure Mom, I'll help." I found a tissue to wipe my eyes. It dried my face but couldn't wipe away my sadness.

I bought a tree grown on the island and strung it with tiny white lights and ornaments from Rome, and made a swag of local greenery, cones, and berries gathered in the woods for the front door. An arrangement of white candles and greenery set off with red ribbon decorated the fireplace mantel.

The whirlwind continued with shopping for modest gifts: a new robe and slippers for both my parents and practical sweaters for Jenna and Sophie, and a simple video game for Jacob. If Sophie didn't show, I'd mail them. But what did people in the aid business want? As Jenna had suggested, a book for Tyler would be the safest choice. I found one with short stories by African writers. The shopkeeper assured me that if he didn't want it, he could select another in exchange. I wrapped the gifts, adding a small donation for Tyler's non-profit organization. Christmas was a week away.

****

Tyler arrived in Seattle on the twenty-first of December, the winter equinox, a day which always lifted my spirits with its promise of longer days to come. He'd called from the airport to ask if he could stop by before going to his hotel. He wanted to introduce his friend. I was delighted he'd make the effort to visit the island immediately after the long flights from South Sudan. He accepted my invitation for an early dinner.

An hour later two people stood on my doorstep: my dear Tyler and a slender young woman with straight black hair and bangs cut even with her brows. Tyler introduced her as Mai, a pediatrician at his aid organization. Mai was reserved at first, but she became more animated as we chatted. Her face lit when she spoke of her work with refugees and how much it meant to her because her own family fled the horrors of Cambodia. She didn't offer details, nor did I ask. I'd read about refugee lives with the perils of starvation, rape, disease, murder, and early death. A frisson of disquiet made me wonder again what Martin had seen in Vietnam and what he'd done there.

Tyler told me about the people he worked with, locals and international alike managing medical clinics to care for the suffering. "So many women die in childbirth and so many little children succumb to malaria or malnutrition. Sometimes it's just too late to help. We don't acknowledge how lucky we are here."

I agreed. "Yes, sometimes I need to step back and consider how fortunate I've been."

"The miseries are endless. A month ago, a clinic I oversee was sacked by some marauders who wanted our drugs to sell on the black market."

"Oh Tyler, please be careful." I blotted out a picture of him dead, blood seeping into the sand.

"I shouldn't have said anything. I'm sorry. Please don't worry, I can take care of myself."

I looked at him, the shock of brown hair falling over his forehead making him seem boyish. But there were sprinklings of prematurely silvering hair and his face showed sun wrinkles around the eyes—a kinder and gentler version of his father. He'd chosen a hard but worthy path and I was proud of him. But now I'd be even more concerned than in the past. To break the spell, I said, "I'll check on dinner."

The mood lightened when we took our chairs at the table. Tyler's descriptions of the land and peoples in the countries where he'd worked made me wish I'd been more adventurous in my younger life—to have heard harp music in Mali, and seen the Dinka cattle herders with their lyre-horned white animals in Sudan. As he talked, Tyler looked at Mai for validation. I watched as she tilted her head toward him and smiled. It was obvious he was in love with this lovely and intelligent woman and she felt the same toward him.

After dinner, Tyler came into the kitchen. I was washing platters and bowls which didn't fit into the dishwasher.

"Mai's catching up on some emails. I'll dry and I want to tell you something."

I peeled off my rubber gloves. "Let's sit down." I motioned toward the old kitchen table, worn by heavy use over the years. We sat close together.

He poured a splash of wine from a nearly-empty bottle left over from the meal before he continued, "I want to apologize for waiting so long to tell you, but you should know I will always remember the good care you took of me for the years I was home. I know I spent most of my time trying to ignore you and Dad. He wasn't loving or interested in me. He hardly ever came to my games like you did. I don't know how you put up with it for all those years."

I felt a rush of gratification he and I had bonded so strongly after the first hiccups. "I would never have withheld my support. Never."

Tyler finished the wine but still held the glass, rolling the stem back and forth in his fingers absent-mindedly. "I would not ever treat my partner the way he treated you. And I'm quite sure Mai will be the person. I want someone to be with, someone who truly cares for me as I for her. We're trying things out now. We want to be sure we make the right decision before we marry. We'll likely remain in Africa for some time. I believe I can contribute and she does too."

I was about to offer thanks and also congratulations

when he shifted in his chair, his face flushed.

"There's more. I'm glad we can talk, just us."

The mood in the room shifted. His focus fell directly on me. I tried not to appear uncomfortable.

"When I saw the photo you sent of you and Jenna over Thanksgiving, I realized something I subconsciously knew all along: she looks nothing like either me or Sophie or Dad." He brushed his hair off his brow and drew in his breath before continuing.

I waited, too, not sure I was ready to respond.

"Jenna is so beautiful. She…she looks Italian, like one of my old girlfriends."

My heart beat faster. He knew the truth. I was not upset or worried because it was a sign he felt comfortable enough to open up to me about anything, even a revelation that could hurt someone.

"If it's true, I hope whoever he was, he was a great guy. If you did want to be with him, I'm happy you didn't leave Sophie and me."

I looked at the coffee rings, gouges, and burn marks on the old table, so many it almost had a personality of its own. The implication that I was courageous wasn't accurate. It was the fear that Martin would have separated me from Tyler and Sophie.

"Sometimes things happen you don't expect. He was a wonderful man but we lost touch many years ago."

"Maybe Jenna will meet him sometime. I'm sure he'd love her."

I scratched at a burn mark to reveal new wood, thinking about how I dropped a pot when the hot handle burnt my fingers the day Alessandro and I parted.

"She's thinking about contacting him. I'm trying to imagine how it might play out."

"If she needs support, she can contact me to talk."

"Thank you, Tyler." I grasped his work-roughened hand. "Now you should return to Mai. I don't want to leave her sitting alone. Let me know what time you will arrive for Christmas dinner when your schedule is set. It will be wonderful to have you here."

CHAPTER TWENTY-FIVE

Jenna collected her grandmother late afternoon Christmas Eve to arrive on Vashon after I returned from work. We'd already exchanged possible recipes until we agreed on salmon for Christmas Eve as the main course for our dinner. The dinner was congenial with my mother more lucid than she'd been lately.

The Christmas sun rose over a frosty scene, dusting the garden with gold and silver glitter as if by magic. A yearling buck appeared in search of breakfast. I was on my second cup of coffee when the phone rang. It was Sophie. My heart beat faster with hope.

"I managed to get away after all. It was such a rush I didn't call earlier. We're in Chicago now waiting for the next flight. I'll be there for dinner with Jacob and a friend."

"Marvelous. I'll be so happy to see you both and to meet your friend."

"Hope Jacob will manage. He's on some new meds. It's hard to get the dosage right."

"We'll help care for him while you're here."

"Gotta go. We're boarding. We're staying near the airport so Jacob won't have too much stimulation with all the people around."

I sat for a moment to stare out the window at the deer as it placidly chewed my shrubbery. It was time to make breakfast inside the house too. Today would be one I'd longed for with the family together except for my father. I'd found the box of panettone, imported from Italy, at the local grocery. The picture on the box of fruit-studded bread took me back to Christmas in Italy with all the colorful boxes stacked in stores and bars. Each box had a little handle to tote it home or to friends.

I sliced the bread to make French toast, a recipe I'd found in an American magazine. The sweet smell of bread dipped into milk and eggs frying in butter filled the kitchen. Maple syrup warmed on a back burner.

"*Buon giorno! Buon Natale*! The salmon last evening was wonderful and I think grandmother loved it too." Jenna was showered and dressed. She looked full of joy.

"And to you." I gave Jenna a kiss on both cheeks plus one extra. "Sophie and Jacob will be here after all with someone else I don't know. And Tyler and Mai—you'll love her."

Jenna hesitated a moment, her face dimming, before she said, "It'll be super to see Tyler after so long. I'll help you take care of grandmother, and try to entertain Jacob too if I can. Poor kid. I guess you never know, do you?"

"No, you never do know what's just over the horizon."

"I've never seen him. Maybe he won't be as bad as you think."

"I keep praying." I did pray but I also researched treatments—not that I discussed them with Sophie who'd never been interested in my opinions or suggestions. In bleaker moments I anguished over the years of care he might require.

Jenna poured coffee. "On a happier subject, I wanted to tell you my news. I found Alessandro with no problem. Like you said, he's a big-time doctor in Rome. She paused to drink. Would you really come with me if I met him?" She wrung her hands.

"I don't know if it's a good idea, but I know you must." In reality, I couldn't let her go alone, but saying "yes" was a leap over a wide emotional chasm and I might fall. So many things could go wrong and I wasn't sure I could support her or make things worse.

"I won't contact him about the meeting until you decide." I saw her apprehensive look as if she too recognized the mission might end in disillusionment.

How would I go with Jenna to Rome for introductions yet stay away from him?

"I'd have to inquire if I could work extra hours to pay for airfare and to make up for the time off, if the care facility would even allow it. I can't afford to be fired." Even if I could scrape up the money, returning to Rome had an element of pure foolishness. Why open up the past? But the need to support her won out. It would be a Christmas present. Giving extra love was what the season required.

"Yes. Yes, I will if he agrees. We could go on spring break for just a few days if I can get the time off and you can find cheap flights. Two students on the loose in Rome." I tried to sound far more enthusiastic than I felt.

Jenna ignored all the "ifs" and responded by wrapping her arms around my neck. "The best present ever, Mom. We'll have a wonderful time. I'll start checking for flights. And, I meant to tell you earlier, I got a part-time job as a lab assistant to help pay for my expenses. Anyway, we can talk more later. I'll get grandmother going."

My mother was bright after a long sleep the night

before, beaming happily at the Christmas tree with its packages beneath, a glow of childlike sweetness lighting her face.

Tyler called to wish me a Merry Christmas and to say they'd arrive late afternoon. I fussed around the house, laying the table, preparing snacks and setting out sandwich fixings for lunch, mindlessly rearranging the gifts under the tree, and wondering what would happen when Sophie arrived.

It was afternoon when Sophie texted. "Ferry arriving." Twenty minutes later, I watched an unfamiliar car park near the house. Sophie was driving. A woman sat in the passenger side with Jacob in back in a car seat.

"He's exhausted after the flight." Sophie said, as she unbuckled her seat belt and opened the car door. The boy's eyelids drooped.

Her face was drawn, complexion muddy, making her look older than twenty-five, near the age I'd been when I'd arrived in Rome. I recognized the strain of leaping feet-first into adult life with all its possibilities and setbacks was taking a toll.

Sophie introduced Annette as a paralegal from her office. She was plump and giggly with curly blond hair and round glasses with electric blue frames surrounding equally blue eyes. Sophie looked at me with an expression that seemed to be saying, "I dare you to say anything." But I was delighted she'd found some companionship. Perhaps the shell encasing her heart was cracking open and ready to receive love. It would be the best Christmas gift ever.

When Annette unlatched Jacob from his car seat, I picked him up and kissed his hair. The boy was lethargic, heavy in my arms. It was frightening to imagine the future if he didn't improve enough to be independent. Then what? I'd ask Sophie how I could aid in his future care if she needed help. If Sophie would talk to me, that is.

"Annette is fantastic with him," Sophie said. "She reads to him every evening after we put him down. She's as good as his therapist or special ed teacher at preschool. He was diagnosed as on the lower-end of the autism spectrum. It could have been much worse and some days are good. Others aren't. Can I put him down somewhere to wear off the meds? And I'd rather we opened presents while he's asleep. Don't want him to get over-excited." Sophie took Jacob from my arms.

"Please use my room upstairs." I led the way. I put my arm on Sophie's thin shoulders when Jacob was settled. "It's been a long time."

"Yes, I guess it's been too long, Mom." For once Sophie didn't pull away.

"But you're here now. I've missed you."

****

I heard a knock on the front door: Tyler and Mai arrived from an island tour, unwittingly interrupting the possibility of further conversation between Sophie and me.

After introductions, I opened a bottle of chilled Champagne in the kitchen and carried it with a napkin around the neck, to the living room. "A happy and healthful Christmas to all. It's marvelous to have you all here with me. I hope it becomes a tradition for the family to be together." I raised my glass and everyone raised theirs in response even though Mom's was filled with water.

I passed out gifts from under the tree. Sophie wasn't

sure about the game for Jacob. She'd ask his therapist for advice and exchange it if it wasn't suitable.

Mom, who'd ignored everyone despite my efforts to remind her who they were and introduce her to Mai and Annette, fondled the robe and slippers, smiling and nodding as if she was immersed in some better time in her life. I momentarily envied her. Did she understand what was happening, and which was worse, knowing or not knowing?

I'd bought a second book of modern African short stories for Mai to compliment the one for Tyler. They both looked pleased and Mai said she was delighted to be included in the gift exchange although it was unnecessary. They gave me a generous gift card. Tyler teased I needed back-to-school short skirts, bobby sox and saddle shoes, like in some old sitcom.

Jenna gave me a child's backpack as a joke and a set of luxurious soaps and bath salts inside. Sophie handed over tourist trinkets looking like purchases from an airport gift shop. I didn't care.

There was a moment of awkwardness with no gifts for Annette.

I said, "Please accept my apologies. We didn't know Sophie would bring a guest until too late. I hope you feel welcome anyway."

Sophie said, "Sorry," although she looked defiant.

Annette broke the tension with a giggle, "No problem. I love Champagne."

I found another bottle. For a few minutes I thought the scene looked like a Norman Rockwell painting except the previous father of the house and my own father were deleted from the scene. But Sophie refilled her glass a third time. Her face blurred and her eyes reddened more with each swallow. I had to get a spare bottle of pinot grigio stored in the refrigerator even though no one else had had more than a half-glass of the Champagne.

To ease the tension, Tyler told Jacob, who'd run into the living room after his nap, about the lions and giraffes he'd seen. The child was wide-eyed, repeating "lion" dozens of times. Annette was about to pry him away from Tyler when he spotted his great-grandmother who was still running her hands over the bathrobe's plush fabric. He wormed his way in beside her. The two sat together, lost in their own dreams, content to be close even if they couldn't know each other.

Tyler told Jenna and Annette about his life in the African bush, about how he'd recently set up the medical clinic in South Sudan, and about the people he worked with. Annette asked in-depth questions.

I wondered about her relationship with Sophie. Annette behaved more like an adult, although they appeared to be the same age. She obviously had a strong relationship with Jacob, for which I was grateful. Maybe Sophie was simply mentally exhausted from work and child care worries.

When dinner was ready, I called everyone to the table. Tyler poured the Nebbiolo—a bottle I'd had shipped from Rome in the hope there would be a special occasion. I passed the bowl of risotto with mushroom and peas before taking my place at the head of the table, playing mother and father.

"Merry Christmas, one and all." The others raised their glasses again. Sophie poured more, emptying the bottle, before she joined in the toast.

"So how's the little Italian girl?" Sophie, now truly

drunk, glared at Jenna before she turned to me. "I saw the photo on your desk. But I knew all along."

"Sophie! What's wrong with you? It's Christmas." I half stood, clutching the table edge with white knuckles.

"Mama's little golden girl. The one who gets everything. You all know what I'm talking about." She waved her sloshing glass in Jenna's direction before chugging it down.

Jenna dropped her fork on her plate with a clang and ran from the room. Tyler, next to Sophie, put his hand on her arm to quiet her, but she ignored him. Mai stared at the tablecloth. My mother looked frightened. Jacob slipped out of his chair. He turned in circles, arms outstretched until Tyler managed to calm him.

I was about to tell Sophie to be quiet, but Annette intervened. "Sophie darling, I'm afraid you've had a little too much and are imagining things. Let's go outside for some air."

Sophie bobbled her head back and forth trying to focus on Annette. After a long pause, as if she was contemplating whether Annette's comment was accurate, she said, "Yes, too much." They moved outside. After a few minutes, they returned to the table where Tyler and Mai stared at their cooling food. Neither said anything but Annette looked embarrassed.

"Would anyone like seconds?" My attempt to capture the earlier mood was unsuccessful, plates still laden with half-eaten servings of risotto. With no takers I removed them from the table. All were silent until Tyler said, "I'll get the turkey."

"Let me find Jenna." She was weeping in my office. "Oh, honey, I don't know why she's like this. Please come back to the table. We need you."

"I'm going back to my apartment. I'll stop by for some leftovers tomorrow morning and take grandma home." She grabbed her jacket from the pile on the upstairs hide-a-bed and shut the front door quietly. As I watched the brake lights flared before she put the car in gear. I knew Jenna would surmount obstacles but my poor mother was on a predestined downward glide. All I could do was to support them both as well as Sophie to keep my family together.

****

Jenna's vacant place dominated the silent room. I put out clean plates, side dishes, and a bottle of dry Riesling. Tyler carved the turkey he'd carried from the kitchen. I ate a few bites of white meat, but they tasted like damp cardboard. The others pushed food around their own plates and, except for Sophie who poured a sip, ignored the wine. No one wanted dessert, my almond cake.

Tyler and Mai departed, saying they needed to be up early to shop for items they couldn't get in Africa and gifts for their African friends. Tyler promised to keep in better touch. Mai held both my hands when she thanked me for inviting her and said she hoped we'd meet again.

I led Mom to the bathroom and then the guest room to tuck her in. Annette took Jacob for a short walk to see if there were any deer out on the cold moonless night before they left to return to their hotel. I seized the opportunity to face Sophie directly as we stood on the deck. She leaned against the railing, one arm supporting the other as she rapidly moved her hand to her lips to take a drag on a cigarette and blow the smoke into the still, frigid air. After a few minutes, she flicked the butt into the grass and turned to me. She'd sobered up so quickly

I wondered if the dinner table exhibition had all been an act. I wanted to let my anger run wild but kept silent until I was sure I had control.

"Do you want to talk about Jenna? You're right, I did have an affair, but it didn't affect my love for you. Please don't ever forget."

Sophie frowned. I waited for another one of her rejections. Instead, she said, "We need to go. I'll call her tomorrow to apologize."

I took Sophie's hand with its ragged fingernails. "Wait please. How are you doing with Jacob? It must be terribly difficult. I want to know if there's anything I can do to help." I wanted to ask if she'd ever considered therapy for her anger but was afraid it would make our estrangement worse.

"I don't know. There are days when I want to roll over and give up but I'm so lucky to have Annette. She's super supportive and we love each other. We talked about having a child but will have to wait to see if school and therapy will continue to help Jacob. He does sometimes seem like he's improving but…oh, Mom, it's so hard. And you know I still mourn Dad. I know he loved me."

I saw my daughter's eyes glistening with unshed tears. Did Martin ever really love her? I couldn't help but wonder.

"Yes, he did and I love you too. I'm happy you have Annette. I'm sure she loves both of you."

"I don't earn a lot, but it's enough to get along. What I keep thinking about is what would happen if…if, you know, something happens to me. I try to set aside some money but it's difficult. I don't know why I bought the car. It cost a fortune. There was nothing wrong with the old one and now the insurance is way more expensive. I'm going to sell it. I guess I was upset after Jacob had a bad day and about Dad's death. Most is set aside for therapy but it's fantastically expensive. I do have health insurance, but it's not comprehensive. But what would happen if I lost my job?"

"Do you want me to see if I can arrange something for the future? I haven't yet got all my finances straightened out but you know I'll always be here for you both."

"We'll see." She slipped her arms into her coat.

I wanted to tell her all would be fine even though it was an empty promise. The moment was broken when Annette returned with Jacob. She thanked me for the hospitality and said to Sophie, "I'll drive."

Sophie buckled Jacob into his car seat and climbed into the passenger side without a further word.

I picked up the cigarette butt and shut the front door. Later, I sat in my usual place by the fire, thinking about Tyler and Sophie. Tyler, the wanderer, had found his life's work and most likely a companion to share it with. Over the years we'd become close friends instead of stepmother and stepson, the age difference diminishing to irrelevancy, the opposite of my relationship with Martin.

The familiar sense of failure as Sophie's mother overwhelmed me with a tsunami of sadness although I was thankful for the small opening. Perhaps with Annette's support she was more able to open up. At least it was a flicker of hope.

After years of solely blaming Martin for Sophie's personality, I knew I must have played a role when I'd unconsciously favored Tyler and Jenna. Sophie, the middle child, the one who always felt left out. I'd wanted a baby right away. I'd been lonely as a child and thought it would be nice even though I was still learning to adjust to seven-year-old Tyler.

A terrible memory swept into my consciousness: Sophie was about a year old and down for a nap. Tyler was at a schoolmate's birthday party. Martin and I were still in love, or at least in lust. We took advantage of the quiet. But Sophie, always hypersensitive, woke and started to cry. She cried so hard she was hiccupping. Martin and I couldn't stop. After that, I grabbed some clothes and rushed to Sophie's cot to comfort her to no avail. She calmed when she was too exhausted to even whimper.

At least she now had Annette who appeared steady and competent but, remembering the incident, I still felt guilty of selfishness, guilty of neglect. Even now, I could feel shame.

Whatever the cause for Sophie's slight opening after the dinner disaster, I was thankful for the gift. But it came with a high cost to Jenna.

CHAPTER TWENTY-SIX

I spent a sleepless night reliving the dreadful dinner and the brief but possibly hopeful conversation with Sophie. Relieved I wasn't scheduled to work until tomorrow, I woke Mom to ready her for the return to the assisted living facility. But what to say to Jenna? I subdued my unease to avoid transmitting the mood to my mother. I needn't have worried because the previous evening's drama was forgotten.

When Jenna arrived, I watched as she composed her weary face with shadow-ringed eyes into one with a forced smile as she opened the front door.

"Hi. How's Grandmother? I won't stay because I've got some reading to catch up on."

"Jenna, come sit for a moment. Please, honey."

"I'm okay. I hope I never have to see her again." Jenna looked at the cold fireplace.

"Oh, Jenna. I'm so sorry about this. I don't know why she's so jealous. It must be my fault."

"I doubt it. She's always been mean to me. I guess some people are just born that way. Anyway, let's forget it. And something good happened. When I got back to the apartment there was a Christmas email from my dad after I contacted him. He wants to meet and he'll pay for my travel."

"How wonderful!" I tamped the butterflies in my stomach.

"He didn't say much else but I'm going to write back to see what we could arrange. For you too."

I could feel my heart rate increase, fear fighting anticipation.

After Jenna left with my mom and a large package of leftovers, I cleaned the house to take my mind off the previous day and the unsettling prospect of meeting Alessandro again. I dumped the congealed risotto and froze the turkey remains for soup before climbing the stairs to change sheets and put away blankets I'd used on Mom's bed. The box with Sophie's journal caught my eye. I gave in, my need to find clues to her behavior overcame guilt at the coming intrusion.

****

The first page was titled "My thoughts." Below was a date, the year she'd entered ninth grade. I carefully turned to the next page, afraid my fingerprints would betray me when I gave it to Sophie. "Forgive us our trespasses," I said aloud as if she would hear me.

I leafed through the journal, picking pages at random. Most entries were what I'd expect of any teenager: angst about her hair, complexion, weight. A page filled solely with "blah" scribbled a hundred times was dedicated to some teacher she'd disliked. There was an entry where Sophie had been tormented over a crush on some older girl named Christa who must not have reciprocated. I breathed a sigh. Everything was normal. Then I found other, later, entries.

Mother hates me!!! All she cares about is her little snot Jenna.

I can't stand her. She thinks she's so smart and beautiful. Why don't I look like her? She doesn't look like Dad. I can't wait to get out of here.

Why doesn't Dad love me? He's never around. He doesn't want me either.

I'll give her credit. She actually told Miss Perfect to go do her homework. Big shock.

I was horrified and stuffed my fist to my mouth to block a cry even though there was no one but me in the house. I put the book aside and sat on the floor until I calmed enough to flee to the labyrinth. The journey was a waste as I stumbled a couple of times despite my slow steps on the path. I gave up and returned home, compelled to finish the diary.

There was more of the same interspersed with other schoolgirl complaints. I turned to the last page.

I saw them again; I know I did. It was Dad and the tramp I'd seen him with before. He's robbing the cradle for sure. He didn't see me but I was with the drama class when we went to see Pirandello. At intermission he bought champagne and then kissed her. And it was a big kiss. The kind with his disgusting tongue. No wonder he doesn't care about me and I'll bet my mother's at it too with one of her Latin lotharios. They make me puke.

I polished, mopped, scrubbed, and dusted to keep my mind focused on the mundane even though I felt like puking too. My daughter had seen me as a whore and my suspicions about Martin were confirmed although I no longer cared about his philandering. But the diary entries revealed Sophie had somehow known Jenna wasn't a full sister for many years. Could Martin have planted suspicion? However she'd found out, the depth of Sophie's misery was bottomless. Perhaps the small exchange at Christmas would produce a positive turn in our relationship. After all, Sophie had called me "mom," instead of "mother." Maybe calm Annette would eventually help her overcome her anxieties and fears. But right now, I was shattered. I had to do something, but I couldn't think what. I sat alone in a chair staring out the window at the gray and cold water.

****

My phone rang on December 30. It was Betty Jo with a last-minute invitation for dinner on New Year's Eve. I accepted, happy for a distraction from the incessant and unproductive thoughts about Sophie.

I hadn't been invited to the writer's home before though Betty Jo had stopped by my place without notice several times, no doubt hoping for coffee and conversation, which I offered, and maybe to snoop. I'd surmised the woman was awkward around others, preferring to hide away and write where she could invent friends and slay enemies. So I was pleased to be invited—assuming Betty Jo saw me as a friend rather than a potential victim in a novel.

It was easy to see why she wrote cozy mysteries: the living room was crammed with books and knick-knacks, a nightmare for anyone attempting to dust. It was obvious no one tried. A green-eyed black cat, who must have been the inspiration for her novels, greeted me before it padded off to another room, tail straight up in annoyance at the interruption of its nap. The room was cold, the fireplace a dead black square. Betty Jo told me to take a seat, saying dinner wasn't ready. She needed to work in the kitchen and it wasn't big enough for two people. I picked cat fur off my white wool slacks and sweater.

My hostess returned once to hand me a glass of white wine and hobble off again. I wished I'd stayed home with a book in front of my fireplace although if I had I would have spent the time going over the terrible contents of Sophie's diary. I looked at my watch: nine o'clock. I yawned and closed my eyes trying to replace visions of the diary with the cat detective.

"Soup's on."

I started, trying to remember where I was. Betty Jo pointed me to the tiny dining room. I hoped my sleepy eyes and hunger pangs weren't obvious.

An ancient food-spotted crocheted tablecloth, made for a table for ten, covered the table and hung down to a worn Persian carpet. I sat at an angle to avoid the broken springs in the middle of my chair. Betty Jo carried two plates in one hand making me wonder if she'd worked in a restaurant one time. She placed them on the otherwise empty table. On each was a slab of forlorn meatloaf with a side of colorless mixed peas and carrots looking like they came from a can. "Sorry, I forgot to buy potatoes. Do you want ketchup?"

"I'm fine. Been eating too much Christmas food earlier today." A social lie because I'd skipped lunch in anticipation of a large meal and gone for a long walk to work up an appetite.

Betty Jo looked at me sharply, not at all convinced. She was a careful observer.

She talked about her next book while I ate the tasteless meal and interjected encouraging remarks. When she took the plates to the kitchen, telling me to wait in the living room for dessert, I checked my watch again to see how much longer I needed to stay. It was ten. Still too early but did I have to stay until midnight? I concentrated on a funny scene from my walk earlier in the day: two donkeys sporting Santa hats standing in a nearby pasture. They were probably tucked up in a stall by now while I was alone in front of a dead fireplace.

My hostess returned with a surprise, canceling thoughts about how to gracefully depart. "Sorry, I guess you can tell I don't do much cooking any more, but I hope this makes up for it." She held a tray with a bottle of vintage Champagne in a silver ice-filled bucket and two crystal flutes. She winked and said, "Don't worry, I washed them today after I found them in the back of a cupboard. Been a long time since Harry used to come here once in a while for a tot even before his wife left. Didn't tell you about that part, did I?"

Betty Jo placed the tray on the coffee table before hustling off to the kitchen again, her arthritis either forgotten or improved with the prospect of Champagne. She returned with two porcelain plates, each with a large chocolate éclair set on frilled paper. She took brightly polished silver forks and monogrammed linen cocktail napkins out of her apron pocket. "Oh dear, I guess I better take this off. But let me light a fire first." She knelt in front of the fireplace armed with kindling and matches. A warming fire crackled.

"Used to be a Girl Scout." Her knees creaked loudly as she struggled to stand.

She lifted the napkin-wrapped chilled bottle from the bucket, removed the foil and untwisted the wire cage protecting the cork. "Hand me a glass."

The cork flew into the air with a satisfying pop. She poured expertly, ensuring the foam didn't overtop the rim. I handed her the second glass; she poured again and raised it to mine. "Here's to a Happy New Year, my dear. I know it's hard but you'll do well with your good looks and brains. I'm sure some appealing man will come along if it's what you want. But don't hurry. Get the right one." Her blue eyes sparkled between smudges on rimless spectacles.

The cat padded back into the room and leapt into my lap, evidently deciding the fireplace warmth was too attractive to waste even if the lap was unfamiliar. The animal purred, a contented hum I loved, cat fur or not. I'd make a trip to an animal rescue place next week.

"Tell me about your life. It must have been different in the past with these beautiful glasses." I held my flute to the firelight to watch the cut glass sparkle.

Betty Jo poked the fire and added a log. "I will if you will talk to me about yours. Promise you won't show up in a book." She grinned but I could not detect if it was sincere or not.

"There wouldn't be much to tell."

"Oh pooh. Everyone has a story. Anyway, eat your éclair. Obviously, I didn't make it and there are more in the fridge. Drink your Champagne too. My family always said it cures all ills. My arthritis is much better today just looking at the bubbles."

I followed her instructions and watched the bubbles rise to the surface between sips of golden vintage and bites of the divine éclair. It was true. I did feel more hopeful about my relationship with Sophie after our brief conversation. The hangover would be fierce but I held out my glass for more as New Year 2014 arrived with promise and peril. I decided it would be the year of "yes." Yes to Sophie, yes to the trip to Rome, yes to new friends, and yes to a positive beginning of my career. A tall order.

****

When I didn't hear from Sophie after Christmas, I was uncertain about what to do to maintain the brief opening. As before, it was too intrusive to suggest a video call and a text would be too informal to begin. A personal letter could be unopened. I couldn't sleep and found it hard to concentrate during the day. When yet another day passed without a word, I found flights to Boston and booked a cheap redeye.

My fingers could barely press the keys as I wrote.

My dearest Sophie

For many years I've wanted to understand what the reason for our difficult relationship could be. I now realize I must have not been the mother you wanted or needed. I'm so terribly sorry. I want to restart our relationship. Make amends for unwitting wrongs. To do this I've booked a flight for a weekend stay. I won't force myself on you but will be available. I do hope you will come to my hotel to start anew.

With much love,

Your mother

I added my travel details in a P.S.

By this time, I was so overwrought even the labyrinth didn't calm me. Several days passed, and then a few more. Finally, there was a response: *If you insist.*

I felt like I'd been punched in the face but packed anyway. I placed Threadbear and the diary in my carry on and chewed several antacids before throwing in a change of clothes and my toiletries.

****

Redeye flights have never agreed with me and this one was hell: crowded, a miserable infant in the next seat suffering from the change in air pressure, and rough weather. I texted Sophie from the airport to say I'd like her to meet me for breakfast at the hotel if she could. Neutral ground seemed best.

"Well, here I am." She slid into the booth I'd picked for privacy. She didn't unzip her puffy jacket or take off her beanie. She shoved the menu aside. "I'm not hungry."

Her belligerent attitude wasn't promising but I wasn't going to give up. "Sophie, we must talk. I cannot go on like this. It's breaking my heart to be cut out."

She sighed, long and heavily, as if past injustices might be forgiven. I took this to be an acknowledgement she'd at least hear me out. While I searched for a way to further the conversation, she said, "I sold the car."

"I hope you got a good price. You must have been sorry to see it go."

"Nah. But I felt like a big shot for a while. I was stupid." Her laugh was bitter.

"Sophie, you are *not* stupid."

She tossed her head in disbelief at my remark but didn't say more.

The silence was leaden until I broke it. "I have something for you. Actually, two things of yours I found when I unpacked."

Sophie clasped and unclasped her hands as I put a plastic bag on the table. "First, here's your old teddy. I never could bear to throw it out. Would you like it? Maybe someday you could tell Jacob about it."

She put out her hand to take the bear. Her eyes were shiny. "Thanks, Mom. I'd forgotten how much I loved him." After a pause, she added, "And when I tried to kill him. It was ghoulish and I don't know why I did it."

"You were upset about the move. It was a hard time for all of us. And anyway, he's all patched up."

Now it was time for the other thing. Maybe a bombshell or maybe just an unwanted memory of her younger days. I pulled the diary from my bag. "And I found this too." I held my breath hoping I hadn't pushed things too far, too fast.

Sophie stared at her chronology of an unhappy year. "Did you read it?"

"I read some. I'm so deeply sorry I didn't understand earlier."

She took it from my hand to riffle through a few pages and handed it back. "Throw it out."

Seeing my no doubt surprised and relieved expression, she added, "I've started going to a therapist. She's helping."

"Do you want to tell me about it?"

"Just to say, I've come to terms with a lot of stuff. You and me, Jenna, and Dad." She picked up the bear again and stood.

I did the same. "Please remember, I have always loved you, even if I couldn't make you see it in a way you could understand."

She slid out of the booth. I followed. We embraced and I could feel the need through her thick clothing. After a minute she stepped back.

"Thanks for coming Mom but I have to get home now."

"Talk soon my dear."

She hurried up the street toward a car park. I was woozy with the aftereffects of the meeting combined with jet lag and lack of sleep. I changed my flight to return in the afternoon rather than staying over but it was too early to return to the airport. The Boston Public Gardens promised some peace. I threw the diary away in a municipal trash can near the Gardens before watching the swan boats until it was time for the airport shuttle.

As my relationship with Sophie opened up, so did the spring season. When I'd arrived on the island it was silent at night except for the occasional bird cry or animal rustling in the garden, but the mild winter prompted a new clamor outside: the insistent high-pitched *kree-eek* of tiny emerald green tree frogs calling in unison in a frantic search for a mate.

I turned my thoughts to Rome.

CHAPTER TWENTY-SEVEN

The plane floated over the Alps before it banked to head south. Jenna, in the window seat, leaned back to let me see snow-covered peaks towering over valleys, lakes and villages. The wings leveled—the mountains replaced by distant views of the flat Po River plain.

The cabin attendant walked down the aisle to ask if anyone wanted more coffee. "How much longer 'til we land?" Jenna asked.

"Less than an hour now."

She held out her paper cup and said, "Oh, Mom, I'm so excited. I've waited for this day now for months. I miss Italy. It's not easy to live in the U.S., and it sure doesn't feel at all like home yet. I know I'll have a great time here and hope you will too."

"You will." I hesitated for a nanosecond before adding, "We both will."

"Really, truly? I mean about you having a good time?"

"It'll be fine. Promise. I'm looking forward to the museums and food." It was all a white lie to comfort Jenna. In reality, my stomach had enough acid to power a car battery. What would happen when we met, and would he and Jenna be able to connect emotionally? What would I do when I saw him? What do you say to a long-lost lover? Maybe I should send Jenna off alone. No, that wouldn't be right either. I picked at a ragged cuticle wishing I'd had a manicure before we left. As if he'd care.

The seatbelt sign illuminated as the plane descended over the Tuscan then Lazio coastline. Twenty minutes later, the plane rolled up to the gate after a rough touchdown and a long taxi. Jenna and I were in the cheapest seats in the back, waiting our turn to leave the aircraft, stand in line for immigration, and reclaim our baggage.

We took the train to Stazione Termini and then a bus to a modest hotel on the second and third floors of an old palazzo in the *centro storico*. Jenna said she'd told Alessandro I was coming too. We'd meet him at the sunken ship fountain near the Spanish Steps in Piazza di Spagna two days from now after he returned from Berlin where he was presenting a paper.

The city looked the same after my eight months absence—the mess of sacred and profane, trash and glory. I was stabbed by splinters of pain from the past and anxiety for how the next few days would play out in Jenna's life.

She visited her old school to talk with some of her former teachers and share lunch or coffee with schoolmates who remained in Rome. I called Maggie to let her know I'd arrived. She invited me for tea but warned Orazio hadn't been well.

I experienced a moment of nostalgia when I passed the door to my former apartment building. The *portinaia's* former desk was deserted. I climbed the stairs, stopping at my old door. The names by the doorbell were now Nocera and Mosconi instead of Carlisle. I hoped they were happy together whoever they might be.

Maggie stood in the doorway to her apartment to

welcome me with open arms. I could feel slack skin and ribs through her dress as I responded. When I stepped back, I saw my dearest friend hollowed out with gray skin and wrinkles.

"So wonderful to see you my dear. But be prepared for a shock. Orazio was recently diagnosed with late-stage pancreatic cancer. He's foregoing treatment, Stoic to the end. He spends his days reading classics in Latin and Greek."

"But why didn't you let me know earlier?"

"I didn't want to burden you knowing you were busy trying to settle on your island. And having you worry wasn't going to help anything. The family is rallying round, a godsend."

I thanked God I hadn't bothered Maggie with my own problems, minuscule compared to hers, as I followed her down the hallway to the living room. Orazio was in an armchair, eyes closed but erect as ever. An open book rested in his lap. A walker was propped against the chair. A side table held medications and a glass of water. He managed to open his eyes and smile when he heard my voice. I kissed him with care and turned back to Maggie who shrugged with her hands open in a gesture of resignation.

We chatted over tea and pastries but Orazio drifted off after a half-hour, the painkillers canceling his efforts to be polite. I prepared to leave, not wanting to intrude further in the distressing situation even though I longed to have time with Maggie. She held my hands. I said I'd call her every week but wondered if I'd ever see her again.

I was battered by a wave of depression at the thought of losing others either by death or distance. Signor

Boncompagni in the junk shop, Franca, Maggie and Orazio, and so many other people I'd known, all lost to me. I wiped my damp eyes as I lingered a minute in front of the apartment building. Without anything more to do while Jenna was busy with friends, I took the Metro to Martin's former office to thank the young woman who helped me after Antonella left the scene. But the guard in the lobby told me the firm went bankrupt a month earlier. The premises were now rented to a company importing cosmetics from China. Another remnant of my past gone, but I counted myself lucky I'd received any of Martin's severance pay before the company collapsed. I spent the afternoon strolling down nearby Viale Europa, browsing the expensive shops. I found a pair of summer sandals at a sidewalk stall, last year's design, inexpensive but still high style, a positive note after the unhappy start to my stay.

Although neither of us mentioned the meeting with Alessandro, I sensed Jenna's level of unease matched mine when we met at the hotel late in the afternoon. We stopped for a prosecco at a bar near the hotel. Jenna sat silently, chewing a strand of hair. I picked at a bowl of peanuts telling myself if I'd survived the change from wife to widow, managed a relationship with Sophie that changed from cold to lukewarm, entered the job market, and became a student returning to school after so many years, I'd survive tomorrow's meeting too.

Jenna roused me from my reverie. "Shall we get a pizza at the place I used to like over in Trastevere?"

We set off on a bus across the Tiber to walk through the old cobbled streets to a place Jenna had often visited with school friends. But neither of us could eat more than a slice of our too-rich Pizza Quattro Stagioni while awaiting a meeting to change Jenna's life forever one way or another.

Later, the noise of young people's talk, buses and motorcycles, police, fire, and ambulance sirens outside the hotel interrupted my sleep. Memories seeped into my consciousness like the fine grains of red sand which had entered our apartment through the rattling wood window frames when the sirocco blew into Rome from North Africa.

****

Rather than pace around the piazza where we were to meet Alessandro, we stopped at a bar to wait. I watched Jenna pleat her silk skirt, fingers working the fabric without cease. I stirred my cappuccino without drinking while looking at each passing pedestrian in the hope I'd see him before he saw me so I could prepare myself.

"There he is!" Jenna jumped up, nearly knocking her chair over. "He looks exactly like the picture he sent me."

I put coins on the table and stood. My mouth was dry despite repeatedly swallowing. A stray hair caused me to blink. Jenna, suddenly shy, retreated to stand a half-step behind me.

"Nicole! Sorry I'm late but an insistent student would not stop asking questions. Like I used to do." Alessandro enveloped me in an embrace. "So beautiful still," he murmured before he let go and turned toward his daughter.

"And Jenna! I recognize you from the photo you sent." He embraced her tightly. "I've longed for this day."

I stared at the paving stones, immeasurably relieved

he'd easily accepted her and relieved I hadn't had to say anything yet because the lump in my throat would have made it impossible. How alike they were: Both tall, both brown haired and eyed. Her eyebrows followed the same arc as his, but with a more delicate line. Her lips copied his slightly crooked smile. What a waste it had been to keep Jenna from her true father.

Alessandro was still trim and youthful, though his face showed smile-wrinkles and a sprinkle of silver in his freshly-trimmed hair. He was the perfect picture of an upper-class Italian, neat and conservatively dressed, polished handmade shoes. I could not keep from a comparison to Martin, who'd traversed the years ungracefully, one of those men whose clothes never hung right, shirttail out, tie carelessly knotted, even if he was wearing a hand-tailored suit.

"Help me catch up on everything I've missed. I never heard anything about your childhood. You said you were in university in your email. What are you studying? Any boyfriends in the picture?" His words tumbled out.

Jenna overcame her initial trepidation but responded in a more measured fashion. "I'm thinking of majoring in marine biology. Seattle's on saltwater and I'm interested in orca conservation."

The two walked away to engage in animated talk. I watched Jenna repeating her father's arm and hand motions. My Italian daughter. I pretended to window shop until they returned from circling the piazza. He wore the same grin as he had in the old photo and Jenna was also wreathed in smiles as he held her hand.

"Let's have Champagne to celebrate. I know a place where we can talk."

My rapid heartbeat slowed with relief at this successful beginning.

We threaded through the masses of tourists on the Spanish Steps up to a restaurant at the top. The day was warm, spring rapidly advancing toward summer. The white marble steps were lined with pots of azaleas laden with red blossoms, a waterfall of color, a sight I'd paused to enjoy so many times in the past despite no one to share my pleasure.

We sat outside at a table set with white napery with the city and its churches and piazzas spread out before us, the dome of St. Peters in the distance. Terracotta flower boxes filled with scarlet and white cyclamens rimmed the terrace railing. I concentrated on the view of the Eternal City.

Alessandro and Jenna continued to talk in a mix of Italian and English, each telling the other about their lives, Jenna now talking as fast as she could about university, Alessandro now more measured. I learned he was married with two children, the girl in first year at a prestigious high school, already concentrating on science. His bookish son was in grade school, aiming for a more traditional classical education. His wife, Beatrice, was a psychiatric pediatrician, and the family lived in Parioli not far from his consulting rooms.

How different our paths were, me proud of being a food blogger while waiting for freedom from an unhappy marriage and a new beginning; him a success in every way and married to a professional. I winced while thinking his wife might have helped Sophie when she was a child.

Alessandro turned to me. "I've never seen your part of the country, but I know about the medical school and research facilities in Seattle. Perhaps I will visit at some point."

Jenna sparkled, but I kept my voice steady. "It would be lovely for Jenna to be able to see you again."

Jenna interjected, "I'd like to come back here this summer. And I can meet your other family, can't I?"

I heard the slightest hesitation before he said, "Yes, I'll arrange it."

How easily Jenna accepted her father, but I was wary. I would warn her his family might not know about her or wouldn't be accepting.

At Alessandro's question, I offered an abbreviated description of life on Vashon Island, telling him about the little town and about the ferry. I described the deer looking in my windows and if I ever found time to garden, a high fence would be the first priority. I left out the part about starting back to school in middle age after learning about his accomplished wife. But when I mentioned the absence of constant noise, he interjected how difficult Rome was now. If he ever retired, it would be to his country home near Cortona where peace prevailed.

When there was a pause, Jenna took the cue and left the table to stand at the railing to take in the view. I seized my chance to ask the question always in the back of my mind from the moment I found his address on the paper in one of Martin's pockets.

Before I could ask, Alessandro leaned toward me to say, "Is there any chance we could meet for a few minutes before my first appointment tomorrow? I know you are leaving the day after and my schedule is tight but…"

I looked at him, a few years older than me,

successful and apparently happily married. Time could not run backward. Lives could not be relived with different outcomes. I knew now I didn't want to anyway. Our time together was the best part of my life and it was important to keep it encased in amber. A lost love to be treasured. Now it was Jenna's time to be with him.

When I didn't respond, he persisted. "I'm not asking for a date. All I want to talk about is what happened to you after we parted and why you never told me about Jenna's life. It would have made such a difference to me to know." His tone was formal. I recognized he, too, was keeping a safe distance.

"I'm sorry. I thought I was doing the right thing. I know now it was wrong and I have much to atone for. I'll meet you, but I'd also like to learn what you've told your family. I don't want Jenna hurt." And I'd ask the question haunting me: How had Martin gotten his office address?

"When Jenna first contacted me, I told them. As you can imagine, they were even more surprised than I was. My wife is supportive. After all, our relationship was long over when she and I met, but it took a while for the children to accept. Fortunately, they've come to look forward to meeting their new American family member. I'm sure they'll get along well even though she's older. It will be fine."

I smiled in relief. He sounded just like a doctor.

When Jenna returned Alessandro invited her to a father-daughter dinner for our last night in Rome. Her face was radiant with anticipation.

CHAPTER TWENTY-EIGHT

Alessandro stood in welcome at a table outside a bar near my hotel. My stomach somersaulted as if the contents were fermenting. He pulled a chair back for me. The legs screeched against the pavement adding to my distress.

"Please sit down. What can I get you? There's so much I want to know."

I ordered a latte macchiato and a *cornetto*, the kind I'd tasted when we first met. When he returned to the table, I kept my head down contemplating the pastry filled with custard and memories.

"I cannot tell you how happy I was when I received Jenna's email. She's a wonderful young woman and I'm proud of her. I so wanted to make contact, but when you broke our relationship, I believed you never wanted me to be part of her life. She said her stepfather had died while you were here."

I looked at him and saw the reflection of Jenna in demeanor and appearance again. "Obviously, Martin and I weren't happy. I was lonely and lost when we arrived in Rome. When I signed up for Italian conversation in exchange for English, I had no intention of, of, of…" I raised the coffee-flavored milk to my lips. "The pregnancy was the tipping point. I could not leave Tyler after his birth mother died, or Sophie, who was having difficulty adjusting. I'm sure Martin would not have allowed me to keep them if I left with Jenna. And you were caught up in your education. We would have been a burden. The years passed and I didn't want anyone to know about Jenna's parentage so I could keep the family together."

I paused to sip again. "I did want you to know about Jenna's life, but I was absolutely sure if I let you two bond it would be a disaster for the other children. Avoiding the issue for so long let it build and build."

"So how did this Rome visit come about?"

"In a way, because of Martin's death from a heart attack up near Cerveteri last summer. Jenna first found my copy of the photo I took of you both while we were packing up to leave Rome, and then, when we unpacked in my new home, the baby shoes she'd worn in the picture appeared. I'd saved them all those years. I'd kept the photo in the poetry book you gave me and it was peeking out from the *Infinity* poem. There was no point keeping the truth from her any longer."

I blotted my eyes with the paper napkin from underneath the *cornetto*. I was done with the story forever.

"I appreciate your candidness, but this is hard for me too. You are right we could never have made a life. But in our months together, you taught me about all the possibilities of love. And I would have supported my daughter somehow."

His hand trembled as he stirred his cappuccino. The spoon clattered to the pavement. He bent to find it and then said, "Let's talk no more about our past. It's done and we'll move forward."

"Yes, but there's another thing. About my late husband. After he died, I found a note with your address.

It wasn't in his handwriting. A few days before I left Rome I went to see where it was. It's the building where your studio is located. Was it some sort of bizarre coincidence?"

"As I'm sure you know, your husband was in poor health. His regular doctor in Rome referred him to me for a consultation on the heart issue some years ago. I did an exam. His heart was bad—enlarged. I gave him several prescriptions to relieve symptoms. He needed to receive advanced treatment, even a transplant if he was strong enough. I advised him to retire and return to Seattle."

"Poor Martin. He never told me." A man with too big a heart physically but too small emotionally.

"I didn't know who he was at the time, but I had the sensation that he wanted to see who I was and not just for medical advice. Perhaps he recognized me, though I am sure I'd never met him before. We were careful, weren't we? He was so much older, so I never connected his name with you."

I finished the latte to ease my still-constricted throat. "Why did you think he knew about you?"

"It was his body language, as if he had confirmation. He actually said, 'Oh yes,' and nodded when I entered the exam room. I know I've changed over the years, but might he have seen the photo you took of me with Jenna?"

I remembered the time I'd noticed the photo wasn't marking the *Infinity* poem. "Maybe. Once I found it in a different place than where I usually kept it. I thought I'd just made a mistake."

"Maybe he'd hired an investigator or maybe it was just an odd coincidence his doctor referred him to me since I've built up a clientele of English-speaking expats because of my language and training in the States. You did know he had a vasectomy a number of years ago? I believe he entered a year on the questionnaire I use for new patients coinciding with the birth of your other daughter."

"Pardon?" I wasn't sure I'd heard correctly. I had a vision of years of pointless birth control pills lined up in a row. Except for the time I was with the man sitting with me now.

"I'm sorry. I assumed you were aware of this. Didn't he ever confide in you?"

I put my head face down on the table. The warmth of Alessandro's hand on my shoulder a moment later steadied me. "He never confided about anything. How stupid of me not to guess. I did want another child and now I wonder if he even wanted Sophie."

"It doesn't matter now."

"No, it doesn't. We had a fight when he found out I was pregnant with Jenna. He must have wanted someone to care for his children more than he wanted to divorce me. I think he lost the ability to truly love after his first wife died—if he ever had it to begin with. I suppose the information about a vasectomy was in the autopsy report, but I didn't read it carefully."

"Everyone is entitled to love, even if it can't last."

"Yes, but I did betray him, and I'll give him credit for never saying anything to Jenna. And for financially supporting her."

Alessandro glanced at his watch. "I need to leave now or I will be late for a consultation. I'll pick up Jenna at seven thirty this evening. We will develop our relationship as it should be: father and daughter. If you and she want, I'll help with her tuition for next year, and for each year until she finishes school, even if it's graduate work. Maybe she'll take after me and go to medical school instead of marine biology."

I wanted to fall into his arms in thanks but instead said, "Neither of us will ever forget your generosity."

He looked pensive for a few moments and then flashed his lopsided grin. "And to think all we originally wanted was to improve our communication skills. I hope you agree my English has progressed. I do remember I was a poor student, at least in languages." He rose and leaned over to give a quick kiss on the top of my head before collecting his briefcase from under the table. He walked away without looking back.

I remained at the table. True, Alessandro hadn't been a stellar English student, but he taught me more valuable lessons: the language and meaning of love, the importance of simply being with someone who wants you, walking hand in hand without a destination, or sharing a glass of wine without a need to talk in any language. Elements of an authentic life. I replayed the scene in the park where he'd confessed love, the couple in the rowboat, the early spring day, and my agreement to go with him to his room. Were his lessons never to be applied to anyone else ever again?

The roar of a motorino passing close to the table jerked my thoughts back to the present. I checked to be sure my handbag hadn't been snatched. It hadn't. What to do for the rest of the day? The sun had warmed the air. I draped my jacket over my arm and set out to find the bookstore where I'd bought a book of Italian poetry so many years ago. The streets were crowded with noisy vehicles and pedestrians on cell phones. The peace of

The Measure of Life

Vashon was far away. How quickly I'd adjusted to my new island home after all.

After a few false turns, I found the store, still dim and dusty but loaded with shelves and tables of temptation. I told myself I could buy one book. I needed to study instead of spending money on novels. I browsed the English language section before turning to Italian. There was a prominent display of Elena Ferrante's first three books of the Neapolitan Quartet with a sign saying the final volume would be out soon. I hadn't yet read any but they were on my mental list. I leafed through the first volume, *My Brilliant Friend,* then the other two. I liked the substantial feel of paper in my hands. My resolve weakened. After all, I hadn't bought anything on the trip except the sandals.

But in penance for the sandals, I carried the first volume instead of two or three to the cash register. A young woman perched on a stool reading the most recent Strega prize winner. No one was in line and when the clerk looked at the book, she took the opportunity to give me a mini-book review followed by a question about how it was that I read Italian.

"I lived here for many years, and I often visited this bookstore. It was owned by an Englishwoman, Primrose. She had a cat. Did you know her?" I pictured her sweater and the cat.

"She was my *nonna!* I'm sorry to say she passed away several years ago when she was over a hundred. She read every book in the shop before it went on sale. Orwell the cat died when he was twenty, poor creature."

We chatted in Italian a bit longer before another customer wanted to check out. The exchange made me miss Italy and all the serendipitous moments I'd experienced in Rome over the years.

****

Aimless again, I toted the bag along the narrow streets. I passed by the red-rimmed ocularium. This time the dial pointed toward *bello*, reflecting the sunny weather and my hopes. The city's mellow-colored walls glowed in the sun. I felt like a tourist, overwhelmed with history and beauty.

Near lunchtime, I found a bar with an empty table outside. When the waiter arrived, I asked for a panino with slices of Parma ham and cheese with a glass of a Sicilian white wine before I opened my new book. Immersed in the story of two brilliant Neapolitan children, I started when an American voice said, "Do you mind?" He spoke slowly and in a loud voice. I looked up. An overweight man in a faded "I love NY" T-shirt, jeans, worn sneakers, and a baseball hat, stood beside my table.

I waved at the empty chair opposite me and continued reading.

"There isn't any place else to sit." He spoke with a Brooklyn accent.

I put the book aside to look at him. Middle aged, maybe fifty-five, short brown hair, stomach draped over his belt.

Under scrutiny, the man said, "I escaped from a tour. Name's Art. My friends call me Artie." He looked expectant. When I didn't respond he continued. "I just got here on a tour and don't know why I signed up. I should have gone to Atlantic City." He smiled showing stained teeth. "Divorced in case you were worried."

I blinked in surprise. "I wasn't." How dare he ruin my lunch.

"Women always assume I've got a wife lurking in

The Measure of Life

the background. I'll be quiet." He was until the waiter brought my order. Then he said, "I'll have a burger and a beer. American."

The waiter looked baffled. I told him in Italian my tablemate would have the same sandwich as I ordered and a local beer. He stalked off as if yet another tourist season would be more than he could handle.

My appetite vanished. Was this what dating would be like if I ever got around to it? I turned my attention to the people walking along the street in an effort not to engage him. Rude, but not too rude.

"I'm a tax preparer. Have my own business."

"Must be interesting."

"Yes, but I needed a break after, you know, the wife, I mean ex-wife and everything. So, I'm on this tour. First time in Europe. Once is enough."

"Oh."

"Say, you wouldn't want to show me around, would you?" His hopeful look reminded me of Zucca, my calico cat, begging for a bite of my dinnertime salmon filet.

"Sorry, but I don't have the time."

Artie got the hint and waved for the waiter. "The bill for both of us."

"This is unnecessary. I want to pay for it on my own."

The waiter slapped the bill on the table. Artie's Adam's apple jumped up and down as he glugged his beer. He found a wad of euros in the front pocket of his worn jeans. "Keep the change." He left.

I ordered another glass of wine and opened my book but couldn't concentrate. Would it ever be worth the effort to meet someone?

It was still too early to return to the hotel to pack. To

pass time, I strolled along Via del Babuino to look at the antiques displayed in shop windows. A marble statue of Janus, the two-faced Roman god of beginnings and endings, attracted my attention. He was the gatekeeper who looked both directions. But I needed a god who looked to the future alone. The past was past.

I turned my steps toward the Corso to walk among the crowds until I came to one of several small museums housed in old *palazzi*. One had a show of Italian Renaissance paintings from someone's collection. Not a blockbuster exhibition with many dozens of canvases, but a more intimate display where it was easy to contemplate the paintings without being hurried along by others wanting to take a five-second glance.

The canvases welcomed me into the brilliant Renaissance world: The jewel colors of clothing, architectural conceits of arches, black and white checkerboard floors in exaggerated perspective, brilliant blue sky, greensward dotted with wildflowers. I delighted in the vivid background landscapes filled with hill towns, lakes, cypress trees and umbrella pines, and merchants leading pack animals.

I paused in front of an Annunciation. Mary, cloistered from the outside world, held a book, but cast her eyes down to an already swelling belly, knowing of a future filled with pain.

My mind was on my own pregnancies when a male voice said, "What do you think of the angel? Could he or it really fly?"

I turned to see a man next to me looking at the same picture. He had a crew cut and a twinkle in his eyes, one of which was green, the other brown.

"Uh, I don't know. I can't imagine it."

The Measure of Life

He smiled. "Sorry if I startled you. What I like about these paintings is the detail, especially the ones with carpets. But the angels always get me. Can you imagine if one flapped into this room right now?"

I let out a snort of laughter in spite of myself. The museum guard shot a disapproving look in my direction.

"Shall we sit over there for a moment? My feet are tired. Museum feet I call it. Never do get used to marble floors." He pointed to his feet clad in stylish sport shoes and to a nearby unoccupied bench.

"All right. I could use a rest but…" I let the remainder of my thought hang in the air, unsure if I wanted another distraction on this overwrought day.

"Let me introduce myself. I'm Robert, go by Bob. I'm from Vancouver and I teach European history at the University of British Columbia. I come to Europe for a week or two every year on my spring break. You?"

"I'm here with my daughter."

"And?"

"I'm a widow. She's visiting her father." I'd said more than I intended and called myself a widow in spite of my resolution not to use the dreary description. The word made me sound as if I wasn't a person in my own right. I removed one shoe to massage my own foot wondering if this is how you meet people—both with the same ailments?

"Sorry, I was prying."

"Yes."

"Okay, let me try again. Would you mind if I walk along with you? I'm bored being here alone. I had a wife once. But I found she liked Italian men in the flesh instead of in old paintings in museums. Anyway, I'd like someone to talk to for a few minutes, nothing more."

"I'm leaving tomorrow." What was I doing, talking to yet another man? But he seemed companionable, not like the self-centered jerk at lunch. "All right, let's see the exhibition. You can describe the iconography if that's the right terminology. And my name is Nicole, Nicki for short." I was surprised at myself for being so open. But the companionship was welcome on this stressful day.

We walked through the gallery, pausing for his brief lecture at each painting. I found myself at ease with him.

When we arrived at the gift shop and cafe, he said, "How about coffee?" He signaled for a waiter.

"Yes, how about it, but I'll have tea at this hour."

The young man's delicate appearance set off a new discussion of angels. I said, "What if one, a blond with a page-boy hair style and a robe, did fly around, feet trailing behind like a heron? There would be panic with all the women worried they were pregnant and all the men trying to be macho and bag the beast.

Bob added, "When someone downed it, people would be snatching feathers as souvenirs. In the end, it would look like a plucked turkey."

I laughed so hard tears welled.

"Hey, please don't be upset. You must have had a rough day." His twinkle vanished and he got out his handkerchief and offered it.

"Not the best time. Anyway, thanks for the tea and talk. I needed it." I waved off the handkerchief.

"No problem. But before you go…"

I looked at him. Now he was bashful, boyish.

"Is there any possibility you might give me your email address? Here's my card. I promise I won't call you unless you call or email me first. Promise. I'm not one of those fake guys on social media."

I hesitated before I took his card and wrote my full name and email address on a paper napkin. "If I respond, I promise I won't be crying."

He studied the paper before he put it in his inside jacket pocket and smiled.

****

The check-in time for the first leg of our flight home, Rome to London, was before dawn. The hotel breakfast room wasn't yet open. We grabbed a coffee in the airport. The coffee was bitter, the *cornetti* yesterday's stale leftover. Neither of us were in the mood to talk.

Even with the caffeine, I alternated between dozing and trying to separate my tangled thoughts as the plane tore through the air to take us away from Rome. I didn't want to ask Jenna about her meetings with her father. She'd tell me when she was ready. I didn't yet know what I made of it or how the course of her life would change. It would be changed. I hoped it would be for the better.

And the man with the kind green and brown eyes, Bob? I looked at his business card tucked in my wallet when Jenna brushed past me to use the toilet. Was it a reminder of another serendipitous exchange like in the bookstore or just a piece of paper? I tucked the card away where it wouldn't be lost.

The clouds parted an hour into the flight. I could see the tidy fields of France, many carpeted with bright yellow rapeseed flowers grown for cooking oil. The coastline came into view. Freighters and ferries floated in the English Channel's cold waters. All clearly defined and orderly.

The flight from London to Seattle was rough as

storms battered the North Atlantic, Greenland, and the frozen wastes of northern Canada. Nature, not humans, was in charge when the plane hit air pockets. The seatbelt sign illuminated. I tried to immerse myself in the turbulent emotional lives of the characters in my new book, but it was too rough to read. I found an in-flight movie, but the headphones didn't work. While I was fiddling with them, Jenna leaned toward me. "Mom, thank you. I love you."

I gave her a kiss on the cheek. "Love you too," and made a silent prayer that she would find someone loving and true as a partner when she was ready.

"I'm sorry I was angry when you first told me about my father. I was so mad I wasn't paying attention and rear-ended someone on the way back to my place. But I understand now. He told me all about your relationship and how much he'd loved you and how it could not be. The best thing is he said he saved the old photo of him and me. He said I could call him dad and introduced me to his other family before we went out to dinner."

She paused for a breath. "He took us all to Pierluigi and it was fabulous. We sat outside in the piazza and I ordered *Frittura di Calamari e Gamberi.* His wife's amazing. Chiara and Gigi are super. They even said I look a little like him. I hope they can come to Seattle. I'd love to show them around. Maybe we could all go to the San Juan Islands together."

I smiled at all the gushing and the impossible suggestion.

We parted after immigration. Jenna said as we hugged goodbye, "Oh Mom, I couldn't have done it without you."

I boarded the ferry back to Vashon Island at sunset.

The glorious apricot clouds were rimmed with gold, the sea a pale lavender. My hair blew wildly in the wind but my mind was at peace. The sunset promised better times. I was home from a trip too fast for jet lag but nevertheless transformative. The year of "yes" was proceeding.

CHAPTER TWENTY-NINE

Spring quarter flew by, and I signed up for summer school and fall quarter at the community college. I also applied to the University's Tacoma Branch for winter quarter when I'd have enough credits to enter my junior year for a BA in Social Work. I negotiated a raise and worked more hours to get experience and increase my income. A photocopy of my first larger paycheck rested on the bulletin board above my desk next to Bob's business card.

I'd been tempted to call him several times but hesitated. Maybe I'd be ready in a few months to find out if he might be the "appealing man" Betty Jo assured me would turn up. But first, I'd have to decide if I needed a man of any variety.

The raise increased the likelihood I'd have enough to keep myself afloat until graduation with a smaller student loan than I'd feared. My biggest concern, Jenna's school costs, was diminished now Alessandro said he would support her studies. He was an honorable man.

Another reason for my improved mood was Sophie and I had begun to video every two weeks. Her conversation was always measured. I recognized a warm mother-daughter relationship like I had with Jenna would arrive at the end of a long road, one probably marred by setbacks. Even so, I found relief with each small step forward. Going to Boston had been the right thing to do.

Also, I noticed Sophie looked happier. The reason was obvious when she called to say she and Annette were getting married and wanted me and Jenna to attend the late-summer wedding in Boston. Thrilled, I accepted the invitation instantly. Jenna took a week before agreeing solely in the name of family unity. We flew to Boston for the ceremony in a judge's chambers. Annette's father held Jacob as the two women said their vows. The boy was calm and looked brighter than at Christmas. He even said a few simple words. I dared to hold some hope for his future also.

Annette looked like the traditional bride in a simple white dress. Sophie selected a white pantsuit to flatter her slim figure. She glowed in happiness. I dabbed my eyes with a mother's traditional emotion.

The small reception was held at an Italian restaurant with the attendees from her law office along with a few Family Court judges. After the cake was cut and glasses raised, the newlyweds left for a short getaway, a one-week cruise to Bermuda. Jacob stayed with his new grandparents.

****

Jenna was immersed in something on her phone on the flight home until the plane crossed the Cascades and began the descent to Sea-Tac. At the point I could sense the plane's angle change, she pulled out her earbuds and said, "Mom, can I tell you something?" I could see she was looking anxious.

"Yes?" I held my breath.

"I hope you won't be upset, but Dad is going to help me get Italian citizenship. We talked about it when I was there last month, and I've been thinking ever since. I might want to live in Europe for a while after I graduate."

When I saw she was apprehensive, I undid my seatbelt to give her a hug. "I'm not surprised, and I think it's great to have options." Inwardly, I couldn't quell a spreading sense of sadness. All my children would be far away. My mother must have felt the same when I'd told her about moving to Rome. The box of rejected gifts I'd found under my childhood bed came to mind.

Jenna brightened up at my outward support and changed the subject. "Just so you know, Sophie and I talked before the wedding. She did apologize. We've agreed to be sisters, but I know we'll never be really close."

"I'm glad you talked. Maybe you will grow closer over time. Now, tell me hon, what Marine Biology courses are you taking next?" Those were my words but I was thinking no matter how old your children are, a mother's worries never end.

****

The summer weather lingered with perfect sunny warm days though it had rained a bit the previous week, a reminder fall was coming again. The flowers on the deck were still exuberant, matching my mood. Summer school was over, I'd been admitted to the U starting in January, and I had a few weeks to take a break when I wasn't working before my last quarter at community college. I snatched a little time to read for pleasure and to paint the front door Pompeiian red, a color reminding me of Rome. Still in a painting mood, I found an old can of black paint in the garage. It was rusted and had a thick layer of dried paint but enough underneath to dip a brush in and hand letter CARLISLE above the numbers on my mailbox near the entrance to my driveway.

The Measure of Life

The fig tree I'd noticed when Martin and I had been house hunting was laden. I picked a few and found a package of prosciutto in the supermarket. Memories of meals on Maggie's terrace flooded back.

Another day, the blackberries, fat and sweet from late summer sun, tempted me to make a cobbler to share with Betty Jo and Deirdre. I threw on old clothes and found the colander. I thought of Tyler, who'd loved to help me pick strawberries for jam before we'd moved to Rome.

As if marriage was contagious, he'd called the day before to say he and Mai had married. The civil ceremony was in Kigali, Rwanda, where they'd recently been assigned. He promised to get time off for Christmas again and would stay longer than last year. He sent photos from his phone. They both looked happy. I was certain they would be a team pulling together through life.

I carried the full colander into the kitchen to wash the berries. While they were draining, I checked my email to see if Sophie had sent the results of a meeting with a new specialist who'd examined Jacob. There was no message from her, but there was one from Maggie.

I looked at the subject line: "Some News." I opened the message expecting to hear about her children or Orazio.

Dearest Nicole. Hope all is well. I don't know if you see the Italian papers or any of the news magazines any more but you might want to know there was an article in Panorama and also Corriere della Sera I think you might want to read. They are about the company I remember you said Martin worked for. I'm attaching them. I'll send you an update on the family soon but do want you to know blessedly Orazio is still with us. Much love. Maggie

My fingers hovered above the keyboard. Open the attachments or not? It was a year since I'd last seen Martin alive and it was almost hard to remember his face. But, unable to resist, I opened the first one. It was a clip from a national paper about an investigation into the relationship between Martin's former company and various arms dealers, some associated with terrorists. The investigation had started several years earlier. After I read it a second time, I was sure the other attachment would mention Martin. I fled to the kitchen in fear he was returning from the dead to dominate my life again.

I filled a mug, holding it tight to still my shaking hands. They shook anyway, spilling coffee to the floor. I set the mug on the counter, flexing my hands to help them relax. They looked uncared for with purple blackberry juice embedded under my nails, stains on my palms and a long scratch from the thorns on the back of my hand. Zucca, rubbed against my legs and meowed. I leaned down to fondle her ears and was rewarded with an invitation to tickle her tummy. At least somebody in my life had no worries.

But the email couldn't be ignored. I climbed the stairs back to my office to finish reading. The attachment was from an investigative magazine in part quoting Italian authorities, or former employees—all of whom denied wrongdoing. There were diagrams showing the network of relationships and arcane details about armaments, none of which I understood. But I learned a former company executive, the elegant Federigo Dante, was under arrest for arms trafficking and fraudulent bankruptcy.

Another section of the article gave me further shock: Hunters had found a body in a smashed vehicle at the bottom of a ravine east of the archeological complex a few months before the story was written. The car was in an isolated area, the body mutilated by ravenous wild boars. Dental records eventually identified the corpse as Karl Trench. The authorities had been looking for him after some of those arrested mentioned him when they were questioned.

The article continued: One employee had died of a heart attack before he could be questioned. Martin's name was not mentioned. But a sodden briefcase belonging to the former employee was discovered near the mouth of the Tiber River. The case contained papers from his firm—partially waterlogged but clear enough to read copies of contracts for the sale of weapons, along with several containers of medications for heart and a tranquilizer, a framed photo of what might have been his family, and a luxury Swiss pen and pencil set.

I slammed the laptop shut. Who had my husband really been? The same old question with no answer.

I crept downstairs again to watch the uncaring world, hoping it would distract me. A regatta was in progress with brightly colored spinnakers vivid against the sapphire-blue water laced with small whitecaps speeding the boats along. An outbound freighter glided by, giant propellers pushing the ship toward its destination. Japan, Korea, China? Wherever, I wished I was on it.

The compulsion to finish reading the documents made me turn back to the screen. I read on until I reached a paragraph where the journalist reported the authorities found a thumb drive hidden in Trench's vehicle containing weapons specifications from Martin's company. The journalist's source said they'd been downloaded not long before his death. One set of fingerprints on it belonged to Trench, the other to the deceased man named Martin Carlisle.

Maybe the day he'd died, his heart couldn't take the stress of telling Trench he wasn't going to cooperate anymore. At least I'd like to think he had some backbone. It all must have started when Trench showed up in Seattle and began Martin's ruin and the downfall of our marriage. Thinking about his remarks about aces and sweet smoke made me think they must have been involved in a racket like drug dealing during the war. Trench would have had the upper hand after Martin started work in the defense industry where he needed to maintain a security clearance. I was ashamed for him and of him but I'd never know the full truth about his double life.

It was no use seeking more information because it wouldn't change anything for me now or ever. There was no point telling the children unless they asked. After I thanked Maggie, I deleted the email and attachments.

I swiveled my office chair to face the window. Trees and water swung into view. A car passed by on the road, the motor's whine rose and faded interrupting my effort to decide what to do with Martin's remaining earthly possessions and his ashes.

I found the baggie where I'd stashed Martin's watch, wallet, wedding ring, and gold cufflinks. The watch face was broken. Neither Tyler nor Sophie had wanted it when I'd asked earlier. It was inexpensive and could be discarded. What to do with the cufflinks? I tossed the links from hand to hand. Keep or not? They had no personal association, and with the price of gold so high I'd sell them the next time I was in Seattle.

But the gold ring? I'd had it engraved, "For MC from NC forever." How meaningless was "forever." I'd sell it too.

I'd look through his wallet later.

His ashes remained in the closet where they'd rested since I'd picked them up at the airport a month after my arrival in Seattle. There was a small columbarium at the labyrinth. But I didn't want him nearby when I walked the circle to find peace.

I took the box in my hands. *Who were you, Martin? I thought I knew, but I didn't know you at all. Did you even know yourself?*

After a long evening walk, I sat by the window to watch the flights arrive and depart. A half-moon played peekaboo as it dodged ragged clouds, concealing and revealing the light as the north wind drove them. It must also be shining on passengers as they either began to read their paperbacks or devices for a journey or gathered belongings to face whatever challenges the new destination would present as the plane landed.

****

The following morning after I threw out the blackberries now fuzzed with mold, I called Jenna to ask if she would participate in a small ceremony to remember Martin and dispose of his remains near the old lighthouse on the island. With her new relationship with Alessandro and his family, she never mentioned Martin, whether for care about my sensibilities or because she wanted to forget him, I didn't know and it was no longer relevant.

"Sure, but what about Sophie? Do you think she'd

want to come?"

"I called her the other day. She told me to do whatever I thought best. I was sure she'd want to have a say but she's moved on. Tyler isn't able to come home. I talked to him too and he agreed with the plan."

"That leaves us, I guess."

I found Martin's billfold still sitting on my dresser and opened it. If it held money the day he'd died, someone had taken it. There were a few of his business cards, several expired credit cards—one issued by his former company—his Italian identification, and driver's licenses.

I was about to toss all of it into the garbage when I pried open an inside pocket and found a photo. It was creased and faded but I could see the image was of a beautiful young woman with a lot of curly dark hair in a style worn in the 1980s. I turned it over to look for some inscription. The ink had blurred but I made out, "To Martin with all my love, Yvette." What had their life together been like, first as a couple, then with Tyler? They must have been happy or he wouldn't have kept her photo all these years. How strange it was both Martin and I had hidden photos to memorialize people we wanted to be with but could not.

****

The mist over the water lifted to reveal a tranquil and sunny Saturday morning in September two days before classes got underway again for both of us. Jenna, saying she needed exercise, was to bike to the Fauntleroy dock and then to the lighthouse park.

I drove to the lighthouse well before our meeting hour. It was already difficult to find a parking spot. Couples and families had arrived early for one more outing in the warm weather before the fall rains dampened enthusiasm. Children ran ahead to find beach treasures or to the lighthouse where they could climb the steps to look at the old lantern with its many-faceted Cyclops eye, blinded when an automated light replaced it.

I placed my backpack containing the plastic bag of ashes, two glasses, and a bottle of chilled prosecco below a storm-thrown log on the beach. I parked my Roman sandals next to the bag and walked toward the icy water while I kept an eye on the weathered gray log in case someone should try to claim it for a picnic. I entangled myself on a long strand of bull kelp, detached from its hold on the seafloor by the last storm. It was the kind I'd played with as a child when my parents took me to the beach. So many memories of a childhood I'd been too eager to escape.

I returned to the log to wait. More memories of all the people who'd supported me in my journey to the life I'd longed for rushed into my thoughts: The two supportive children and Sophie who'd mellowed, the old antique dealer who listened to my heart's sadness and helped me to the right choice, dearest Maggie who was always there for me, later Countess Franca, my friends and clients, and maybe Martin who'd unwittingly offered me a chance to meet Alessandro. They'd joined together to make me who I was and point me toward an authentic life of service to others and deeper communion with my precious family wherever they were.

Jenna rushed towards me, face damp with perspiration.

"Finally! The ferry broke down. We had to wait forever." After a few deep breaths, she added, "Are you ready?"

"Yes. Let's do it. The bottle's here." I pointed to the backpack. "I don't know if we're supposed to have alcohol here so be quick. We'll pretend we're Italians and don't know the rules."

Jenna balanced the glasses on the log and pried off the gold foil around the bottle's cork.

I took the plastic bag and waded into the water, undoing the tie when cold wavelets wet my knees. The fine gray ash poured into the water, a residue of dust rising until it, too, settled softly. I added the photo of Yvette, Martin's true and only love. The ashes and picture floated away together on the outgoing tide before they sank out of sight in the green waters. "Martin, your life's tortured journey is over. May you find peace at last."

When I heard the cork pop it was time to turn toward shore to grasp a flute of golden wine. I raised my glass to the sun to watch the bubbles rise.

PASTA ALLA PUTTANESCA
Nicole's version

INGREDIENTS:
1 pound linguine
3 tablespoons extra virgin olive oil
4 anchovy fillets, chopped into small pieces
3 cloves garlic, peeled and crushed
1 28-oz can crushed Italian tomatoes
½ cup pitted and halved Kalamata olives
2 tablespoons capers
Red pepper flakes to taste
Fresh ground pepper to taste
Optional: garnish of basil or parsley

METHOD:
Heat 2 tablespoons olive oil, add garlic and anchovies in a large fry pan. Cook on medium heat, stirring occasionally until garlic is golden.

Add tomatoes along with salt and ground pepper to taste. Cook for about 10 minutes. Stir in olives, capers, and red pepper flakes. Reduce heat to simmer for about 10 more minutes to bring out flavors.

Bring a large pot of salted water (6 – 8 quarts) to a rolling boil. Add linguine. Follow the cooking time on the pasta package for al dente texture after the water returns to a boil. Stir occasionally to keep strands separated.

Drain into a colander and pour into a heated serving bowl. Add sauce along with the tablespoon of olive oil. Toss to distribute sauce and adjust seasoning if necessary.

Add garnish if desired. Serves 4

A word about the author…

Judith is the author of a memoir, Coins in the Fountain, recounting stories from ten years in Rome working for the UN World Food Programme. She is an avid traveler, having visited well over 100 countries. She holds a JD cum laude from Lewis & Clark Law School in Portland, OR. When she isn't writing, she serves on committees related to literary arts and public services. She and her family live in the Seattle area. https://judithworks.net

Acknowledgements

To Elena Hartwell, my original developmental editor, who set me on the right path.

And Najla Mahis who did the polishing.

To Kathryn Schipper who always found just the right word.

Also, many, many thanks to Tori Peters, Laura Moe, Harriet Cannon, and Susan Ferguson who took time from their busy lives to read the manuscript closely and offer detailed substantive comments.

And, finally to those who served as readers and commenters over the time it took to bring the story to light: Anne Johnson, Susan Frederick, Mary Jane Cryan, Kizzie Jones, Beverley Cresswell, Margaret Jessop, Nicki Harbo, Judy Slattery, Mindy Halleck, and Vivan Murray. Apologies to anyone who I have neglected to mention who lent their time and energy to help bring the story to life over its long period of gestation.

A big thank you to all!!

Thank you for purchasing
this publication of The Wild Rose Press, Inc.
For questions or more information
contact us at
info@thewildrosepress.com.
The Wild Rose Press, Inc.
www.thewildrosepress.com